I0761688

Advance Praise for

THE WRITING ROOM

"*The Writing Room* is a timely and compelling portrait of people who rise above broken families and oppressive systems to find belonging and solidarity with one another. Through the eyes of the well-rounded and unique character of Maya Mitchell, Mickelson explores with deft and unflinching craft the racism and anti-immigrant fervor directed against Latines and other communities of color. But more than the ongoing fight against bigots, *The Writing Room* confronts head-on the confounding and deflating betrayal by the very ones who once declared themselves family and allies, people who seemed to love and value the marginalized but who turn on us the moment it's expedient. Still, Maya finds purpose and strength alongside others who refuse to be broken in a beautiful bildungsroman anchored by a sweet, slow-burn romance. Daringly defiant and achingly hopeful, *The Writing Room* is an essential book that speaks to this moment with clear vision and powerful prose. Not to be missed!"

—David Bowles, author of *They Call Her Fregona*

"As emotionally gripping as it is heartfelt, *The Writing Room* is a powerful novel about family, finding your voice, and the potency of first love. Mickelson masterfully weaves trauma and tribulations with hope and healing, affirming the necessity of making space for yourself alongside and within your community."

—Jessica Parra, author of *Rubi Ramos's Recipe for Success* and *The Quince Project*

"An inspiring story about learning what's important to you and finding the inner strength to stand up for it."

—Ismée Williams, author of *This Train Is Being Held*

THE WRITING ROOM

MARCIA ARGUETA MICKELSON

MINNEAPOLIS

Carolrhoda Lab®
An imprint of Lerner Publishing Group, Inc.
241 First Avenue North
Minneapolis, MN 55401 USA

For reading levels and more information, look up this title at www.lernerbooks.com.

Image credits: Matej Kastelic/Shutterstock (fire escape); aga7ta/Shutterstock (scribbles); maxstockphoto/Shutterstock (brick); nattha99/Shutterstock (background); Stmool/Shutterstock (graphic).

Main body text set in Janson Text LT Std.
Typeface provided by Adobe Systems.

Library of Congress Cataloging-in-Publication Data

Names: Mickelson, Marcia Argueta, author.
Title: The writing room / Marcia Mickelson.
Description: Minneapolis : Carolrhoda Lab, 2025. | Audience term: Teenagers | Audience: Ages 13–18. | Audience: Grades 10–12. | Summary: "After eighteen-year-old Maya is kicked out of her wealthy dad's NYC home, she is grounded by a shared writers' workspace where she finds her voice—and the courage to stand up to her dad" —Provided by publisher.
Identifiers: LCCN 2024050173 (print) | LCCN 2024050174 (ebook) | ISBN 9798765627716 (library binding) | ISBN 9798765673195 (epub)
Subjects: CYAC: Family problems—Fiction. | Fathers and daughters—Fiction. | Self-actualization—Fiction. | Writing—Fiction. | LCGFT: Novels.
Classification: LCC PZ7.M581924 Wr 2025 (print) | LCC PZ7.M581924 (ebook) | DDC [Fic]—dc23

LC record available at https://lccn.loc.gov/2024050173
LC ebook record available at https://lccn.loc.gov/2024050174

Manufactured in Guang Dong, China by Dream Colour Printing
1-1011937-52145-3/6/2025

To my sister and bosom friend,
Claudia Armann, for a
Lifetime of friendship

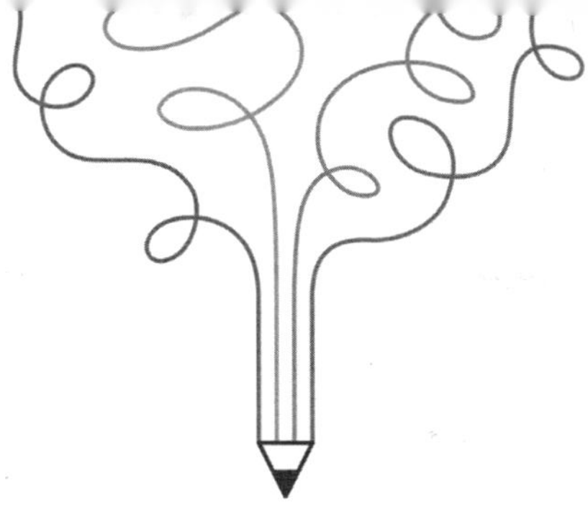

CHAPTER ONE

I'm in the back of a BMW, which is the last place you'd expect to find a homeless person, but that's what I am. For eighteen years, I've known this would happen. Even so, I'm still in shock.

Today I'm moving out of the home I've lived in my whole life. Not by choice. This is just what my father has always done when one of his children graduates from high school. He's committed to paying for four years of college, which he considers essential, and absolutely nothing else. We've been told this from a very young age. My brother, Daniel, would usually interrupt the childhood lecture by breaking into song, belting out "The Bare Necessities" from *The Jungle Book*. It seemed funny back then.

Ernie, our family's driver, is taking me to stay with my friend Yoly and her husband, Ricardo. I'll live with them temporarily, until I start college in the fall and figure out this whole adult thing.

Ernie pulls the car to the curb in front of Yoly and Ricardo's building. It's a beautiful two-story brownstone with bright red shutters on a quiet, tree-lined street in New York's Morningside Heights neighborhood. I know I could do a lot worse for temporary lodgings.

Ernie's eyes glisten as he opens my door. He's been working

for us since Victoria was seven, Daniel was two, and I was in utero. "Maya, you should talk to him again," he says.

"No. It won't make a difference. This is how he wants it." I sling my messenger bag over my shoulder and pull my suitcase from the trunk.

"Why don't you call your mother?"

Even if it would help to talk to her, I don't think I'd reach her in the western highlands of Guatemala. "No, Ernie. I'll be fine. Victoria was fine and so was Daniel."

"Yes, but they're tough. You're the baby."

He means I'm the weak one. Victoria had a paid internship lined up even before she moved to California for college, and she's been climbing the journalism ladder ever since. These days she runs her own women's lifestyle magazine that covers everything from fashion to finances, with a monthly print edition and a popular website. Daniel stayed closer to home but didn't play it safer: he moved into a tiny one-bedroom apartment with five drama club friends, left his college money in the trust, and waited tables while auditioning for plays. He's currently on a cruise ship playing one of the T-birds in a traveling production of *Grease*.

Me? Yoly helped me line up a paying job at the library, where I've been volunteering since sophomore year. I'll work full-time over the summer, then switch to part-time once my classes at Columbia start. My mom insists on sending me whatever money she can spare, and I'm hoping I can earn the rest of what I'll need through freelance writing gigs. At the end of the day I know I'm the least impressive Mitchell. If my family were the Bennets from *Pride and Prejudice*, I'd be bookish, boring Mary, the one with the fewest prospects.

Ernie frowns, probably reflecting that I'm incapable of

handling anything as well as my siblings. He pulls two cardboard boxes from the trunk and sets them by my suitcase. Yoly and Ricardo live in a studio apartment with very little space, so this is all I've brought for now.

Yoly bounds down the brownstone's steps, her curly black hair bouncing behind her. In her yoga pants and baggy T-shirt, she could pass for one of my peers, though she's actually well into her twenties. She throws her arms around my shoulders, almost squeezing the breath out of me. "Maya, it's going to be okay."

"I know," I say with a smile I don't feel. "Thanks for taking me in."

She grabs a cardboard box from Ernie, who's watching us with the eyes of a sad puppy. "I'll take this upstairs. Be right back to grab the other one."

With his hands free now, Ernie reaches into his back pocket and pulls out two twenties. "Here, Maya. In case you need it."

I shake my head. "No, Ernie. I can't take your money. I'm going to be fine. My new job as a library page comes with a paycheck. So does every article I write for Victoria's magazine, and soon I'll have more writing jobs too."

Victoria, who is not opposed to nepotism, started paying me to write weekly pieces for her magazine about a year ago. They're *not* fashion articles, given my complete lack of expertise in that department. Exhibit A: the black ankle boots I wear with almost every outfit. Instead, I review books—specifically, classics that I think deserve to be rediscovered by a new generation of ambitious, intelligent women.

"Seriously, Ernie. Don't worry about me."

He stuffs the money back into his pocket. "You call me, Maya." He's sweet, but I doubt I'll take him up on that offer.

Now that I'm not part of Dad's household, Ernie doesn't get paid to take care of me anymore, and I don't want him to feel like he has to do it for free.

My smile falls as he drives away. I'm going to miss the rides to school with Ernie. Every morning, we would pick up coffees and the *Times*. I would read him the headlines as he drove, and he would tell me which articles to circle for him to read later. That's over now. A lot of things are.

Yoly's back. She grabs the remaining box at my feet. With my suitcase and messenger bag, I follow her inside, up to one of the second-floor apartments.

"Here's your bed." She points to the couch. It has a pillow with a lace-edged pink case that looks new, judging by the fresh creases. Clearly, Yoly sees me as a little girl. It's probably the way I seemed three years ago when we met at the library. I was just a nerdy fifteen-year-old who wanted to start a book club focusing on the classics. I'm now a nerdy eighteen-year-old who just graduated high school trying to somehow figure out life with a mother who's three thousand miles away and a father who's a million emotional light-years away.

Yoly has set my two boxes in the corner of the room next to an olive-green lounge chair that looks like it was salvaged from a junkyard. She motions for me to do the same. "Ricardo's picking up pizza from Enzo's, and I made a cake, so happy graduation!"

"That's so sweet of you. You didn't have to go to all that trouble." I manage a smile so she doesn't feel like her efforts have been wasted, but nothing about this day feels celebratory to me.

Yoly crosses to the kitchenette and picks up a plate with a lopsided chocolate-frosted cake.

"That looks amazing." A lie, but I'm grateful for her effort, even as the image of last month's three-tiered birthday cake comes to mind. I never wanted that cake—it was Dad's doing, and I'll never understand why he spent thousands of dollars for my eighteenth birthday party only to abandon me on my graduation day.

Yoly puts the cake on the coffee table in front of me. I sink down into the couch that is now going to be my bed.

The door, which Yoly hasn't locked behind us, opens. Ricardo walks in carrying two pizza boxes and whistling the commencement song. Right behind him, propping the door for him, is a young woman I don't know—about my age, with brown hair in a ponytail.

"Welcome, Maya," Ricardo says as he sets the pizzas next to Yoly's cake. To Yoly, he adds, "Look who I ran into on the stairs," right before the girl asks, "Oo, is this the friend with the fancy car?"

"Hi, Katie," Yoly says, like the girl's appearance is the most normal thing in the world. It reminds me of old sitcoms I've seen, where characters are always barging into each other's apartments. "This is my friend Maya. She's going to be staying with us for a few months, till she starts at Columbia in the fall."

"Hi, Maya," Katie says. "I live in the downstairs apartment. I saw you from my window when you drove up." She puts her hand on her hip and says half-jokingly, "Was that your Beamer outside?"

"Not anymore. It belongs to my dad, and he just kicked me out." What's the point of mincing words? I don't want this girl to presume I have wealth that's no longer mine.

"Oh. I'm sorry." Katie reaches to touch my arm. "Let me know if I can do anything."

That's a kind offer, but short of presenting me with an exact replica of my childhood bedroom, there isn't anything she can do for me. "Yoly and Ricardo have been great to let me stay here for the summer, so that's a big help."

"We're celebrating Maya's graduation," Ricardo adds. He opens a pizza box, pulls out a slice, and takes a bite. I look around for plates or napkins, but there are none. No one makes a move toward the kitchenette to get anything to serve the pizza on. I've never eaten pizza straight out of the box, but it seems like a convenience I can get used to.

"Cool," says Katie. "I graduate next week and I'm actually super nervous . . ."

Ricardo points to the box and asks Katie, "Want to stay for pizza?"

"Oh, that sounds great, but I'm heading to Jersey to see my family this evening. In fact, that's why I stopped by—to borrow an egg. I want to make them cookies."

"Sure thing," Yoly says. "Check the fridge. I'm pretty sure we have some."

"We do," Ricardo says. "Still had half a carton left this morning after I made omelets."

Katie walks to the refrigerator. "Thanks! I'll totally pay you back."

Ricardo takes another bite of pizza and turns to Yoly with a raised eyebrow.

Yoly stifles a laugh as she sits on the couch, grabbing for the pizza box. Neither of them seems to find it weird that a neighbor is freely helping herself to their fridge contents.

Katie heads toward the door, egg in hand. "Nice meeting you, Maya. Maybe later this week we can hang out."

I fake a smile and say goodbye. I really don't feel like

becoming instant besties with this girl I just met. Everything feels so messy and scary and stressful right now.

The pizza, at least, is a bright spot in this otherwise dismal day. Yoly remembered that I love Enzo's and that their veggie combo is my favorite. That's at least as much thought as my family has spared for me.

Mom messaged me two days ago, saying she would be away from service for a while but would be able to call me later this week. This morning Victoria Venmoed me five hundred dollars with a short message, and Daniel emailed me a gift card. And my dad? He came to my graduation ceremony, took some pictures with me, and handed me a typed inventory of items I could buy back from him. All the expensive gifts I've received throughout my life—jewelry, books, artwork. They're all catalogued and waiting in a safe, available for me to purchase for myself when I have extra tens of thousands of dollars.

I don't foresee that happening anytime soon. Dad has been very clear that he won't be giving me a cent over my tuition money. He's letting me keep my phone, laptop, and e-reader for college, but he cautioned me that if I need to replace any of them, that'll be on me.

For help with living expenses, I'm supposed to ask my mom. His exact words were, "God knows our dollars have been going to her country for years; it's time some money flows back to this country for once." I wonder what he would've said if Mom were from Norway or Italy instead of Guatemala.

At any rate, I don't want to have to ask Mom for money every time I need it. My goal is to use my article-writing money for everyday expenses and save up enough from my library paychecks to mostly cover the cost of student housing for my first semester.

We finish the pizza and have some of Yoly's cake—which actually tastes pretty good, much better than it looks. Ricardo lets out a long sigh and pulls himself up, taking the empty pizza boxes to the kitchenette counter. Just past the kitchenette is a dark green curtain hiding Yoly and Ricardo's bed from the rest of the apartment. They'll be sleeping just on the other side of that thin curtain. It hits me that my presence on this couch every night will have an impact on their intimacy, and guilt and embarrassment wash over me along with this dose of reality.

Yoly stretches her arms over her head. "I'd better throw some towels in the wash if any of us wants to shower in the morning."

"I can help." I get up and follow her to the closet by the kitchenette.

She opens the rolling doors to reveal the tiniest washer and dryer set I've ever seen. "Check it out—our pride and joy. This is a huge luxury for a New York apartment. Will you grab the two towels hanging over the shower rod in the bathroom?"

"Sure." The bathroom's another two steps away. I bring the towels to Yoly, who stuffs them into the little washing machine along with other towels she pulls out of a laundry bag.

Melinda, our housekeeper, did the laundry at our house. I've occasionally done a load when I needed something right away and she wasn't around, so I know how to operate a washing machine, but I'm not in the habit of washing clothes every day or week or however often most people wash their clothes.

"Oh, shoot. We're out of detergent." Yoly shakes a small bottle of Tide. "Can you run downstairs and see if Katie has some we can borrow?"

"Um. Sure." I've never been sent to a neighbor's home to borrow something, but it doesn't have to be a big deal.

I pull the apartment door closed behind me and slowly descend the stairs, running my hand along the smooth oak of the banister. After idling in front of the door a few moments, I knock.

The door opens slightly, and a young man with wavy dark hair and Katie's eyes pops his head out. He's wearing a T-shirt with the image of Andy Warhol's soup cans. "Yeah?" he says brusquely.

Malcriado, my mom would call him. He is in severe need of her "tienes que saludar" lecture, which taught me to politely greet every person who came within my orbit. "Hi," I say, thrown off by his curt greeting. "Um. Is Katie here?"

"No."

I wait for a follow-up statement, but there is none. Where did she take that egg, if not here? "Oh. Well, I'm Maya. I'm staying with Yoly and Ricardo. So, Yoly asked me to come borrow some laundry detergent."

"Wait." He disappears.

I wait, wondering if he's capable of saying more than one word at a time. He comes back with a small yellow bottle of detergent. "Here."

I take the bottle. "I can bring it right back."

"No," he says. "Don't worry about it. There's less than half a bottle in there, and I bought another one yesterday. Besides, Katie's borrowed close to ten pounds of sugar and several dozen eggs from them." A smile creeps into his brown eyes but doesn't quite make it to his lips.

I return his almost-smile with one of my own. "Fair enough. Thanks."

"Welcome," he says, returning to one-word answers. The door closes.

Back upstairs, Yoly starts the laundry while Ricardo makes a phone call. I huddle in the corner where we've put my stuff by the green chair. But, practically speaking, I can't actually unpack anything: There's no dresser, so my clothes will have to stay in the suitcase and one of the cardboard boxes. Same for my toiletries, since the bathroom medicine cabinet is already packed, the old-fashioned sink has no counter, and the claw-foot tub has only a narrow rim. And I might as well keep my laptop, e-reader, and notebooks inside my messenger bag until I need them.

For a moment, I hold the bag close. It was a gift from Mom, handmade by a woman she knows and sent to me not long after she moved back to Guatemala. I always feel just a little bit closer to her when I have this bag in my hands.

I sit down cross-legged and flip open the lid of the cardboard box that holds my favorite books. It was painful to leave the rest of them behind. For my twelfth birthday, Dad had floor-to-ceiling bookshelves built for me, complete with a rolling ladder like Belle's from *Beauty and the Beast*. Now, all I have is this twelve-by-twelve box with a fraction of my collection.

On top is an illustrated copy of *Pride and Prejudice*. At the bottom is my prized possession—a signed first edition of *Charlotte's Web*. A couple of years ago, Ernie drove Dad and me to a rare books store in Midtown to pick up this book. Dad had been searching for it for months and proudly presented it to me on my sixteenth birthday.

Finding rare first editions of classics is kind of our thing. Ernie has driven us to many bookstores, as far away as Boston, so we could add to the collection. That same day, Dad also picked up a first edition of *The Grapes of Wrath* because he couldn't resist buying *himself* something for *my* birthday.

Still, book-hunting has always been something I loved doing with him, something that made me feel connected to him in a way I imagine some daughters connect with their fathers on a regular basis.

Almost as if he's summoned by my thoughts about this lovely book in my hands, Dad's face appears via FaceTime on my phone.

He looks tired. Gray is prominently sneaking into his trimmed beard, and his ice-blue eyes are narrowed at me. "Maya, did you take the *Charlotte's Web*?"

Not the greeting I was expecting. "Uh, hi, Dad."

"Did you take it?"

"It's mine. You gave it to me."

He sighs, turns away from his phone, and runs a hand down his face. "And what? You're going to sell it to pay your rent?"

"No! I would never sell it." Not to mention that Yoly and Ricardo aren't charging me rent. "I love that book."

"Just like Victoria pretended to love all her jewelry. I have the most ungrateful kids." He shakes his head and narrows his eyes at me again. "I picked out every piece of jewelry for her myself, taking the time to find just the right one for every birthday, every Christmas. And what does she do? She sells all of it and uses the money to start a rag with a name that sounds like a criminal enterprise."

He means Victoria's magazine. It's called *Latina at Large*.

"And now you sneak off with that special copy from my collection," Dad goes on.

"*Your* collection? You gave me that book for my birthday. It's mine."

He takes a deep breath. "Did you sell it already?"

"No!" I show it to him. "I told you, I would never sell it."

"Ernie is coming to pick it up."

"What?"

"He'll be there in fifteen minutes."

"I can't believe you."

"You have to make your own way, Maya. You can have that book back when you can afford to pay for it. No more handouts from me." And he's gone.

I turn around, and Yoly's right behind me, her hands clasped together. Lowering herself to the floor, she puts her arms around me, and I start crying. I let go of every emotion I've kept at bay all day. Every fear I've had, every flash of self-pity I've tried to suppress, culminate in this moment. I can't stop crying.

"I'm so sorry," Yoly says, gently patting my back.

I shake my head. "I shouldn't be surprised. He's always been up front about his expectations."

Yoly looks like she's physically restraining herself from responding to this. All she says is, "Want me to go downstairs with you?"

I nod, and we both get up off the floor. She directs me to the tissue box on a small shelf by the door. I wipe my eyes and nose, then wash my hands in the kitchen sink before picking up my beloved book. Even though it will no longer be mine, I want to keep it in good shape.

In silence, we walk down the stairs and out into the warm evening. We don't say anything; there's no need for words. Yoly knows how sad and hopeless I feel, and nothing she can say will make me feel an ounce better.

Ernie double-parks and turns on his hazards. He's out of uniform now, wearing sweats, and I know Dad pulled him out of his own home after he was off the clock to fulfill this petty quest. What makes it even worse is that Dad knows Ernie uses his evenings to take care of his sick wife, after other family members have taken turns staying with her during the day.

Ernie looks ashamed as he approaches us. "I'm so sorry about this, Maya."

I nod and don't say anything because I don't think my tears are done. I hold the book out to him, but he doesn't take it. He pulls me into an embrace and kisses the top of my head. "I'm so sorry." In all the years I've known Ernie, it's the first time he's hugged me.

I know, and he knows, that this is about more than just a book. The book is important; of course it is. But my dad is sending me a message that he is one hundred percent not there for me.

Finally, Ernie takes the book. He was there the day I received it. He saw how happy I was to get this generous gift from my father. "I could come by later this week. We can get coffees, and I'll take you to the library for your shift."

I shake my head. "He'll find out. I don't want you to get in trouble."

Ernie nods and looks down at the ground. "You take care, Maya. Okay?" He looks over to Yoly with a grateful half smile.

"I will, Ernie. Don't worry about me. You take care too."

He turns toward the car, and Yoly places a guiding hand on my arm as we head back inside.

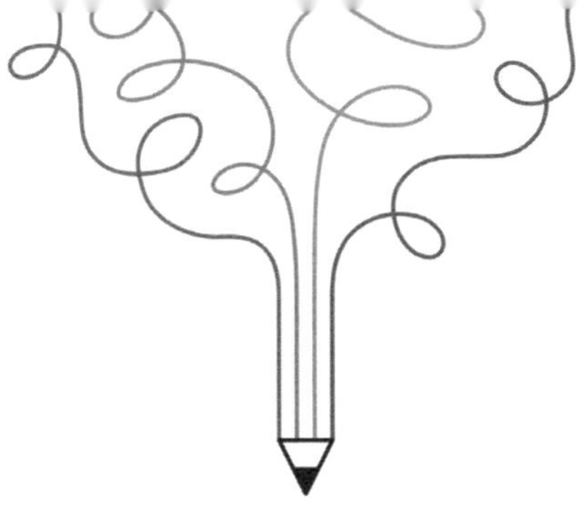

CHAPTER TWO

It'd be ungrateful to say so, but this has been my worst night of sleep ever. The discomfort of a thrift-store couch that's not long enough to hold my whole body, coupled with recurring doubts about how I'll support myself financially, resulted in about three hours of solid rest. I open one eye and stare into the bright pinkness of the too-starched pillowcase grating against my face. Faint sunlight streams through the tiny slits of the wooden blinds. Outside, the city is buzzing with traffic sounds, a new morning stimulant for me. In my Upper East Side home—or rather, my father's Upper East Side home—soundproof walls kept out any hint that we live in one of the noisiest, busiest cities in the world.

I hear the shower going, and I suppose I'll be the last to get a turn in the bathroom. That's fine, as I have only one thing on my to-do list today: meet my best friend, Layla, at our favorite coffee spot.

My phone buzzes with an email from Dad. It's a link to my phone account with information on how to make payment changes. The next payment is due in two weeks. I guess it'll come out of the money I get for my *Latina at Large* pieces, which I'll now be spending on necessities instead of on books and outings with friends.

Ricardo steps out from behind the curtain and into the kitchenette, tying a yellow tie around his neck. "Morning, Maya. I'm about to make oatmeal. Want some?"

I pull myself off the couch's pink sheets. "That sounds great."

We sit at the small table and eat steaming bowls of oatmeal. Yoly emerges from the shower in a bathrobe with her hair wrapped in a towel atop her head. Ricardo hands her a cup of coffee and kisses her on the lips before hurrying out to work.

She takes a sip of her coffee. "You sleep okay?"

"Yeah." It's not the first white lie I've told her and likely won't be the last. "Thank you for letting me stay here. I'm sorry to be such a burden."

"Don't worry about it. I promise you, that couch has had so many guests sleep on it. We almost always have someone staying here." The thought that countless people have slept on that very couch doesn't make me feel any better, but I'm going to have to get past it. I know Ricardo and Yoly are involved in a community mutual aid group that focuses on helping neighbors in need, and that people frequently crash here when they need somewhere to stay. Now I'm the one benefiting from that generosity, and I inwardly chide myself for being squeamish about it.

"In fact," Yoly says, "you may be the last guest we host in this studio! Our neighbors across the hall, Daisy and her son Lorenzo, are moving out of their one-bedroom at the beginning of September, and they're going to sublet it to us. Which means *we* can sublet *this* place to someone else. Though the couch will be coming with us," she adds with a chuckle.

"That's great," I say, vaguely aware that it's hard to find a reasonably priced apartment in New York. "And in the meantime, I can pitch in with rent. My mom will send me some money each month, so with that and my paycheck and my free-lance work for my sister's magazine . . ."

"Don't worry about it, Maya," says Yoly. "Focus on saving up to pay for your dorm in the fall. You don't owe us anything."

Her hand on my arm calms every cell in my body that's telling me I'm going to flop on my face my first full day of being an adult. "Thank you."

She goes back to the bathroom to finish getting ready, while I clear the table and put the dishes in the sink. It takes me a second to register that there is no Melinda to wash them. The chore will fall to one of us. I've seen Melinda put dishes into the dishwasher, but I've also seen her wash some in the sink. How does one decide which to do?

Growing up, I did dishes every summer in Guatemala when I cooked with my abuela, Mamá Juana. My mom came from a middle-class family; they had a young woman who came in every day to help in the kitchen and do the laundry, but we all did our share. So I've washed dishes in the sink, but never in the dishwasher. Mamá Juana is a firm believer in hand-scrubbing.

I opt to do as she would do, hand-washing all the dishes and putting them on the drying rack. I'll have to ask Yoly later how to use the dishwasher.

Victoria's FaceTime call comes in just as I dry my hands on a kitchen towel. "What are you doing up?" I ask her. "It's so early there."

"Yoga." Victoria is sitting cross-legged on the floor, her phone propped nearby. Her long black hair is pulled into a tight bun atop her head. "How was your first night free of Dad?"

"It was okay. Yoly and Ricardo have been great."

"Still makes me nervous that you're basically staying with strangers. Like, how well do you even know them?"

"I told you. Yoly and I work at the library together. She's a librarian. She's very cool, and she's only six years older than me." Closer to my age than Victoria, in other words. "We're friends."

"What about the husband?"

"He's an immigration lawyer, and he's really sweet and not remotely creepy, if that's what you're worried about. And Morningside Heights is a very safe neighborhood, so you don't have to worry about that either."

"Crime's been on the rise there the last few years," Victoria says in a cautionary tone. "There've been issues with unhoused people, drugs—especially in Morningside Park, from what I've read. You should just come here. Go to UCLA. Live with me. I have an extra room. It could be yours for free."

"No, Vic, I already told you. I'm not going to freaking California. That's your thing, not mine. I love this city. It's home."

"New York will chew you up and spit you out." A crease forms between her two perfect eyebrows. "Sorry I couldn't be at graduation yesterday, but you understand, right? That city equals death. I will never go back."

"A little melodramatic, don't you think?"

"I'm sorry." Victoria hasn't returned home to visit since she left. I've had to fly to California to see her, or we've met up over school breaks and weekends in non-death cities.

"That's okay," I say even though it really wasn't okay that only Dad was there to see me graduate. Mom couldn't get away from patients who needed her, and Daniel's in the middle of the ocean somewhere. Victoria, on the other hand, had no real reason not to show up.

"Well, I'm going to send you a couple of names and email addresses. Editors at two teen magazines. Get in touch with them; mention my name and see if you can get started on some freelancing with them. Pitch them some articles—maybe something about applying to colleges or top ten things for teens to do in the city. Human-interest stuff like you did for your school paper."

"Okay. I'll do that. Thanks, Vic. I'll talk to you later."

"Bye. Love you, sis."

I start to feel more at ease. My paycheck from the library won't be much on its own, but the money I get for my weekly pieces, along with these new opportunities Victoria has presented me with, should be enough to pay my bills. My financial situation isn't nearly as dire as it could be. It'll just take some getting used to.

I take a short subway ride to meet Layla. Dad always thought I should stay away from the subway, but Layla and I would use it sometimes to go to museums or shows. Sophomore year, when I joined the school newspaper staff, I volunteered to write a piece about tips for riding the subway, and Layla helped me with my research. We told our families we had "mandatory Spanish club meetings" after school, when actually we were figuring out how to enter a subway station on the correct side of the street, how to pay our fares with our phones' digital wallets, and how to blend in with the other riders. Our lie went undetected until we made the fateful mistake of taking the express train uptown, which meant we were forty minutes late getting back to school. Our drivers showed up to find the building's doors locked and no evidence of a Spanish club in sight. Layla's parents grounded her for three months. Ernie covered for me, not telling my dad but making me promise to stop riding the subway.

Well, now I have no promises to keep—not to Ernie, not to Dad. Whatever Dad thinks is not relevant anymore. I can do what I want.

Layla's waiting at the entrance to our coffee spot. "Maya, oh my gosh. How are you holding up?" She puts her arm around my neck as we walk into the building together. "I'm so sorry about everything."

In January, I started plotting where to live after kick-out day, aka graduation day. Layla offered her home, and her parents happily agreed to have me stay with them. When Dad found out, they quickly changed their minds. They never gave Layla and me an actual reason, but I know Dad got to them somehow.

He's a master at manipulation. It's why Mom finally left him after twelve years, and honestly, I never blamed her. After the divorce, in which he cheated her out of a good settlement, she moved into an apartment not far from home. We'd stay with her half the time, and I loved that time. But two years ago, she moved back to Guatemala to start a humanitarian nonprofit that serves the Mayans in the western highlands. She says she made the change because Mamá Juana is getting older and needs someone to look after her, but I know it was partly to get away from Dad.

Even with her gone, I created a safety net for myself—and Dad just knocked it out from under me. I don't know if I'll ever understand that.

"I feel so bad about you not being able to stay with us," Layla says now. "It sucks, and I'm still mad at my parents about it."

"Don't be mad at them. It was *my* dad who was calling the shots." We're pretty sure he threatened to get Layla's mom kicked off the nonprofit board she sits on. It's literally her whole life.

Layla shrugs and steps up to the counter. "They could've stood up to him—like, grown a spine or something. I'm paying," she announces to the barista, waving her credit card at both herself and me.

I pull my wallet out. "You don't have to do that."

She pushes my hand away. "Don't worry about it. Come on, Maya. It's just coffee."

The gold card in Layla's hand serves as a reminder that even though we're best friends, the differences between us are as vast as the park that separates where we live now. I smile my thanks, but uneasiness creeps in. I'm not used to being in this position, being in Layla's debt. I used to have a magical card that paid for everything I wanted when we went out. Now, my bank account holds exactly five hundred dollars, Victoria's graduation gift, which will have to cover my food and transportation expenses, my next phone bill, and anything else that comes up until I get a paycheck. From now on I'm going to have to keep track of every dollar I spend.

We sit at a cushy bench with our coffees and check our phones. This was our daily routine before school—scrolling through our social media and sharing what we think the other person will find interesting. Our latest obsession is ChitChat, an app for videos and photos. To follow an account, you have to pay ten cents, and then every time you like or share a post, you pay another cent. On the flip side, *your* account accrues money with every follow, like, and share from other users. I've never actually posted anything, but I figure that even in my newly precarious financial situation, I can afford to part with a few cents each day.

"You really should be more active on here," Layla tells me. "If you draw a decent following, it could be an extra source of income for you."

I snort. "Way too much work for way too little payoff. Ten cents from a new follower here, twenty cents for some likes there. I could make it my full-time job and still barely bring in enough for this coffee. Especially if I'm still liking all *your* posts!"

Layla is the queen of selfies—one for almost every new outfit. I'm more comfortable looking at pictures than being looked at.

I show her my brother's latest post, captioned, *Doing Grease in Greece tonight.* Daniel and his boyfriend, Adam, are backstage in full costume.

Layla clutches her heart. "Ahh! Goals."

I haven't seen Daniel in four months, and it'll be another two before he's done with the cruise ship tour. I sure could use one of his hugs right now. When we were younger, Daniel was my comforter, consoling me every time Dad yelled at me. But he also seemed to bear the brunt of Dad's wrath—the wayward heir, more interested in show business than the family business.

I pause in my scrolling long enough to like a post from our friend Lucinda Blalock, captioned, *Fashion show in Paris.* Lucinda was my best friend until high school, when modeling and fashion became her priorities. I don't blame her for quitting school at sixteen to follow in her mother's footsteps. Lucinda is, after all, divinely beautiful, as Anne Shirley from *Anne of Green Gables* would say. As kids, we both adored that book. We often debated Anne's question—"Which would you rather be if you had the choice: divinely beautiful or dazzlingly clever or angelically good?"

Even at age ten, there was no question that Lucinda was picking the first option. I, on the other hand, wore my limp black hair in a ponytail and had crooked teeth that only two years of braces could fix. We agreed that my sister, Victoria, was the most "dazzlingly clever" person we knew. At seventeen, Victoria had already amassed a secret bank account of over twenty thousand dollars by quietly selling off all her jewelry. She was ready for Dad's eviction, and she never looked back.

That's what Dad wants—for us to make our own way in the world, just as he did. He came from nothing and built a multimillion-dollar business. He raised us in the good life, with the best of everything, so that we would come to appreciate it, crave it when he took it away from us, and work to earn it back for ourselves.

I sigh and close the ChitChat app. I'll never be as clever as Victoria or as beautiful as Lucinda, which I guess leaves the "angelically good" option. Who wants to be angelically good? I'm certain that would've been Anne Shirley's last choice.

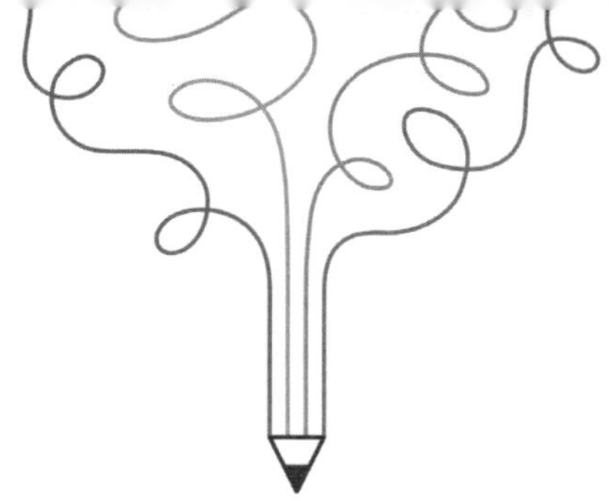

CHAPTER THREE

I spend the day with Layla. She shops for college clothes with her graduation money, and I dutifully hold her purse while she tries things on, since a new wardrobe isn't in my budget. After we part ways, I take the subway back to Yoly and Ricardo's.

Katie is sitting on the front steps with a black-haired boy around our age. They both have open laptops balanced on their laps.

"Hi, Maya," she says when I approach. "How was your first night at Ricardo and Yoly's?"

People keep asking me this question. How am I supposed to describe my first night couch-surfing in a studio apartment with a married couple? Embarrassing, uncomfortable, awful? Those all seem ungrateful. "It was okay."

She gestures at the boy. "This is Lorenzo, my boyfriend." To him, she adds, "Maya's the one who's staying with Yoly and Ricardo."

"Nice to meet you," he says.

I recognize the name. "So you live across from Yoly and Ricardo?"

"Till September. Then my mom and I are moving to Princeton."

Katie closes her laptop. "We're both going to Princeton in

the fall. I'm staying in the dorms, and Lorenzo and his mom are getting an apartment near campus. We're looking at classes right now, trying to figure out if we can have any overlap in our schedules."

"Your mom is going to college with you?" I ask Lorenzo, perching on the step in front of them.

Lorenzo laughs. "Yeah, she's kind of overprotective. She's a nurse and got a job at a hospital over there."

I can't help staring. The idea of a parent picking up her whole life to follow her child to another state is foreign to me. My mother wasn't even at my graduation.

"I know it's weird." He rolls his eyes.

"No. It's not weird. It's wonderful." How would that kind of parental love feel? Something like heartbreak stirs inside me. "Your mom sounds amazing. My parents would never do something like that. My dad just kicked me out, actually. That's why I'm staying with Yoly and Ricardo."

Lorenzo's smile fades. "Kicked you out? Why?" He quickly shakes his head. "Sorry if that's too personal."

"No, it's fine." I look down at the cracked sidewalk. "It's just what my dad does—he kicks out his kids when they graduate, so we can go out and make it in the world on our own."

"But isn't your dad rich?" Katie asks. "I saw that BMW you showed up in."

Pushing away the feelings of heartbreak, I pull my gaze off the ground. There's no sense in trying to hide the truth. "A bit of irony, right? Millionaire Robert James Mitchell kicks his daughter out of the house and sends her away in one of his nicest cars."

There, I've said it. It's the closest I've ever come to criticizing my dad in public.

"Wait. Your father is Robert Mitchell?" Lorenzo asks. "*The* Robert Mitchell?"

"Yep."

"Woooow," Katie says.

Everyone in New York knows who Robert James Mitchell is. Well, anyone who has ever been on Park Avenue and passed the huge M on the side of Dad's building. He built the Mitchell name himself. He didn't come from money. He put himself through college and eventually created revolutionary medical software. There's probably not a single medical facility in the state that doesn't use Mitchell MedTech. From MedTech, his empire expanded, and I can't think of many fields that Mitchell Enterprises doesn't reach now.

"Sounds like your dad sucks," Katie adds.

Layla—the friend who knows the most about my relationship with Dad—would agree. But Dad would insist that he's doing his kids a favor by making sure we don't turn out soft and entitled. "Well, anyway," I say, still stretching for a casual tone, "that's why what your mom is doing, going to Princeton with you, seems pretty cool to me."

Lorenzo gives me a half smile. "Yeah, she's not so bad."

"And she makes the best lumpia," Katie chimes in. "Did Yoly tell you about Sunday dinners?"

"No, what's that?"

"Once a week everyone from the three apartments in the building gets together for a potluck, and each of us takes a turn hosting. This week it'll be at my place. Next time it's at Lorenzo's, then Yoly's. Hopefully you can come!"

"I don't really have anywhere else to go, so yeah, I'll be there." That came out wrong. I quickly add, "It sounds wonderful."

"My mom always brings her lumpia. No matter what, you can count on that," Lorenzo says.

"What's lumpia?" I ask.

"Oh my gosh!" Katie says. "Lumpia is the best. I can't believe you've never had it."

"You've been missing out," Lorenzo agrees. "It's a spring roll, kind of like an egg roll but a hundred times better. They're from the Philippines, where my mom was born."

"I can't wait to try it. Thanks for the invite." I shift my bag on my shoulder and stand up. "I'd better head inside. Nice to meet you, Lorenzo."

"You too." He gives me a small wave, and Katie says, "See you later, Maya," as if we've known each other for years.

I go up the stairs, fishing the key Yoly gave me out of my purse. As I reach the landing my phone buzzes with a notification. I've got a new follower on ChitChat—Katie Canales. She really is going full-tilt with the friendliness. I feel obligated to follow her back, so that we at least break even and she hasn't wasted ten cents following a lurker account.

Across from Yoly and Ricardo's door is Lorenzo's apartment. Several pairs of shoes are lined up neatly next to the door. I'm eager to meet Daisy, this mother who would drop everything to follow her son to college just so she can be there for him. Meanwhile, here I am trying to navigate this new stage of my life feeling so, so alone.

I turn the key and am greeted by the smell of garlic wafting through the air and guitar music streaming through the speakers. "Hey, Maya. Come try this stir-fry sauce I'm making."

I drop my bag on the couch and walk to the stove, where Yoly feeds me a spoonful of sauce. "Yum, that's so good."

She hands over the large wooden spoon. "Here, keep stirring. I need to do some chopping."

I stare at the spoon, which was in my mouth a second ago. I drop it into the sink, take a clean one out of the silverware drawer, and start stirring.

"So heads up," Yoly says, "tomorrow night, some people are coming over for a meeting. Sorry, we're going to be using your bed. It won't run too late, I promise."

"Of course. This is your place. I'm just grateful you're letting me stay here."

She chops pieces of broccoli and tosses them into a saucepan. "It's for a group that meets a couple times a month to talk about issues affecting our community. We usually host because all the other people in the group live with roommates and have even less space to share. It can get crowded here, but I like having people around."

"Oh, speaking of having people around, Katie told me about Sunday dinner."

Yoly's smile widens. "Sunday dinner is the best. I love our neighbors in this building. It feels like a little family."

I like the idea of a little family. At the moment, I'm feeling like I have no family at all. "I met Lorenzo."

"Love Lorenzo. He's brilliant. He and Katie both are. They're like number one and number two in their class. I forget who's number one and who's number two. They're both so, so smart."

"I can't believe Lorenzo's mom is leaving her job and her home to follow him to Princeton."

Yoly shakes her head. "Daisy is like the world's biggest helicopter parent. It's fine with me, though, because that means we get their apartment. It'll be so nice to have an actual bedroom."

Ricardo comes home, and we eat the stir-fry with rice. It's a cozy setup, reminding me of nights when Dad wasn't home and I'd have dinner with Melinda in the kitchen. In fact, in the years since Mom and Daniel moved away, I've probably shared more meals with Melinda than anyone else. I think wistfully of our afternoon debriefings over veggies and her homemade dip, when I filled her in on all the mundane details of high school and she dispensed the latest building gossip.

After dinner I volunteer to do the dishes, and Yoly gives me a quick tutorial on how to use the dishwasher. I want to call my abuela, Mamá Juana, and tell her it's a must-have time-saver.

Ricardo and Yoly take glasses of wine to the couch. Across the room on the olive-green lounge chair are my pillow and neatly folded sheet. I didn't put them there; I'm used to Melinda making my bed each day. I suppose that's a luxury that comes with your rich dad hiring a live-in housekeeper, but Yoly and Ricardo are not my housekeepers. I'll need to remember to clear off the couch every morning when I wake up.

Yoly puts her feet in Ricardo's lap while they talk about their day. Suddenly I feel like a third wheel again. I am most certainly in their way.

I sit at the small table with my laptop to work on my weekly piece for Victoria and the pitches I want to send to the teen magazines. I reach into my messenger bag for my brainstorming notebook, the one where I jot down ideas I'd like to write about.

It's not there. I must've left it in my desk, back in my room at Dad's apartment.

I need that notebook. In my two years of reporting for the school paper, all my best articles have taken shape on those pages. I still have lots of good ideas in there, germs of longer pieces, even some preliminary research notes.

I'll have to make do without it for now. I can at least finish the book review for Victoria. My notes for that are in a different notebook, one I do have with me, and the draft is saved on my laptop.

Dutifully I flip open my other notebook, with my running list of possible books to review and my many musings on them. I like using pen and paper rather than a digital option. Ink seeps into the fibers of the page, making my thoughts permanent instead of easily erasable with the tapping of my fingers—more likely to materialize into something real than typed letters on a screen.

". . . and ICE was right there, waiting for their shift to start," Ricardo is telling Yoly. "They picked up six people from Martin's Meats, and they're just sitting in detention."

"That's awful. I hope you can help them," Yoly says. "Ugh, that reminds me—have you heard anything about a guy called Bernard Wright? I saw his name floating around social media today, and it didn't sound good. Some politician spewing anti-immigrant vitriol . . ."

"Doesn't ring a bell. Is he local?"

"He's in the state legislature, I think?" Yoly swipes across her phone screen. "Yeah, state assemblyman. He's from Greene County, owns a resort up there. Seems like he's been getting some high-profile coverage lately."

"I'll look him up," says Ricardo. "Might be worth talking about at the group meeting tomorrow. Julissa's really plugged into state politics; she can probably bring us up to speed."

I've made zero progress on my book review. I put in my earbuds and try to drown out my hosts' voices with music, but I work best in silence. And seeing Yoly and Ricardo right in front of me makes them hard to ignore.

I've been spoiled, I guess. I'm not used to working with other people around. The last few years, I've had practically the entire apartment to myself, with Mom, Victoria, and Daniel gone and with Dad perpetually at work. Melinda would be in and out, between her various errands, but she always gave me plenty of space when I needed to focus on something, and the place is big enough that I could easily forget she was there.

I shouldn't resent my lack of productivity, though, given that I have a roof over my head and will very soon be able to crawl onto that lumpy couch for the night.

CHAPTER FOUR

Two days after graduation, I take the subway to the Midtown library branch for my first day of work. My shift starts at ten, slightly later than Yoly's, so I'm commuting on my own. Mom used to bring me to this library for story time when I was little; I'd sit on her lap on the royal-blue carpet listening to stories come alive. In high school, I was thrilled to line up the volunteering gig two days a week. Now, for the first time, I'm getting paid to be here. As I put on my new nametag, I feel different, more grown-up.

In practice, my job isn't that different from my volunteering routine. I spend several hours shelving books and tidying up the children's sections. Lunch catches me by surprise because I'm not used to working a full-time schedule. Yoly has me clock out for my break, which gives me just enough time to grab a sandwich from the library café. I'm going to have to plan better by packing a lunch, because I cannot afford an overpriced sandwich every day.

Yoly and I both get done with work at six, just as the library's closing. Though it's not even dark yet, I'm glad to have her company on the short trip back to Morningside Heights. After she's asked how my first day went, we make plans for next week's meeting of our classics book club. Yoly helped me organize this group last year, and we facilitate a meeting at the library once a month. This month we'll be discussing *Go Tell It on the Mountain* by James Baldwin, one of my favorites.

As I sit next to her on the subway, Yoly reaches into her purse and pulls out a magazine, folded open to a short story titled "In Justice We Trust."

She says, "I want you to read this. It's the library copy, I've checked it out for you."

I take it and flip to the front cover. This is a magazine I haven't heard of, one that seems to publish mainly crime fiction and thriller stories. "I don't really read this kind of thing."

Yoly snorts. "You mean anything written in the last fifty years? Let me see what's in your bag. I bet it's some book we were all forced to read in freshman English."

"Classics. They're called classics, Yoly. Tell me again why you were an English major."

"I like some classics, but I'd much rather discover something new than reread *Pride and Prejudice* for the millionth time."

"Agree to disagree. *Pride and Prejudice* is the best book ever written."

"Hey, I love it too, but interesting stories still get written and published every day. I really think you'd enjoy Junior Vega's work." She taps the magazine cover. "He's been published in several literary journals over the past year or so. And he has a huge following on ChitChat. He shares one new paragraph on his ChitChat account every day."

I shake my head. "ChitChat? Are you for real, Yoly? You're letting a social media app shape your literary taste?"

"You're such a snob, Maya. If a white person didn't write it a hundred years ago, it's not valid?"

"I didn't say that." In fact, I've read plenty of recent YA

books that Yoly has recommended to me, and I've even liked some of them. "But I read *literary* fiction. I doubt this guy is for me."

"Look, Junior Vega is writing some really genre-bending stuff. He's got this intricate prose style, and he tackles straightforward themes in sophisticated ways. People are calling it vengeance lit because it's about settling scores, righting wrongs—stuff that would usually get dismissed as pulpy."

I read the first few sentences. "This is kind of creepy. Kind of dark and sinister."

"It *is* dark and sinister. That's part of what makes it interesting." Yoly takes the magazine back and shoves it into my messenger bag. "I want you to give it a try."

"Fine, I'll take a look," I say, which probably means I'll read a few more sentences and then return the magazine to the library. But considering how much I owe Yoly, the least I can do is indulge her questionable literary taste a little.

Yoly kicks her shoes off the minute we walk into the studio. "Mmmm, smells good." She kisses Ricardo, who has a pot of soup simmering on the stove, and grabs some bowls from a cabinet above his head.

"I can put those on the table." I take the bowls from her and clear mail off the table. When Ricardo brings the pot over, we all sit down. "I love how you two take turns cooking," I tell them.

Yoly blows on her spoonful of hot soup. "Wait until you taste his arepas. He's making them for Sunday dinner."

"You know, I can take a turn cooking too," I say. "My abuela showed me how to make a couple dishes when we visited her in Guatemala every summer. It's been a few years since I've been there, but . . ."

"That would be awesome," Yoly says. "And I can teach you a few other easy recipes."

"I'd love that. Thanks." I should also offer to chip in for groceries, especially since I'll need at least some basic sandwich ingredients for my weekday lunches. I never thought about how much planning Melinda must do for our meals at home, even though I was used to her regular grocery runs and the hours she spent in the kitchen.

Yoly remarks, "I didn't know you had family in Guatemala."

"Yeah, my mom was born there. She came here on a student visa to go to medical school. That's where she met my dad. When we were little, my mom would take us every year for summer vacation. And then one year, right before I started high school, my dad just didn't let us go. I don't know why. He told her she couldn't take us anymore. He's always called the shots in our family."

Yoly and Ricardo look at each other. "And she's living there now?" Ricardo asks.

"Yeah, she moved there about two years ago."

Yoly reaches out and puts her hand on mine. "I'm sorry, Maya. I'm sure that's very hard. You still need her."

I wasn't expecting the sudden onset of emotion, but I do need her. "Well, I understand why she left. The indigenous people in that region need medical care, and she felt they needed her more than New Yorkers. Plus, my abuela has been having medical problems and Mom wanted to be closer so she could help take care of her." Above all, though, she was trying to get away from Dad. Even after the divorce, he was still trying to tell her what to do.

"Two things can be true at the same time," Ricardo says. "She's doing great service to people who really need her *and* it's hard to have your mom be so far away."

I try to lighten the mood. "I guess the polar opposite is that your mother can move in with you when you go away to college." I force a laugh for good measure.

"Oh boy!" Yoly laughs. "Daisy and Lorenzo. There is no one like them. I love them."

"I'm going to really miss them," says Ricardo. "I'll be the only guy at Sunday dinner. We'll have to make them come visit once in a while."

"Doesn't Katie's brother come to Sunday dinner?" I ask.

"Jake? No, not really," Ricardo says. "Sometimes if it's at their apartment, he's around, but he keeps to himself."

Yoly puts her hand on Ricardo's arm. "But Katie, Daisy, and Lorenzo are all leaving. That means Sunday dinner will be down to just us."

Ricardo makes a face. "I think we have to make new friends, love."

"What about your friends who are coming over tonight?" I ask.

"They're more like acquaintances we do community work with," says Yoly. "They're cool, but we don't really hang out just for fun."

Ricardo checks his phone. "Speaking of which, Brady and Julissa just texted that they're walking up now."

"Sorry, Maya—we're taking the couch, aka your bed." Yoly hastily grabs our bowls and brings them to the sink.

"Don't even worry about it. This is your place." I've barely finished saying this when my mom's face pops up on my phone. I almost forgot she'd promised to FaceTime me tonight. Yoly tells me I can take the call on their bed behind the curtain.

I sit cross-legged on the bed, and the curtain offers a little privacy, but I can still hear their community acquaintances filtering in.

Mom's hair is pulled back in a loose braid with a few strands framing her face. She's not wearing any makeup, and she looks tired. "Mija! I'm so sorry I missed your graduation, linda. I just couldn't get away. How are you?"

"Hi, Mom. I'm doing all right. How are you?"

"So busy! I just got back from my trip up to the mountains. So many people there need medical care. I saved a mother in labor who almost bled to death. And she already has four kids. Can you imagine those four kids without a mother?"

"I kinda know what that feels like right now," I say before I can think.

"¡Ay, hija! Really? That's what you think? That you don't have a mother? I'm right here." She points to herself.

"I'm sorry. It just sucks having you so far away."

"I know, Mayita. It's hard for me too. My kids are scattered so far from me. But I have to be here. Some of the people I'm reaching have never seen a doctor before. I'm making a difference here. I wish you could understand."

"I do understand. That doesn't mean that I can't miss you and feel a little sorry for myself."

"Why don't you come visit me this summer? I'll buy you a ticket. El monstruo can't stop you now that you're eighteen." That's what she calls my dad—the only thing she's called him since the divorce.

"I don't know, Mom. I need to save money for student housing this fall."

"Bueno, think about it. And let me know how much you're going to need for the residence hall."

"Well, I don't have to pay the first installment until September, and I'm going to save all I can."

"I know it's hard now, but it's so much better that you're out from under that roof. Ese hombre es un maldito. The only thing he was good for was giving me mis tres hijos. I love you, mija. Call me if you need anything."

"Bye, Mom. Love you."

Her face disappears from my screen, and I feel so alone. The small area behind the curtain is suddenly stifling. I get off the bed, slide the curtain over.

Two men and two women, along with Yoly and Ricardo, turn to look at me. Yoly makes quick introductions, and I wave as I walk to the one chair left at the table. I pull my laptop from my messenger bag, hoping to finish this week's book review and start writing the pitch letters. I don't want to interfere with their meeting.

Five minutes later I find myself checking out the prices of noise-canceling headphones online. The good ones are pricier than I would like, considering my current budget. But my earbuds aren't cutting it.

One woman, whom Yoly introduced as Julissa, is talking quite loudly. She holds a tablet in one hand and gestures with her other hand to emphasize her points. "So, this is Bernard Wright." She shows the others a picture on her tablet—a generic middle-aged white guy with dark hair and a crisp suit. "He owns the Hilltop Ski Resort in Upstate New York. He's been in the state assembly for the past twelve years." She scrolls to a video and presses Play.

A deep voice fills the room. "New York has been overrun

with illegals. It could be an illegal doing your dry cleaning, serving you coffee, cleaning the lobby of your apartment building. Local leadership does nothing. They're inviting them in, protecting them from law enforcement. We need state leadership to stand up and do something about it."

Julissa pauses the clip. "He just started an exploratory committee for the governor's race. And he has a *lot* of money backing him. I've looked into it. His state assembly campaign fund received waaaay more contributions than it got last quarter, and if he does decide to run for higher office instead of reelection to his assembly seat, all that money can be transferred to his next campaign."

"Where's the money coming from?" asks a young blond man with glasses—I think his name is Brady.

"Nobody knows, because he's not required to disclose that information yet. But it feels fishy, and it makes me nervous. Here's another sample of his greatest hits from a fundraiser a few weeks ago." She scrolls to another video clip. Part of me wants to look away and focus on my work, but I just keep watching.

Bernard Wright is at a podium. "What they're doing is simple—they're bringing them in from other countries. All illegals. They're giving them jobs, a place to live, so that they and their offspring can replace those of us who have been here for generations. If we don't do something now, all of these illegals will be voting soon. They're being groomed by the liberals to vote for liberals, and once they start replacing us, we will never win another election."

Brady grimaces. "This is basically 'great replacement' theory he's describing here. It's very disturbing ideology."

"We're aware," Ricardo says with the slightest undercurrent of irritation in his voice.

Brady doesn't seem to notice. "And he's seriously thinking of running for governor?"

"Sure looks like it," says Julissa grimly.

Brady scoffs. "Well, with talk like that, he stands no chance. Not in our state. This is New York."

"We can't discount him," Ricardo says. "It's easy to say, 'That can't happen here,' until it does."

"Agreed," says Yoly. "We have to get this out there. If people know what he's saying, hopefully they'll realize how dangerous he is and make sure he doesn't stand a real chance."

Julissa nods. "I'm forwarding this to all of you. Share it on your socials. Get loud about it."

I think I'm with Brady on this one. No way would people in our state take this ridiculous man seriously. I turn away from the group as they continue their discussion of Bernard Wright. I've got my own work to do.

CHAPTER FIVE

Sunday dinner prep is a bit chaotic. Ricardo assembles the arepas, Yoly makes brownies, and I wash the dishes they've used, almost like I'm an expert at it now. Yoly wants the kitchen completely clean before we leave so we don't come home to a big mess. Luckily, we're not going far—just down the stairs.

"Hi, come in!" Katie opens the door for us. Lorenzo is sitting on her couch with a petite middle-aged woman who must be Daisy. She has straight black hair in a short bob and a scrutinizing smile.

Ricardo and Yoly go into the small kitchen to put their dishes down. Daisy gets up and gives them each a hug before turning to me. "Hello, Maya. Lorenzo told me you moved in across the hall. Welcome to the building."

"Thank you. It's really nice to meet you."

After we've all filled our plates, I end up sitting on the couch with Yoly and Ricardo, while Lorenzo and Katie sit cross-legged on the carpet and put their plates on the coffee table in front of them. Daisy sits in a recliner by the door.

"So your father kicked you out of the house?" Daisy asks me.

"Mom!" Lorenzo yelps.

I look from Daisy to Lorenzo and back. "Yes, it's his family tradition."

"Terrible. What a terrible thing. So much money and won't take care of his own children." Daisy shakes her head and takes a bite of one of Ricardo's arepas.

"Sorry," Lorenzo mouths to me.

I shake my head to let him know it's okay. This is part of the reason I've never talked much about my dad's plan for us; I know it will strike most people as outlandish at best and cruel at worst.

That's when Katie's brother, Jake, walks in from another room. I haven't seen him since that day I moved in and he gave me their laundry detergent. He wears light brown corduroy pants, a blue T-shirt with an image of the Puerto Rican flag, and a pair of worn black sneakers.

Katie smiles at him, her dimples showing. "Hi, Jakey. There's plenty of food left if you want some."

"Thanks, I'm good," Jake says, holding up a hand in acknowledgment to the group as a whole. "I grabbed something earlier." He walks to the kitchen and takes a water bottle from the fridge.

Katie whispers to me, "Don't mind him. He can be moody sometimes."

"I have a sister like that," I say and turn back to the group.

Daisy is talking about Lorenzo and Katie. "—and the reason you see them studying on the stoop every day is because they're not allowed to be in my apartment by themselves when I'm at work, and they can't be here if Jake is not here. The last thing we need is for Katie to get pregnant and—"

"Mom!" Lorenzo dramatically hides his head in his hands.

A quick look at Jake reveals a slight smile I didn't know his face was capable of forming.

"What, Lorenzo? If Katie gets pregnant, you will both lose

your scholarships and have to drop out." Daisy turns to the group. "Then Lorenzo won't become a doctor and Katie won't become whatever she's planning to be. What is it you're planning to be?"

Katie shrugs slightly. "I don't know yet."

Daisy leans back in her chair, crossing her arms like Katie's answer tells her all she needs to know.

Yoly changes the subject, telling a funny story from her library shift. The oddest things can happen at the library.

I get up for more lumpia because yum, they're as tasty as Lorenzo and Katie said. As I go into the kitchen, Jake walks past me into another room and closes the door behind him.

Katie's right behind me, serving herself one of Yoly's brownies. "I hope you're having fun," she says to me.

"Oh, yeah. This is a great group, and the food is sooo good."

"Sunday dinners are my favorite." She pops a piece of brownie in her mouth. "You're working at the Midtown library, right?"

"Yeah, plus I write for my sister's magazine, and now I'm trying to pitch articles to other publications."

"That's so cool. Let me know what magazines, and I'll check them out."

I lean against the counter, chewing on my fifth lumpia. "Well, I haven't been able to do much lately." I barely got this week's piece for *Latina at Large* turned in on time, and it wasn't as polished as I would've liked. "I think I need to find a quiet space to get work done."

She raises her eyebrows. "Does the library not qualify?"

I laugh at this very fair question. "Well, most nights it closes just as my shift ends. It's open later on Tuesdays and

Wednesdays, but Yoly doesn't want me staying after work and then taking the subway home late by myself." To be honest, I'm not wild about that prospect either. "Which leaves the weekend, but by then I'm so sick of being in that building . . ." I trail off, afraid that I sound spoiled. There are other libraries around the city where I could go over the weekend, but that would still feel like being at work. It'd be uncomfortable to sit at the patrons' tables when my instincts would be telling me to shelve books. I doubt I'd be able to focus on my writing. I brace myself to be reminded that this is a rich-girl problem.

But Katie's response surprises me. "Well, if you're interested, my brother runs a writing room not far from here."

"A writing room?"

"It's actually an apartment where people go to write."

It sounds a bit strange, sort of like an urban legend. I think I've heard of the concept before, but I've never seen one.

"My brother manages it for the owner," Katie goes on. "I think there's something like thirty people who use it at different times during the day. Jake practically lives there when he's not at his other job. Each person pays a monthly fee that works out to about five dollars a day, and they can go there anytime. If you want, I can talk to him."

On the one hand, I'm supposed to be saving my money, but on the other hand, five dollars a day is less than I'm used to spending on coffee. "Yeah, that does sound like something I'd be interested in."

Katie smiles. "I can take you there tomorrow, and we can talk to Jake."

We return to the studio completely full. Yoly and Ricardo invite me to watch a show with them. The three of us squeeze onto the couch together, but I have a hard time concentrating on the show because all I can think of is this writing room Katie mentioned.

It would be a nice alternative to working at the kitchen table surrounded by non-writing people, or huddling on someone else's bed behind a curtain, or fighting the constant urge to do a work-related task at one of the library branches. Still, entering an unknown apartment with people from all over the city who are complete strangers sounds daunting—and a little ominous. I can just imagine my mom's favorite cautioning words: *ten cuidado*. I wouldn't know a single soul in there, with the exception of the unfriendly brother of my new neighbor.

But I wouldn't need to know anyone or befriend anyone. All I need is a quiet place to write.

I decide to follow through with meeting Katie and checking out this writing room.

On Monday morning before either of us has to be at work, Katie and I walk about ten blocks from our place, and she leads me up the steps of an old prewar building. On the third floor, she knocks quietly on a door, which is opened by a woman who acknowledges her with a nod and lets us inside. The room we enter is sparse in furnishings and decor. The exposed brick wall is bare and the other three walls are painted white, with no embellishments. There are a couple of tables, plus a couch where a middle-aged man in tan slacks and a wool sweater is sleeping. Along one wall are half a dozen cubicles, each with a chair and enough desk space for a laptop. A few of them are filled. A closet-sized kitchen holds a refrigerator and a sink; an even smaller bathroom is wedged beside it. A door on the far end of the room is closed. Just behind the couch is a small window that leads to the fire escape.

Jake sits on the fire escape. A cigarette dangles from his mouth, and he's writing in a little notebook. Katie walks over to the window and knocks on it, which momentarily wakes the sleeping man. Jake takes one final drag on his cigarette and drops it to the ground, squashing it with his sneaker. He opens the window and steps over the sleeping man's head to climb back inside.

"Hi, Jakey," Katie says as he closes the window.

Jake tucks his small pencil behind his ear—something I've never seen a person do in real life—and stuffs his notebook into his back pocket. "Hey, Kate. What's going on?" He eyes me curiously, and I inadvertently reciprocate. He's wearing a black T-shirt that reads "No Newt is good Newt." I'll need to Google that later to see what it means.

"You remember Maya?" Katie asks.

Jake nods and I give him a small wave, which I immediately regret because it looks so goofy.

"She wants to use the writing room. Do you have space for one more?"

"This isn't a study hall." He speaks to Katie, not to me.

Katie makes a face. "Oh, come on. It's a writing room; she would be writing."

"I thought you said she was rich. This is a place for folks who don't have the money to rent an entire office for themselves."

"I'm not rich," I whisper, hoping the others in the room aren't overhearing the conversation.

"Isn't your last name Mitchell?"

Katie pushes him on the shoulder. "Come on, Jake, don't be a jerk."

Jake sighs. "I can give you an application. There's a twenty-dollar application fee. I need three references before I can give you a key. Membership fee is due quarterly. We have some ground rules."

I nod.

Jake digs his hands deep into the pockets of his blue corduroys. "This is the quiet room, and that's the absolute silence room," he says, nodding toward the closed door. "You can talk softly in here, to share ideas or ask each other questions, but keep the volume low. Glen here is our gauge." Jake signals toward the sleeping man. "If he starts stirring, that means it's getting too loud."

Katie chuckles. "I think he's been asleep every time I've come in here."

"In the absolute silence room, there is *no* talking. The only sound allowed is the clicking of keys on laptops. We have high-speed internet in both rooms. Cell phones have to be silenced in both rooms."

It all seems so strict—overly elaborate for such a small enterprise. But the structure of it is almost comforting. I've missed knowing what to expect from my surroundings.

I pull a twenty from my wallet and hand it to Jake.

Jake nods, stuffing the bill into his pants pocket. He walks to the corner that's supposed to be the kitchen and takes a sheet of paper from a drawer. "Here's an application," he says, walking back to Katie and me. "You can bring it back here when you've filled it out, and I'll try to let you know soon."

"Thank you," I say, taking the form.

"I'll see you later, Kate." Jake gives his sister a hug.

Katie holds him in the embrace. "Bye, see you tonight."

Before I can say goodbye, Jake is already crawling back out the window.

Outside, the humid air is filled with the nearby sounds of cars honking and with their accompanying exhaust. It's all familiar, even in a neighborhood I don't know well. Victoria's offer to live with her in LA means stability, but I don't think I could ever leave this city.

"I'm sorry about my brother," Katie says as we head back toward our block. "He's a great person, but he can be kind of cold to people he doesn't know well."

"It's fine. That's just New York. I think we're all like that to some degree."

"I guess so. I just wish he wasn't so . . . distrustful."

I laugh. "Again, typical New York."

"Well, he wasn't always like that. He's had a really hard time since my parents died."

"Oh, I'm sorry."

Katie lifts her shoulders in a not-quite-shrug. "It's been three years. It was hard on me too, but he just hasn't gotten past it. Not that I'm *past* it—I don't think a day goes by that I don't think about them. But with him, not a day goes by that he doesn't relive it."

Katie stops at the end of the block and waits for a line of cars to pass. It's not till we've crossed the intersection that she speaks again. "They were killed in a car accident. It was a hit-and-run."

My hand quickly goes up to cover my mouth. "How horrible. I'm so sorry."

"Yeah. We were all in the car when it happened, but it was at night and I was asleep. I don't even remember it. Jake saw it all."

"I'm so sorry." I'm just repeating myself, but I don't know what else to say. I've never been struck by the cruel fist of death. Everyone in my immediate family is still alive; even seventy-six-year-old Mamá Juana is still making the rounds in her garden taking care of her flowers.

"Sorry to dump all this on you," Katie adds. "I just don't want you to judge my brother for the way he is."

"I don't think anything bad about him. I've got family members who are a hundred times ruder and more bitter, and they don't have any reason as compelling as that one."

Katie smiles, fully showing her dimples. "That's really understanding of you. I hope it works out with the writing room."

"Thanks. I hope so too."

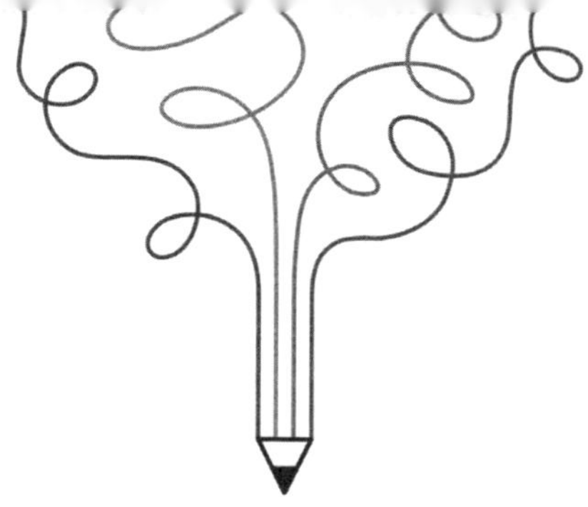

CHAPTER SIX

The next morning, I finish the writing room application as soon as Yoly and Ricardo leave for work. It's quite thorough—three pages, double-sided. It asks questions like what I write, what my goals are, and the hours I plan to be there. For references, I list Victoria, Yoly, and Layla. I also have to pass a background check. It feels like applying for colleges all over again.

When I'm done I have just enough time to take a shower, eat the spinach omelet Ricardo left me, and do the dishes. That's become our routine. Yoly and Ricardo don't trust me with food prep after I ruined one of their pans trying to make eggs. Let's face it, I only know how to make a few things, and Yoly did say she would teach me more recipes, but there really hasn't been time. So each morning, either Yoly or Ricardo makes breakfast and I handle the cleanup. I've at least learned how to use the dishwasher—though last night I noticed Yoly surreptitiously rearranging some of the dishes after I loaded them. Guess the cups have to be turned upside down.

My final task is to slap together a simple sandwich for lunch. As I pack it in my messenger bag, I come across the magazine Yoly gave me, with the story she wanted me to read. I guess I'll have to pick it up eventually, as I did tell Yoly I would.

On my way to the library, I stop by the writing room to

give my application to Jake. Jake opens the door when I knock, but he doesn't invite me inside. He says nothing in the way of greeting, just looks at me expectantly.

"Hi." I smile. His unfriendliness will not distract me from my purpose. "Here's my application."

He scans the pages and looks up at me, almost as if registering for the first time that I am an actual person standing in front of him. "I'll call your references and wait for the background check, then I'll be in touch." He nods slightly before closing the door.

I text Victoria to give her a heads-up about the reference call. Before I've even reached the stairway, Victoria is FaceTiming me.

"What is a writing room?" is her opening line.

I quickly exit the building, not wanting Jake to hear any part of this conversation. "It's a shared workspace for writers in the city."

She rolls her eyes. "That city is so weird. Why can't people write in coffee shops like the rest of the world?"

"It'll be good for me. I haven't been able to get a lot done lately."

"Are your hosts throwing wild parties in their apartment?"

"Nothing like that. But they do have this community group that meets there, and the other night I had to listen to them talk about some creep of a politician." As I walk to the subway, I tell her about the bizarre ideology of Bernard Wright, potential gubernatorial candidate.

Victoria scowls. "Just what New York needs—another unhinged bigot inciting people to commit hate crimes. Can you please just move here already?"

"Vic, are we going to have this argument every time we FaceTime?"

"Yes. I just think you'd be safer here. With me."

"Look, I have to go to work. Can you call me after you get that reference check call? The guy's name is Jake, and I want to know every detail of the conversation."

"Why?"

"Bye." I disconnect from the call and descend to the subway station.

I'm slowly getting used to the subway. I do miss coffee with Ernie and a comfortable ride every morning, but there's a certain satisfaction that comes with this fragment of independence I'm beginning to feel.

There's no cell service in the tunnels between stations, which might be the hardest part of the commute to get used to. Whenever we stop at a station, I use those few seconds to do a quick social media check. Layla posted on ChitChat thirty-two minutes ago. It's a bathroom selfie inside the Previdial Healthcare building. She starts her "summer youth experience" internship today. It's basically a made-up position for relatives of higher-ups at Previdial. Nepotism at its finest. Layla's father is the CFO. Not that I can judge, considering how I got my gig writing reviews of old books for *Latina at Large*.

Layla is so excited about this pre-college internship, even though it'll basically entail getting coffee and making copies. And she looks absolutely amazing in her pink Chanel skirt-suit and high ponytail. I double-tap her picture and add a comment to the current count of eighty-seven. When I scroll down, I see Lucinda's recent post, which is most definitely not a bathroom selfie. It's a professional shot on a beach in Hawaii, Lucinda wearing a bright yellow Calvin Klein bikini that'll probably show up on glossy magazine pages in the near future.

A free suggested post appears under Lucinda's photo—ChitChat does this sometimes to prompt people to follow more accounts. This one is a video that auto-plays before I even register what it is.

Bernard Wright's blistery voice fills my earbuds. "They're calling these people asylum-seekers. This is not asylum. They're not refugees. They're illegals. It's illegals coming over the border illegally, and this government seems to want to help them no matter what. Well, no longer. Not in New York. We have to stand up. Or they're going to replace every last one of us . . ."

The subway car starts to move again, and I lose service, which for once is a relief.

I think about my mom. She wasn't born here; she came on a student visa. I don't know how hard it was for her to get that visa, and I sure don't know the situations of other people who are trying to come over here. I don't understand how anyone can be so hateful toward people who are probably leaving behind very difficult circumstances.

At the next station, I tap the post of Wright's speech clip and select the block feature so I won't have to see anything else from that account. Maybe now I'll be able to put it out of my mind.

When I get off at my stop, I message Layla, wishing her luck on the first day of her internship—and telling her to expect a phone call from Jake. She texts back a kissy face emoji.

Victoria texts me while I'm at work to tell me she talked to Jake, but I can't respond right away. During my lunch break, while I wolf down my sad little sandwich I text her back to thank her.

Victoria: Your Jake-o is a weirdo.

Me: What do you mean?

Victoria: He was overly formal, like he was vetting someone for the vice presidency. Are you trustworthy? Are you someone who follows rules? Am I aware of any outstanding warrants?

Me: Did it sound like he would approve me?

Victoria: Don't know. I told him you freelance for me and need office space to meet your deadlines.

Me: Thanks for talking to him.

Victoria: I looked up that Wright guy. He is deranged.

Me: I hope NY voters agree.

Victoria: Hard to predict. Yet another reason Californians are superior to New Yorkers.

I send her a poop emoji and say bye.

My shift wraps up with the monthly meeting of our classics book club. By the time I make my way to the small, insufficiently lit conference room we use, the usuals are filtering in, talking among themselves. It's a small group, mostly retired New Yorkers mixed in with a couple of women straight off the subway from their nine-to-fives.

Louisa, a retired attorney who wears her long gray hair in a high ponytail, is talking to Gregory, who's already read most of our selections several times. They're joined by Concha, a retired librarian. Her jet-black bob defies her age, but Yoly told me that Concha met Pablo Neruda when he came to New York in 1966 and she was working for the New York Public Library.

" . . . it's not *just* a book for children," Louisa is insisting. "It's much more complex than it seems on the surface."

"Another pitch for *Little Women*?" I ask Yoly, who's arrived ahead of me with her paperback copy of *Go Tell It on the Mountain.*

Yoly responds with a good-natured eye roll. "She's starting to wear me down. I think we've just gotta do it for next month and get it over with."

Louisa is an everytimer, and at each meeting since the book club started last year, she's been pushing for us to read

Little Women. She is, after all, named for Louisa May Alcott, she has reminded us several times.

Gregory, who's also never missed a meeting, remains a hard sell. "What if we read some of Alcott's lesser-known work instead? Like her thriller, *A Long Fatal Love Chase*? Or some of her short stories?"

Louisa snorts. "The potboilers? You've got to be kidding. She wrote those under a pseudonym for a reason. She didn't want anyone to associate her with them."

I guess that worked, because I had no idea Louisa May Alcott wrote thrillers. I glance at Yoly to see if this is as surprising to her as it is to me, but she doesn't seem fazed.

"Well, I think they're actually the most interesting things she wrote," Gregory insists, adding dryly, "not that the bar is very high."

Before Louisa—or I—can defend the nuances of *Little Women*, Yoly gets the group's attention so we can discuss the actual book of the month.

Four days later, I wake up to an email from Jacobo Canales. I know enough Spanish to pronounce *Jacobo* with an *h* sound. Learning Jake's full name feels significant for a reason I can't name.

The intro to the email reads *Dear Applicant*, like he couldn't even take the time to plug in my name. I've been approved for writing room membership, and the email details the hours, code of conduct, and payment schedule. I know Victoria will agree to cover the monthly fee if I ask; maybe it'd even count as a business expense. But I remind myself that it costs less than one fancy caffeinated drink per day. I can handle this.

Ricardo has already left for work and Yoly isn't far behind him, though she makes sure to leave a box of Chex on the counter for me. While I eat a bowl of cereal, I check social media, block two more suggested ChitChat posts featuring Bernard Wright with captions like "True leadership!!" and distract myself from that unpleasantness by rereading Jake's email. At the very end of the message, there's actually a slightly personalized line: he says I can stop by his apartment today to pick up the key to the writing room.

After taking my time in the tiny shower, I put on my favorite jeans and a striped tee—a simple outfit compared to Layla's powder-blue Gucci midi skirt and tank. I wonder if she plans to document her outfit on social media every day this summer.

I slide my laptop into my messenger bag, running my hand over the soft cotton. It has light brown leather trim surrounding bright emerald-green woven fabric with blue and pale yellow diamonds. When my mom sent me the bag, she said that diamonds in Guatemalan weaving represent the four corners of the universe and the path of the sun in its daily movement.

I think about those four corners daily, wondering why my family has to be scattered across them: Mom to the south, Victoria to the west, me to the east, and Daniel who knows where at any given moment.

I'm not sure why I can't seem to include Dad in this universe. Maybe it's because he's physically and emotionally removed each of us from *his* universe, one by one.

I pull the bag over my shoulder and head downstairs. My knock is quickly answered by Katie. "Hey, Maya!"

I greet Katie and Lorenzo, who's lounging on the couch, his legs crossed at the ankles and his feet resting on the coffee table. If Lorenzo is here, that means Jake must be too, according to Daisy's rules.

"We're about to start a movie," Katie says. "Want to join us?"

"I'm actually heading to work, but I was hoping to grab the writing room key from Jake."

"Oh yeah, he told me they accepted you. That's awesome."

"Thank you so much, Katie. It's all due to you."

"Phsh, no big deal. Come this way—he's in his room."

I follow Katie down the little hallway. Jake's door is open, and he's seated at a desk facing a window. Bookshelves cover every inch of the walls. I need an hour in here by myself to investigate his collection. I'd have to bring my Belle ladder to reach the books on the highest shelves, which are just about scraping the ceiling.

He turns around, surprise framing his face, and takes his earbuds out. "Hey."

"Hi. I got your email. Is it okay if I get the key from you now?"

"Sure." He opens a drawer in his desk and pulls out a small manila envelope, smaller than an index card, and stands up to hand it over. I try to make eye contact, but my eyes are also flashing around the room attempting to catch at least one book title.

I take the envelope from him and focus my eyes on his. "Thank you. Can I start going today?"

He shrugs. "Yeah, sure."

Katie smiles and silently claps her hands. "I love it when things work out."

CHAPTER SEVEN

After work, I stop at the apartment just long enough to scarf down some food before I make my way to the writing room.

As I enter, I see Glen asleep on the couch in much the same position as before and possibly in the same clothes, almost as if he hasn't moved since the last time I was here. Jake is perched in what seems like his usual spot, on the fire escape. He holds a cigarette between two fingers and reads from his pocket-sized notebook. The stubby pencil is pushed behind his ear.

I watch him as he places the cigarette in his mouth and starts writing. He looks up for an instant, catching my eye. I look away quickly and find an empty cubicle.

There are only a couple of people working in the room, two middle-aged women seated next to each other at a table. I think about going into the absolute silence room but decide to stay where I am. These ladies won't be too much distraction. And I like the sense of purposefulness in the air, the soft rhythmic sounds of their fingers on their keyboards signaling that they're hard at work.

It's such a relief to be able to concentrate. I quickly get in the zone and create a pitch letter for one of the teen magazines that Victoria recommended. After racking my brain, trying to remember any of the ideas in my lost notebook, I've settled on pitching an article about how teens can get involved in charity work. I offer to outline different ways to contribute, from volunteering in person to making monetary donations. I can also profile a few highly rated charities, summarizing their missions and achievements.

Such a lot of work for just the possibility of writing one article for one small paycheck.

Once I've sent the pitch, I start drafting my next book review for *Latina at Large*. I go through the handwritten notes I took while rereading *A Tree Grows in Brooklyn* by Betty Smith, picking the plot points and themes I want to highlight in my piece.

After a productive couple of hours, I enjoy the fifteen-minute walk back to Yoly and Ricardo's place. The setting sun rests on my back, filling me with more than just physical warmth. I'm feeling satisfied with what I've accomplished. Not having Ernie to drive me around was a shock at first, but now it's becoming routine. I just have to make sure I leave the writing room by around this time, because I don't think I want to walk these ten blocks in the dark.

When I get to the studio, Ricardo is on the couch-slash-my bed, in the middle of a video call on his laptop. He waves and smiles without taking out his earbuds. I can hear the shower going, so I pull out a chair at the kitchen table.

I told Yoly that I would read Junior Vega's short story. Might as well give it a try while the apartment's relatively quiet; Ricardo is doing more listening than talking on his call.

Almost immediately, I'm swept into the story. Somehow the writer puts me inside the main character's head. I'm seized by the words he uses to describe his hatred for the man who killed his wife and sons. Very little page space is spent describing the murders themselves. Instead, the writer delves into Judge Valdez's mind, and I'm surprised at how compelling the character is. I can feel the judge's loneliness, his desperation. I understand his urge to exact revenge on the person who killed his family.

It isn't that I *like* Judge Valdez. I don't think any writer could manipulate me into siding with evil . . . but is it really evil? This character knows firsthand that the criminal justice system doesn't always hold people accountable for their actions—especially powerful people like the man who murdered his family. Judge Valdez feels he has to take matters into his own hands, not just to satisfy his personal desire for revenge but to balance the scales of justice. Of course I wouldn't endorse vigilante justice in real life, but in the context of this story, I do sympathize with him, even root for him.

While I only intended to read for a few minutes, I'm surprised to see that I've polished off most of the story, giving very little attention to Ricardo's long video call four feet away from me or Yoly's blow-dryer buzzing behind me. I yawn but continue reading.

Yoly was right about the story. It's surprisingly powerful. I look up the author online, but there's not much information about him other than that he's published a few other short stories in various literary magazines. I open ChitChat and find him there right away. I scroll through his long feed of posts, none of which actually show his face.

All the images are of short, typed paragraphs that, when joined together, make a story. You have to read each day's post to get the full story. I go to the beginning of his feed and start reading. The prose sucks me in right away, but I can't help being skeptical of social media as a platform for writing. Anyone can just get on an app and post a paragraph. If it doesn't go through a professional editing process, or at least some form of vetting and revision, can it really call itself literature? Even my little book reviews for *Latina at Large* get a thorough copyedit.

I close the app but decide to check out Junior Vega's work in other literary magazines at the library. Those, at least, have been seen by the eyes of editors.

By the time Yoly's out of the shower and making herself some herbal tea, I'm rereading parts of the story. When she sits down next to me and leans over to see what I'm reading, surprise and elation compete for dominance on her face. "Well?"

"Why can't I put it down?" I shake the magazine in the space between us.

She slams her tea mug on the table. "I know! I told you, didn't I?"

"And you were right. The proverbial page-turner."

"So, you love it?"

"I wouldn't exactly say 'love.' It's like one of those things that are bad for you and you know you shouldn't do, but you can't help it. Like eating a ton of junk food or staying up late."

Yoly laughs. She claps a hand over her mouth; Ricardo's still on his call. "That's what's so interesting about Vega's writing. It's propulsive and accessible, but there are also layers to it. He puts you in the character's mind and sort of warps your thinking."

"I know. I feel guilty that I'm rooting for this guy to do vengeful things, but you can almost understand it. It's his family; he's destroyed. So, how do you reconcile that?"

"Well, you're not a bad person because you root for him. That's just a sign of a great writer. Maybe you could write a review of this story in your next magazine column."

"But it's a classic book review column."

"What is so great about the classics?"

"Yoly! Classic books talk about universal themes and stand the test of time."

She takes a long sip of tea, unfazed. "The vast majority of classics were written by, for, and about white men. How many classics are there about people who look like us?" She says the word *classics* with air quotes.

"I don't know . . . There's the work of Jorge Luis Borges, and Gabriel García-Márquez, and—"

"I'm not saying there are *no* critically acclaimed Latine authors from previous eras," Yoly clarifies. "All I'm saying is that there's room to expand the literary canon. And you've got this cool platform through your sister's magazine. Maybe you can think about what kinds of stories will resonate with young people in this day and age. All the books we were forced to read in high school? Or maybe stories that reflect a wider variety of experiences?"

I'm quiet, staring at the last page of Junior Vega's story.

Yoly lifts her mug again but pauses before she actually drinks from it. "I'm sorry. I'm not trying to tell you what to do. It's just something to think about."

She's absolutely trying to tell me what to do. Which doesn't necessarily mean she's wrong. "Yeah, it's something to think about."

I've always been encouraged to read the classics—by my teachers, by my father.

I can't think of any books on my dad's shelves with characters who look like me.

I job-shadow Yoly and Ricardo through their Saturday chores so I can learn enough to help out. I get familiar with the vacuum and the array of cleaning products appropriate for wiping down various surfaces. Yoly makes spaghetti marinara for lunch and teaches me the recipe. After we've eaten, I pack up my materials and head for the writing room.

Settling into the same cubicle I used yesterday evening, I get to work on my write-up of *A Tree Grows in Brooklyn*. I start to tell the story of eleven-year-old Francie Nolan, but my thoughts keep jumping back to Judge Valdez and his dead family. I can't seem to put aside that story. Phrases keep popping into my mind, demanding that I pay attention to them.

I promised Victoria a piece about a classic novel, not about a brand-new short story published in a noir magazine. The comparison brings to mind Tuesday's book club conversation, when Gregory brought up Louisa May Alcott's "potboilers."

I do a quick search online and learn that she wrote dark, pulpy thrillers under another name. She called them blood and thunder tales. They were heavy on deception, revenge, manipulation, and murder, and apparently nobody took them very seriously at the time—including Alcott; she wrote them strictly to support her family. But some modern scholars think they're notable because they talk about real social issues, like the limitations and dangers women faced at the time.

I read half a chapter of *A Long Fatal Love Chase* and close the tab, unimpressed with the writing style and completely put off by the dialogue. Honestly, Junior Vega's style strikes me as far superior.

I shake off the specter of Judge Valdez and keep typing.

I write steadily for an hour. As I pause to save, I look around the room. It's emptied out considerably since I arrived. Glen is still asleep on the couch, and Jake is on the fire escape. I watch him for a second as he lights a cigarette and begins scribbling in his notebook. What does he write? Why does he choose to sit out there instead of inside?

He catches my eye, and I turn around to get back to my own work.

My phone rings. At first I assume it's Mom, since she messaged me earlier and told me she'd be free to talk tonight.

It's Dad.

I duck out of the writing room to avoid waking Glen and answer the call in the stairwell. "Hi, Dad. How are you?"

"Maya, at the end of August, you'll be off my insurance. I wanted to make sure you knew."

"Insurance?"

"Yes, the health insurance policy. You're going to have to get on your own policy."

"But Victoria said I can stay on your policy until I'm twenty-six. She said that's the law."

He laughs. "The law. The law can't compel me to cover anyone else's health expenses. You're an adult now. No adult should be living off of mommy and daddy. You can imagine who even pushed for that kind of law to pass."

I don't know what he's talking about. All I hear is that I'm losing my health insurance, which seems like a big deal. "So what does that mean exactly?"

"It means that you'll have to find your own coverage. Just go online and figure it out. Isn't that what all you kids are good at these days—being online?"

"Why do you have to do this now? Can you just wait until I've had a little more time to save up?"

"These challenges will build resilience. At your age, I was on my own, paying for everything myself. All these entitled brats still living in their parents' homes, relying on their parents for car payments, insurance, tuition—they're freeloaders, they're lazy, and they're what is ruining America. Spending all their money on tattoos and piercings instead of contributing to this country. My kids won't be like that."

"I'm trying, Dad. It's just a lot."

"You can do it. I have to go."

I stare at my phone. One more thing I have to figure out, and I don't have a clue how to even start.

Outside the building, I sit on the front stoop to FaceTime my mom. A small breeze makes the stifling June heat bearable.

Mom picks up right away. "¡Hija! It's so good to see your face. How are you?"

"I'm okay. How about you?"

"Crazy-busy, but good." She walks across the small courtyard of Mamá Juana's house. Mamá Juana sits in an old wooden rocking chair where I spent many summer afternoons reading books. "Mira, aquí está tu Mamá Juana. Say hi."

She looks so much older than the last time I saw her. Her long hair, in the braid that hangs over her shoulder, is now completely gray. "Hola, Mamá Juana. ¿Te está cuidando bien mi mamá?"

She waves a small, bony hand at me. "Hola, Maya. ¿Cuándo me vas a venir a visitar?" She asks when I'll come visit her, and I don't know how to answer. I have the freedom to come and go as I please now; Dad isn't looming over me, forbidding my mother from taking me to Guatemala. But everything in my life is so uncertain. I don't feel like I can leave until things are more settled.

Instead of waiting for my answer, Mamá Juana pulls herself off the rocker with the help of my mom, who puts the phone down for a minute. Next, Mamá Juana wants to walk around the small courtyard, showing me some of the flowers she's been growing. "¿Te acuerdas de la rosa de jamaica? Esta es mi favorita." She fingers the soft petals of a red hibiscus. Mamá Juana and I used to make tea from the petals every summer.

Mom follows Mamá Juana around with the phone as she points out each cluster of flowers, naming them and telling me the care instruction for each one.

She gestures to a cluster of hanging white flowers. "Este es el loroco. Tiene mucho alimento." Mamá Juana walks away to get her watering can, and Mom turns the phone camera back to herself.

"She fell down yesterday, and I had to leave work to take her to her doctor. I can't get her to keep still. She wants to be as busy as she's always been; doesn't want to slow down."

"Is she going to be all right?" I ask.

"She's fine right now. Nothing broken, but it scared me."

Mamá Juana is in the background, watering each cluster of flowers with painstaking care. I know that she's part of the reason Mom moved back—that it wasn't just to get away from my dad—and I'm not bitter about it, but sometimes it's so hard to have her away from me.

"Have you gone back to see el monstruo?" Mom asks.

"No . . ." I don't mention that I do need to go back at some point to retrieve the notebook I left behind.

"Do you need more money?" she presses.

"I have enough for now." It's not her money that I want in this moment. It's *her*. I wish she could be seated next to me, helping me figure out each step of adulthood. "But I think I'm going to need help with health insurance. Dad said he's taking me off his plan."

"Pendejo. Why? You can still be on his policy."

"He said I need to grow up."

"Well, look online and see what your options are. I'll pay for it."

One more expense she wasn't counting on. "I'll figure it out. I'll let you know."

Mom follows Mamá Juana inside the small brick house. Mamá Juana continues watering plants in the kitchen—she has several hanging from the window and a few on the counters. I remember those counters from my summers visiting her. I'd put on a handmade apron and help Mamá Juana make tortillas, taking a mound of masa in my hands and clapping my palms together to flatten the dough.

Mom's eyes drift away from me as she watches Mamá Juana's slow steps around the kitchen. "And have you thought about coming to see us this summer before school starts?"

"I'd like to . . . if I can." I should go. I may not get many more chances to see my grandmother.

"Well, let me know. I'll buy you a ticket."

That's another several hundred dollars, if not more. I can't expect her to be my day-to-day safety net *and* cover extra expenses. But I'll hash that out with her another time.

Mom asks how my writing is going, and I tell her about the writing room. She tells me about some of her recent work. Even though she's two countries away, I feel buoyed by this conversation, by seeing her face, by sensing her concern and love for me.

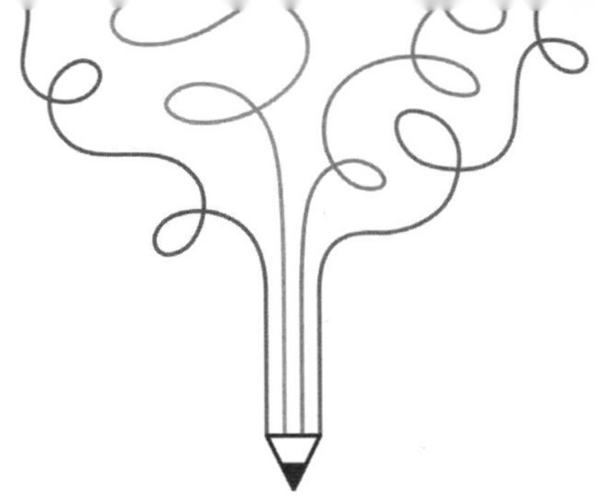

CHAPTER EIGHT

Back in the quiet of the writing room, I research insurance options. Columbia offers a health insurance plan for its students. It's a lot less expensive than buying health coverage through the government. I send the link to my mom, promising myself that any help I accept from her will only be temporary.

For the rest of the afternoon, I fall into a writing groove, eventually pressing Send on my review of *A Tree Grows in Brooklyn*. Every time I submit a finished piece of writing, I feel like a mother songbird shoving her chicks out of the nest. My hope is that the words will reach someone and make a difference to them. In this case, I imagine the readers of *Latina at Large* being intrigued enough by my description of Smith's novel to check it out for themselves. And I like to think that what struck me most about the story—Francie's discovery that through perseverance, happiness can be within her reach, and that happiness can be found in small ways—will stick with new readers too.

I haven't heard back about the pitch letter I sent, so I decide to try the other contact Victoria gave me, reconfiguring my story pitch to fit better with that publication's focus. I'll take a narrower approach, focusing on three specific charity organizations that welcome teen volunteers. This version of the pitch comes together more easily, and I'm pleased with the result. The article itself is starting to take clearer shape in my mind; sentences are forming, waiting for me to join them together.

Reaching out to help others has always been important to my mother, and I like the idea of writing about organizations that try to improve people's lives. It makes me feel closer to her.

Memories of my early childhood are filled with my love of words and her love of service. While Victoria and Daniel were in school and I was in preschool only three days a week, Mom and I would spend every Thursday at the Santa Maria Soup Kitchen, but first we would stop at the library down the street. I would fill my small backpack with books and then sit on a stool behind her at Santa Maria, reading as she helped serve food. People coming in for a meal would often wave at me or ask Mom how old I was. I'm convinced that Mom taught me how to read at the early age of four for this precise purpose—to keep me occupied while she served.

We would both leave feeling full, satiated from spending a day doing what we loved. Her message to me each Thursday was the same: *Cuando Dios te da más de lo que necesitas, compártelo con quienes necesitan más. When God gives you more than you need, share with those who need more.* She would tell me in both Spanish and English to make sure her message sank in. Sometimes it seemed to contradict messages from my dad, who acted as if he didn't have enough wealth, as if *he* needed more.

It was from those hours, spent rereading the same seven books at a time, that I picked up a love of words. I was fascinated by how they could be arranged to make sentences that communicated ideas. And I knew there were messages inside me that I wanted to communicate. I wanted to have the power of stringing words together to tell the world something. Now I have an insatiable need to tell more and more. The idea that someone doing a Google search might come across one of my pieces, might read my messages, gives me unparalleled gratification.

I don't realize how late it is until the clock in the corner of my laptop screen flashes to *9:00.* I look around the emptied room and see that even Glen has made his way off the couch and out into the night.

Darkness has descended on the city. Walking the ten blocks home has been manageable, even enjoyable when the sun offered its safety, but I've never walked home in the dark.

Jake comes inside and shuts the window above Glen's couch. I haven't been entirely alone after all.

"Are you leaving?" I ask him.

He looks at the door and back at me. "Yeah, but you can stay. People come and go whenever they want. As long as you lock the door when you leave."

"I was thinking about heading home now, actually. Can I walk with you?"

Jake shrugs. "Sure."

I follow him out and wait as he locks up. Silently, we walk down the stairs and into the cool night.

I search for a way to break the ice. "So, what are you working on right now? Your writing, I mean?"

"Just random thoughts, I guess."

"What kind of stuff do you write?"

Jake turns to study me. "Why are you being so nosy?"

"I'm just trying to make conversation so this isn't awkward."

Jake shakes his head. "What is wrong with silence? Why do people always think they have to be saying something?"

"Because we're humans, and we communicate via speaking. I'm not talking about some new-age concept here."

Jake sighs. "Sorry. I guess I'm just tired."

I'm tired too, and all I want to do is crawl onto the couch, so I let us both off the hook for the rest of the walk. When we reach our building, he hastily says, "Good night," and I thank him. As the front door closes behind me, I realize he's hung back. Peeking out the little window, I see him turn around and walk in the direction from which we came.

We're hosting Sunday dinner this week. Ricardo's lasagna is in the oven. Yoly cuts up melon, kiwi, and strawberries for a fruit salad, and I'm checking on the one dish I know how to make well—Mamá Juana's black bean soup. The large pot has been simmering on the stove for an hour and a half. It's a simple recipe that Mamá Juana taught us kids when I was seven. She sat the three of us down at the long wooden table in her kitchen with a pile of black beans. We learned how to sift through the beans and pick out any stones. Victoria made it a competition to see who could find the most stones. Then we rinsed out the beans and added them to the pot with the onions, garlic, spices, and water. Back then only Victoria was trusted with a knife to chop the onion and garlic cloves.

Daisy and Lorenzo come in carrying the famous lumpia and a covered dish of something that Daisy calls pancit. Katie follows with a loaf of homemade bread. The guests spread out at the small table and on the couch; I sit by the corner window in the olive-green chair. I've served myself four lumpia and a steaming plate of pancit, which turns out to be translucent noodles with chicken, carrots, and cabbage.

"This soup is great," Katie says from her place on the couch.

"Maya made it," Ricardo says from the table, where he's seated with Daisy and Yoly. It's basically become the grown-ups' table, and they start a conversation among themselves.

Katie gives a spoonful of soup to Lorenzo, holding a hand under his chin to catch any spillage.

"I looked up some of your writing online," Lorenzo tells me. "Oh, that *is* good." He looks at Katie and nods, and then turns back to me. "Your book reviews are cool. Katie said you're looking to write more stuff?"

"That's my hope."

"Have you ever written about food? Like foods from different countries that you can find in New York City?"

"I haven't. That's a great idea."

"Yeah, just look around. You got people from how many places in this room alone? Puerto Ricans." He gestures to Katie. "Filipinos." To himself. "A Mexican, a Colombian." To Yoly and Ricardo.

"Sounds like the beginning of an off-color joke." Katie elbows him in the ribs.

He laughs. "Except Ricardo made lasagna," he says, slightly raising his voice. It carries easily in the tiny space.

"Hey!" Ricardo retorts from the table. "I told you the arepas are special, and they come out only once in a while. Not every time."

"And your black bean soup is from Guatemala?" Lorenzo asks me.

"Yeah, my grandmother showed me how to make it. We used to go there every summer for a month when I was younger."

"That's cool. My mom and I go to the Philippines every year."

Katie shrugs. "And I've never been to Puerto Rico even once. Both my parents were born here, and they never took us when we were little, but I feel, like, this longing to go there. I won't go without Jake, though, and he's very against it."

"I'm sorry. Why is that?" I ask.

She responds with an even bigger shrug. "Reasons. He doesn't really leave the city."

Lorenzo jumps in to change the subject. "So, Maya, if your mom is from Guatemala and your dad is from here, how did they meet?"

"My mom came here on a student visa. They met when they were in med school at NYU."

"That was before your dad became all rich?" Lorenzo asks.

"Yeah. They met at a liquor store when they both tried to grab the same bottle. They talked for a little bit and then he was behind her in line. When she was showing the cashier her ID, my dad looked over her shoulder and memorized her address. Showed up at her door later that night with flowers."

"Whoa!" Lorenzo says.

Katie's eyes go wide. "Major red flags."

"I know." I laugh uncomfortably. "When I was little, I thought it was so romantic, like from a movie, but it really is quite creepy." I haven't even told Layla that story, much less my opinion of it. Somehow, I feel comfortable sharing this with Katie and Lorenzo, letting some bitterness leak out.

Katie winces. "I'm really sorry, Maya."

It's my turn to shrug because what can I say? He's my dad, and I wouldn't be here if not for his creepiness.

"Family. You gotta love 'em no matter how nutty they are," Katie says. "Like, I love my brother even though he's too antisocial to come with me to Sunday dinner. Maya, can I take some soup up to him? He loves black beans."

"Of course. That's so nice of you to think of him."

“I guess.” A serious look comes across Katie’s face, so different from her usual exuberance. “We kind of look out for each other, you know. When my parents died, we both went to live in New Jersey with my aunt and uncle. He would sneak out of the house every night. Every night. He would stay out all night and not come home until morning. My aunt and uncle didn’t know how to deal with it. It was hard for them; they had other kids. So Jake’s had a really rough time. He’s doing okay now, though. We both are. He’s got a steady job at this adorable T-shirt shop, plus the job handling the writing room. Last summer after he turned eighteen, he was able to get the apartment here, and I moved in with him.”

Lorenzo puts his arm around her and pulls her in close. “He’s lucky to have you, Katie.”

“I’m the lucky one. He’s the best brother. Even if he doesn’t want to go to Puerto Rico with me.” Lorenzo kisses her forehead, and she smiles.

What are the qualities that make him the *best* brother? I adore my own brother, but for as long as I can remember, Daniel has defined himself mainly in contrast to Dad’s hopes and expectations for him. Dad tried to mold him into a copy of himself, someone who’d take over the business and carry on the family name. Daniel couldn’t have been less interested in that path. When we kids would visit Dad at the office, Daniel constantly cracked jokes, spun around in the desk chairs until he got dizzy, stood on conference tables pretending they were stages. When Dad wanted him to join the high school debate team, he opted for dance instead. Every choice Daniel made was a disappointment to Dad, culminating in Daniel’s announcement that he wasn’t going to go to college but instead wanted to pursue musical theater.

I'm proud of Daniel, and I know he loves me and wants the best for me. But with my siblings, it's always been a "put your own oxygen mask on first" situation. I don't think I'd ever gush about them the way Katie does about Jake.

Then again, maybe that's because what Victoria and Daniel and I have dealt with isn't nearly as traumatic as what Katie and Jake have been through. I can't imagine what losing their parents was like for them and how it still impacts them.

There seem to be multiple layers to Jake. So far, the only one I've seen is the aloof misanthrope, but somewhere beneath the surface, there is a best brother to Katie. Does he ever let anyone besides Katie see that part of himself?

Lorenzo takes Katie's hand in his and traces circles across it. "I'll go with you to Puerto Rico if you'd like."

"Ha! Can you imagine your mom?" She brings her voice down to a whisper. "She would never let us travel together. I could get pregnant! Then how will you ever become a doctor?" She starts laughing.

Lorenzo looks over his shoulder to see if Daisy has overheard, but she's engrossed in her conversation with Yoly and Ricardo. "I don't even know if I want to be a doctor," he whispers.

Lorenzo's mom is only a few feet away from us, maybe a little too close for his comfort sometimes. I wonder if his dad is in the picture or ever has been. My dad is across the city, not giving me a second thought, and my mom is half a continent away. Katie's parents are dead—suddenly, violently dead at that, though it's clear she still feels loved. Maybe everybody's circumstances are a mix of good and bad, tragic and hopeful. Maybe instead of comparing myself to others, I should focus on what gives me hope.

CHAPTER NINE

Layla's going away with her family for Fourth of July weekend, but she has Mondays and Wednesdays off from her internship, so the Monday before the holiday I'm excited to meet her for coffee on my way to the library. I'm glad she left her Chanel suit in her immense closet because I definitely couldn't have competed with that in my leggings and T-shirt. Today, she's wearing ripped jeans and an oversized tee with her hair in a messy bun.

I give her a tight hug because I'm used to seeing her every day, and all this time apart has been wearing on me. "I miss you!"

"Me too! I miss my real friend. Everyone at Previdial is so fake. Like so fake, Maya. I really needed this day off, away from them."

This time I pay for my order before she can offer to cover it. We find a corner table where we sip on our coffees and scroll through our phones. In Lucinda's latest ChitChat post, she's in a pink Gucci crop top at London's Heathrow Airport, flashing a peace sign. It's a casual selfie, but she looks like she underwent complete professional hair and makeup just to take it.

Next there's a suggested post—a photo of Bernard Wright captioned with "New York needs someone who tells it like it is and stands up to the immigrant invasion." This is getting seriously out of hand. Isn't this guy just some random assemblyman? How did he end up with so many fans on ChitChat and why are their accounts constantly popping up in my feed? Maybe they're mostly bots. I kind of hope so.

To cleanse my palate, I find myself looking at Junior Vega's account again. On ChitChat, you can only view a handful of a person's posts unless you're a follower. I told myself I could save a dime by *not* giving him a follow and just keeping a lookout for his printed work. But now I give in. Ten cents poorer, I scroll to the beginning of his current story so I can read it, one single-paragraph post at a time.

"Ah! Look at this dress, Maya." Layla shows me a post on her screen. "It's so cute, right? I've got to figure out where to buy it." Social media inevitably leads her down a rabbit hole that takes her straight to online shopping.

I take this as my cue to pay more attention to her. "So how's the internship?" I ask, setting aside Junior Vega for the moment. "Besides the fakeness?"

"It's meh. I mean, the work isn't bad. Making copies, getting coffee, filing stuff, taking notes at meetings. But the other interns are cutthroat. They act like they're your friends, but then you hear what they say behind your back."

"I'm sorry."

"Whatever. I'm only there for the summer. How's the writing room thing working out?"

"Really well! Thanks for giving me a good reference. I mean, I'm *assuming* it was a good reference?"

She puts her hand on her chest and blinks fast. "Of course it was. I told the guy who called that there's no one I trust more than Maya Mitchell. Who was that guy anyway? He sounded cute."

I look at the table. "He is cute."

"Maya! Who is he?" She puts her phone down and sits up straight.

"His name is Jake. He and his sister live downstairs from me. She's really sweet. He's . . . broody but interesting." I don't mention my negative first impressions of him. From what Katie has said, I can tell there's more to him than the brusque exterior. Appearances have always ruled my dad and, by extension, us. I don't want to live my life like that.

"Is he an older man?" Layla asks half-jokingly.

"I think he's, like, a year older than us." Katie mentioned him getting the apartment last year after he turned eighteen.

"Maya! Oh my gosh. I need to check out this broody, interesting gentleman! Is he on ChitChat?"

"You know, I can't find him anywhere on social media." Because I looked, last night after Sunday dinner, when I was trying and failing to fall asleep on my couch-slash-bed. "But his sister's posted some pictures of him."

I scroll through Katie's feed and find a photo of her and Jake at Christmas. A selfie of the two of them standing in front of the tree at Rockefeller Center. She's got a huge grin showing most of her teeth, and he's attempting a closed-mouthed smile, but his eyes aren't into it. They're wearing matching blue New York Yankees-branded stocking caps, which is unexpected; I didn't know either of them was a baseball fan. "This is Jake."

Layla grabs my phone and zooms in. "Wowzers, he *is* cute. His eyes are dark and mysterious. I love them. He's got main character vibes. You have to get me invited to one of these Sunday dinners."

I take my phone back. "You're welcome any time, but he doesn't come to them. He keeps to himself."

"I see what you mean about the broodiness. Definitely main character material."

I shake my head at her even as I swipe to the other picture in the post. It's an older-looking photo in front of a different Rockefeller Center tree. A young couple wearing the same Yankees stocking caps are holding a little girl and boy with matching smaller caps. That's when I notice the caption: *Mom and Dad's favorite place to be on Christmas Eve.* I decide against showing Layla. It seems too sacred to share in a gossip session.

We spend another hour catching up before I head to the library and she heads to a boutique down the street to find an outfit for tomorrow. Meanwhile the images of Jake and Katie and their parents linger in my mind, an unfinished story.

The writing room is practically empty when I walk in after work. After all, this is New York City and most people have social lives. Glen isn't on the couch, but there's an older man with a laptop at one of the cubicles. He smiles a greeting when I sit down a few chairs away from him.

I've picked *My Ántonia* by Willa Cather for my next *Latina at Large* book review and brought a library copy with me. After skimming it to refresh my memory and taking notes on the parts that feel most important, I start drafting. I always write about the book's themes first, and then I go back to write a short summary at the beginning of my piece. I tend to get carried away with the themes, though, so I end up having to condense before I submit.

When I need a break, I do some research on charities I might want to cover if one of the teen magazines greenlights my article pitch. I'm especially interested in Revest Reinvest, a nonprofit that helps out-of-work women get back in the workforce, and Votemos Todos, which aims to empower Latine voters. Around me, a handful of people drift in and out, settling in and typing for a while, then heading home. Despite everyone being behind their own laptop screens, buried in individual work, there's a sense of community. A woman in her fifties, whom I heard someone call Madeline, asks to borrow the older man's phone charger. A few minutes later Madeline exchanges laptops with another woman, and I gather from their continued typing that they're reading each other's work and giving each other feedback. But none of it breaks my concentration. If anything, it reinforces what I'm here to do.

I don't come up for air until three hours later. Everyone but the older man has left the quiet room. I say good night to him, as well as a few others who emerge from the absolute silence room and go out into the night. I peek into the absolute silence room; it's empty now. Jake is still on the fire escape, opening a pack of cigarettes. He lights up, takes the pencil from behind his ear, and reimmerses himself in his notepad. I watch him for a moment before getting back to work, giving myself a half-hour cutoff. After that time passes, I begin packing up. I'm hoping he might be leaving soon too. If not I'll brave the darkness by myself.

I guess this is the lesson my dad is trying to teach me—that it's up to me to be responsible for myself. Even though I've never walked home alone in the dark before, the cliché that there's a first time for everything is becoming abundantly clear, and I may just have to embrace it.

The window opens with a loud thud. "You leaving?" Jake asks.

"Yes," I say as I continue packing my messenger bag.

Jake climbs through the window. "I'm leaving now too."

I assume this is an offer to walk home with me. I instantly abandon my internal monologue about being the independent and brave woman my father expects.

On the way downstairs, I decide to take a stab at starting a conversation, even though that didn't work out very well last time. "So, how did you come to be responsible for the writing room?"

"I know the guy who has the apartment. He's living out of town now, but he didn't want to let it go, so he lets me manage it as a workspace for writers. At least the apartment's not just sitting there, and I keep the place up for him."

That might be the most I've heard him say at once. Maybe I can keep the momentum going. "How many people use it?"

"About thirty, but some only come by occasionally and then there are the ten or so regulars. I've never had problems with any of them."

"What is the deal with Glen?" I ask.

Jake laughs; that's also a first. "I know it seems like he doesn't do much writing. He's actually just catching up on sleep at the moment. Last month he was under a deadline and wrote almost constantly—pulled a lot of long hours. Now he's just hibernating until his next deadline, I guess."

"Why doesn't he just sleep at home?"

Jake shrugs. "I guess he feels more at home at the writing room. He lives with his brother, and I don't think they get along very well."

"And what does he write?" I ask, mentally noting that Jake seems to know a lot about the writing room's members.

"Sci-fi, I think."

I'm tempted to ask again what Jake himself writes, but he doesn't give me the chance.

"By the way, I've been meaning to say thanks for the black bean soup. Katie told me you made it."

"Yes, I did. You're welcome."

His eyes are still facing the sidewalk in front of us, but I feel him fully engaged in the conversation. "It was really good."

"Well, you should come to Sunday dinner sometime. How come you don't?"

He looks up at me—and immediately back down at the sidewalk. "I wouldn't be good company. I'd probably just ruin it for everybody."

"Why do you say that?"

He shrugs. "I'm not really a dinner party kind of person. I would make it boring."

"Nonsense. Next time I make soup, you have to come. It's better fresh, so if you skip, I'll just have to tell Katie no when she asks to bring some home to you."

He shakes his head but lets out a chuckle. "So, listen. I want to apologize for how I acted the other day when you asked for an application."

"Don't worry about it."

"I shouldn't have acted so standoffish, and I shouldn't have made assumptions about you just because of your name. Katie told me about your dad kicking you out, making you pay your own way."

"Yep. That's my dad."

"I'm sorry. It was really rude, what I said."

"Thank you for apologizing." I wasn't sure if "sorry" was in his vocabulary, but I'm glad to find that it is. "You weren't wrong, though, about my family name opening doors for me.

My sister pays me to write about classic books for the women's magazine she runs, and she's connecting me with some other publications I'm hoping to write for. That's what I'm working on at the writing room."

I'm hoping this prompts him to volunteer some hint of what *he's* working on, but no luck.

"Well, you must be a decent writer, or your sister wouldn't be recommending you to her connections," he says. "It's one thing for her to give you a job; it's a whole other thing for her to vouch for you with other people in the business."

"Oh, trust me, if Victoria thought I wasn't a good writer, she'd tell me to my face. And then suggest ten to twenty other careers I could pursue instead."

"Yeah, you have to be really good at writing if you want to make a living at it. Really good and really lucky."

"I know. I never would've been able to afford rent in the city this summer if Yoly and Ricardo hadn't taken me in."

"That was really cool of them."

"They're lifesavers for sure. The kind of person I want to be when I grow up."

It's hard to see his face in the dark but I think I catch some warmth in the eyes. "It's probably hard to get much writing done at their place, though."

"It's been hard for *me*, at least. I have a very particular process that works for me. A quiet space, a notebook and a pen for scribbling my ideas . . ."

He raises his eyebrows. "Really? Same. The notebook part, I mean."

"I noticed. But you write in pencil."

He shrugs. "Because I mess up a lot, and I like to erase."

"And why such a small notebook?"

"So it fits in my back pocket. I carry it everywhere—write on the subway, wherever I get a chance."

"So you're not a notes app person? My sister uses that for everything."

"Nah. I like to be able to get to the end of a page, end of a notebook. The notes app is, like, infinite. You could never get to the end of it."

"Yeah." It's a small thing to have in common, but I seize on it. "I've tried it, but it felt too much like texting. So un-special. I like writing to feel special."

The wailing sound of a siren starts behind us, and Jake turns around to see, but it quickly fades in the distance. He falls back into step with me.

Now that Jake is revealing himself a little, I want to keep the conversation flowing. "I'm guessing you're not a Kindle person either, right? I noticed you also have a lot of physical books in your room." *A lot* is putting it mildly.

"Never used a Kindle," he confirms. "I like the feel of the paper, the turning of pages, the weight of the book in my hands."

"Me too. But at the moment, I've been separated from most of my books. So being able to carry around hundreds of books on an e-reader is like still having a piece of home with me, you know?"

Jake nods. "I get that." He doesn't ask what happened to my physical book collection, and I'm glad. I might tear up from just the thought of *Charlotte's Web* sitting unused in the place I've always called home.

We're nearing our building. I haven't minded the walk.

I venture to ask another question. "So, why don't *you* write at home?"

Jake shrugs. Looks like we're back to enigmatic silences.

"I can't imagine Katie makes too much noise for you."

"It's not Katie. It's the apartment. It's just stifling."

"Your room looks quite cozy. Like a perfect place to write. What's stifling about it?"

"The four walls, I guess. Besides, I have to keep an eye on the writing room anyway, make sure everything's okay."

A dark van approaches, slows down, and pulls over beside us. I'm instantly on high alert.

"Hey, Jake," the driver calls.

Jake goes up to the van and shakes the man's hand. "How's it going tonight?"

"Same old, same old," the man answers. He looks at me and waves.

I wave back feebly, still on guard. But Jake's ease around the man seems reassuring.

"I'm headed uptown now—you want a ride?" he says to Jake.

"Sure. Can you wait for me a minute?" Jake asks.

"You can go if you need to," I tell him.

"I think I can manage to walk you another half block," Jake says as the guy double-parks the van.

"It's okay, really. Your friend is waiting."

But Jake keeps walking until we get to the door of the apartment building. We exchange awkward, hasty good-nights, and I watch him make his way back to the van. Part of me wishes I'd asked him where he's headed, but most of me knows he wouldn't have answered.

CHAPTER TEN

I see him again, this time picking someone up on 106th. Now that I've become semi-acquainted with him and his navy-blue van, it's like he's everywhere. Sort of like when you hear a new word, suddenly you see and hear it a dozen times. On Tuesday, he's picking up a girl about my age. Her long, stringy hair hangs limply in her face, and her faded jeans are dirty and tattered. She stumbles slightly as she gets into the van. Is she on drugs? Who is this guy and why is he picking up young people?

And what does Jake have to do with him? Is *he* using drugs? Is this man his dealer? It's none of my business, but these thoughts haunt me.

On Wednesday, I run into Katie on the subway; she's coming home from her summer job at the YMCA. "How was your day?" I ask her.

"Good," Katie says. "It was just a long one. Wednesday's my longest, and I'm starving."

"Me too!" My homemade sandwiches are a poor substitute for Melinda's lunches and snacks.

"I know this great gyro place just above our stop."

"Ooh, sounds good," I say. "Ricardo and Yoly are going to dinner with friends tonight, and I was not looking forward to figuring out what to eat at home." And yes, I'm on a budget, but

I suspect Katie is too, so I figure this place will be reasonably priced.

The Greek restaurant is a tiny hole in the wall, with only a few tables and a small counter. Just as we sit down, I notice the navy van double-parked just outside. The driver comes into the restaurant. Before I can recover from the shock of the coincidence, Katie stands up and says, "Buck."

The man turns around. Katie walks over and embraces him.

"How are you, Katie?"

"Pretty good. How's work?"

Buck sighs. "The same."

They keep talking as Katie walks with him toward the counter to pick up his to-go order, and I can't hear what they're saying. After Buck says goodbye and leaves with his order, Katie sits back down with me.

"Who's that?" I ask.

"A friend of Jake's."

I already knew that much. I want more details—like, is he a drug dealer? And where do he and Jake go at night? Does Jake buy from him . . . or work for him? For the first time it occurs to me that a two-bedroom apartment in Morningside Heights is probably too expensive for the average nineteen-year-old with an hourly-wage job at a T-shirt store and a side gig taking care of a coworking space. Would selling drugs give Jake the money he needs to afford rent?

I don't ask any of these questions. I just eat my gyro as I wonder how much Katie really knows about her brother. For her sake, I hope Jake isn't using or dealing drugs, but I can't come up with another explanation.

Two hours of fine-tuning the previous night's writing is all I can do tonight. I keep yawning, my body telling me that I need sleep. It's almost nine o'clock and probably a good time to stop. As I'm packing up, Jake comes in from the window. He's wearing a Pirates baseball jersey with the number 21. It's a V-neck with buttons down the front, so I catch a glimpse of a thin gold chain with a small cross hanging from his neck.

There's now an unspoken understanding that Jake and I will wait for each other and walk home together, even if he isn't in a sociable mood. Yesterday night, he barely talked, grunting answers to my polite questions. After a couple grunts, I gave up and we walked the rest of the way in silence.

Tonight starts off more promisingly, when I ask him how long he's been writing and he responds right away.

"When Katie and I were little, my mom signed us up for this kids' book-of-the-month club. Every month, we'd get a box of six books and we could keep the ones we wanted and send back the ones we didn't. She used to keep them all; didn't ever send any back. Katie and I read those books over and over. We'd make a fort in the living room with the blankets from my parents' bed and read our books inside. Then I wanted to make my own books. I started writing, and Katie would draw the pictures to go with my stories."

"That's adorable. It reminds me of how my brother used to pretend he was starring in musicals when we were little."

Jake asks about my siblings, and I talk about them for a while. He volunteers a few embarrassing childhood stories about Katie.

"So, when Katie goes to Princeton, will you pull a Daisy and go with her?" I ask.

He laughs, and the sound is so delightful that I vow to try

to think of more funny things to say. "Nah. Katie will be fine on her own. And I don't really leave the city. There's nowhere else for me but here."

"I feel the same way. My sister keeps trying to convince me to move to LA, but I don't want to leave. I'm the one who has to go visit her, though, or we meet somewhere in between. She won't ever come back here."

"Why?"

"She associates this city with my dad, and she hates him."

Jake looks over at me, his eyebrows drawn together in a pained expression, but he doesn't say anything.

I shouldn't have said that. His father is dead—died right before his eyes. Harboring hatred for a parent probably isn't something he can fathom.

Uneasiness settles into me. Neither of us says anything the last few minutes of our walk home.

The apartment is silent; Yoly and Ricardo have gone to bed. I decide to stay up for a while to read. Tired of the couch, I sit in the green chair by the window with the literary magazine I checked out from the library. I'm about halfway through the Junior Vega story that's published in it, and it's just as intriguing as the first one I read, but instead of absorbing the words on the page, I'm dissecting the conversation I had with Jake. I still regret mentioning Victoria's hatred toward our dad. I do like that we share a love of this city.

Our street is fairly quiet at this hour, but not too far away the city is fully alive, burgeoning with action. Through the window, I see a figure cross the street—Jake, walking away from home. I watch him until he's out of view.

On impulse, I call Victoria.

"What's wrong?" she asks immediately.

"Nothing, I'm just wondering how you're doing."

"I'm great. What time is it there? Shouldn't you be asleep?"

"I'm working on that. Trying to shut off my brain, you know? I keep thinking . . . do you have any good memories of Dad?"

She laughs. "*That's* what you're thinking about as you try to sleep? I can see where you went wrong. You need to get into mindful breathing or something."

"It's a simple question, Vic. Come on, humor me."

She pauses for a long moment, considering her next words. "Do you remember the summer he went to Guatemala with us?"

"Barely."

"I have this vivid image in my mind of him wearing one of Mamá Juana's aprons, making tortillas with me."

"Making tortillas? You've got to be kidding me."

"I know there's a picture of the two of us somewhere. When I was in high school, I looked for it everywhere. I wanted proof that I wasn't remembering it wrong. That it actually happened. I never did find that picture." She pauses before adding, "He actually tried to learn Spanish that summer too. He'd ask Mamá Juana, how do you say flour in Spanish, how do you say stove in Spanish."

"I wish I remembered that."

"I try not to think about it too much; it makes the loss feel more palpable."

"Sounds like he was a completely different person back then."

"He was. He was still in love with Mom—he still cared more about people than he did about money. I don't know what happened to that person. He started fading after the first million and completely disappeared after ten million. For a long time I thought he'd switch back. If I could just make him proud enough, if I could just make him *see* me. But he won't, Maya."

"I know," I say, even though I'm wrestling with my own indelible memories. Childhood bedtime stories, comforting hugs, shared excitement over a rare book find. Those moments aren't automatically erased by the way he treats me now.

"Will you be able to get some sleep now, you freak?" Victoria says. "Or do I need to recommend a meditation app?"

"I'm fine—thanks, Vic. Good night."

I'm tempted to stay up until Jake returns from wherever he's gone, but I decide against it.

In the morning, after Yoly and Ricardo leave for work, I finish the Junior Vega story over breakfast, savoring each twisty sentence and each conflicted thought of the protagonist, who keeps critiquing his own actions even as he finds increasingly creative ways to escalate them.

A frantic knock on the door startles me. Maybe it's Katie with a desperate need to borrow eggs.

When I open the door, two elementary-school-aged girls, clutching each other's hands, look at me with wild eyes.

"Is Ricardo here?" asks the older one, who's maybe eleven or twelve.

"No. Can I take a message or . . . ?"

She shakes her head and starts crying, releasing the other girl's hand to cover her eyes. The younger one starts crying too, shoulders shaking.

"Come in." I usher them inside. "What's wrong?"

The older one wipes her eyes and pulls her hair away from her tear-streaked face. She takes a deep breath to compose herself. "Do you know when Ricardo will be back?"

"He's at work. Do you want me to call him?"

She looks at the younger girl and back at me, nodding.

I walk over to the table to pick up my phone. "What's your name?"

"I'm Teresa, and this is my sister, Brenda."

"They took our mom," Brenda says.

"Who took your mom?"

Brenda starts crying again. "La migra."

I look at Teresa for confirmation. She nods. "She was dropping us off at the summer program, and when they grabbed her, she told us to run."

"How did you know to come here?"

"My mom and I used to clean the apartment downstairs, till that person moved out last year. We would run into Ricardo sometimes and he was always nice, and now he's my mom's lawyer. Most of my mom's jobs are uptown now but I still remembered how to get here. Can you please call him?"

I'm barely processing this, but I know it's urgent. "Of course."

His cell goes to voicemail. It takes me a minute to find his work number. An assistant answers, and I ask for Ricardo.

"Can I tell him who's calling?"

"It's Maya, and it's kind of an emergency."

He answers a few seconds later. "Maya? What's the matter?"

"There are two girls here at the apartment, Teresa and Brenda. They said their mom was taken by immigration."

"What's their mom's name?"

I ask Teresa, and she says it's Alicia Torres Hildago. "Do you know her?"

"Yes, I know her. How are the girls? Are they all right?"

I look at both girls, who are clutching each other's hands again. "I think so. They're shaken up, of course."

"Okay, let me check the emergency contacts in their mom's file. I'm pretty sure she has family in the area; I'll call them, but it might take a little while for someone to get to Manhattan. Do you think you could stay with them until a relative can come pick them up?"

"Yeah, of course. And you're going to help their mom, right?"

"We'll do everything we can. We should at least be able to find out where she's been taken. Let me talk to Teresa real quick."

I give her my phone, and she nods as she listens to Ricardo. By the time she hands the phone back to me, the call has ended. I'm on my own.

I gesture toward the couch. "Go ahead and sit down. One of your relatives will be here soon. Do you want anything to eat or drink?"

Teresa shakes her head, and Brenda, taking her cue from her sister, does the same, her pigtails swinging with the movement. They sit as close together as they can on the couch.

"I'm so sorry," I add. "Ricardo said they're going to find out where the immigration people took your mom. Are you sure you don't want something to eat? Did you have breakfast?"

Brenda shakes her head. Teresa elbows her and says quickly, "We always eat at the summer program. They give us breakfast and lunch."

But they didn't make it there. They were on the way there. "Well, why don't you join me for a snack while we wait for Ricardo?"

I bring cereal and three bowls over to the table. They look at each other and seem to come to a silent agreement. To encourage them, I start eating, and they join me.

I replay Teresa's story in my head. She *and* her mom used to clean the apartment that Jake and Katie now rent. This little girl's biggest problem should be school cliques, not child labor. And now she's been pulled away from her mom, left to safeguard her younger sister and find her own way through this nightmare.

When Dad shoveled me out the door, I thought I was too young to be out on my own, but these girls have been forced to fend for themselves at a much younger age, without even knowing where their mom is. I can't even imagine what that must feel like.

After we've eaten, Brenda and Teresa return to the couch, their bodies pushed together as if they fear they, too, could be separated at any moment. Their expressions are layered with fear, worry, and doubt. I suddenly wish I had my copy of *Charlotte's Web* to share with them. Even with its sad ending, the friendship in the book has always brought me comfort.

"I was about to read a book. Is it okay if I read it out loud?" I say to Brenda and Teresa.

The girls look at each other and shrug. "Sure," Teresa says.

I take out my e-reader and borrow an ebook of *Charlotte's Web* from my library app. I start reading, hoping that Wilbur can distract them for a little while.

Eventually, there's a knock on the door; an aunt has arrived to pick up the girls. After they all leave, I'm left wondering what's going to happen to them.

CHAPTER ELEVEN

For the rest of the day, I have trouble focusing. I sleepwalk through work, and at the writing room I sit at my cubicle staring at my laptop screen for more than an hour. The space doesn't calm me or focus me the way it usually does; it only contrasts my safety with what Brenda and Teresa are facing.

On the way home, Jake and I fall silently into step next to each other. He looks over at me once but otherwise keeps his eyes focused ahead.

"You're unusually quiet," he finally says, breaking the silence between us. "No pressing question of the day?"

I shake my head, whispering, "No," as we stop at an intersection to let cars pass.

"Is something wrong?"

It all spills out of me. He doesn't interrupt as I regurgitate every wrenching detail of the morning. When I pause to catch my breath he says, "That's awful. Those poor kids."

"I keep imagining myself at that age, in desperate circumstances, trying to find out what happened to my mom. I would've been so lost, so scared."

"I'm really sorry, Maya. I'm glad you were there to help those girls."

"I didn't really do much. I wish I could've done more."

"It was probably one of the scariest moments of their lives, and when they knocked on that door, looking for help, they got you. They got your good heart, and that's not nothing."

His words pierce the concrete wall of dread I've been carrying around with me all day. I feel a flicker of hope—maybe I did soften Brenda and Teresa's fear, offer them some respite. "My mom's told me about some of the situations some of her patients in Guatemala are experiencing. And how some of them have even had to flee the country in order to save their lives. But it never fully sank in for me."

"Seeing something up close can change your perspective in a way that just hearing or reading about it can't," says Jake.

"I don't know about that. I think I've learned a lot of empathy from stories. But . . . yeah, looking directly into those girls' eyes . . . I'm never going to forget it. I'll never understand how someone like Bernard Wright can dismiss them and everyone like them as basically less than human."

"Who is this Wright person? I've never heard of him."

"I just learned about him recently, from Yoly and Ricardo's community group." I get Jake up to speed.

"Sounds like a scary guy."

"Terrifying."

"I'm really sorry," he says. "Sorry it happened to that family. Sorry it's going to haunt *you* instead of someone like him."

Jake's usual guarded cynicism is absent tonight, and his words are genuine and thoughtful. Talking to him has made me feel just a little bit better.

The next day—July Fourth—Yoly and Ricardo have invited Brady and Julissa for dinner. I help Yoly chop vegetables for a salad while Ricardo makes a chicken-and-rice dish.

"Sorry in advance if we talk shop too much," Ricardo says.

There's a knock on the door, and Brady and Julissa walk in. They greet me, and I'm surprised they remember my name. We all sit at the small table and pass around the food. The mood is pleasant at first, but Brady's simple question of "How's everybody's week going?" sets the conversation on a bleak track.

Ricardo shakes his head. "One of my clients was grabbed when she was out with her daughters."

"Is she okay?" I blurt out. "Did you figure out where she was? Are you going to be able to help her?"

Ricardo hesitates. "Sorry, Maya—I shouldn't talk about details of my cases outside of work. I'm doing everything I can. That's all I can say."

Julissa pushes her fork around on her plate. "ICE is targeting sanctuary cities for raids. They're all over the city, standing outside subway stations, schools, factories."

"Parents are going to be afraid to send their kids to school," Brady says.

"Better not come to the library." Yoly slams her glass down on the table with a force that seems to surprise even herself.

Julissa takes her tablet out of her bag. "Have you heard the speech Bernard Wright gave a few hours ago?" She pulls up the short clip, which shows Wright claiming that undocumented immigrants are being flown from the southern border to Westchester County. He complains that millions of dollars of federal money are being used to transport these people who have no permission to be here. He warns that there'd better be no such planes coming anywhere near his Greene County or there'll be hell to pay. "He wouldn't be doing this if he weren't getting ready for a run," Julissa said. "He's going to run for governor. I just know it."

Brady still looks skeptical. "Nobody had even heard of this guy until, like, five minutes ago."

"Exactly," says Julissa. "He came out of nowhere, but now he's constantly showing up in my newsfeed."

I think of all the content on ChitChat praising Wright, and I see her point.

Julissa shoves the tablet back into her bag and balls her hands into fists. She shakes them out and then spreads her fingers, trying to calm down. "I can't decide what to do about videos like this. Share them so people know what we're dealing with? Or, don't share them—don't give him publicity, the notoriety? What do you all think?"

"Share," Brady says. "We need New Yorkers to know what kind of man is thinking of running for governor. New Yorkers won't put up with this. They'll shame him into not running."

Ricardo laughs and immediately covers his mouth like he didn't mean to. "There are plenty of New Yorkers who are just fine with this."

Brady shakes his head. "But they're outnumbered by those of us who think it's vile."

"Well, Wright's managed to raise a ton of money already, so what does that tell you?" Julissa fires back.

Brady shrugs. "Nothing. It tells me nothing. He hasn't reported where that money's actually coming from, so for all we know it's from people outside the state. Probably one or two ultra-rich shadow donors who are skirting campaign finance laws, trying to prop up some random, obscure guy nobody actually likes. Money doesn't necessarily translate into votes."

"That's bizarrely optimistic of you," says Julissa. "Money buys advertising. Money buys influence. Money buys attention, and *that* translates into votes more often than any of us would like."

"You're both right," says Yoly. "It's too soon to panic, *and* it's never too soon to take this stuff seriously."

After some more discussion, they decide to share the new video clip on all their social media platforms as a warning, so people can start preparing for what might be a long fight ahead. I wonder if I should do the same, but I only have a handful of followers, and of that handful, I suspect only Layla would notice if I actually posted something for a change.

By the time Julissa and Brady leave, the fireworks are starting. I hear their staccato rumblings in the distance as I load the dishwasher.

Since I've just turned eighteen, this is the first election I'll be able to vote in, and suddenly that weighs heavily on me. A candidate like Wright could have a horrific effect on Brenda and Teresa and so many innocent people who are trying to make a better life for themselves. If Wright ends up on the ballot, of course I'll vote for someone running against him, but that thought doesn't bring me much satisfaction or comfort. I feel as if there's more I should be doing, but I don't know exactly what.

On Saturday, after I finish writing for the night, Jake walks me home as usual. I've almost been looking forward to it. He still doesn't talk much, but he's gotten less reserved than he was at first. Gradually I've been able to draw out small details that help me piece together what kind of person he is. Almost like when you read a novel for the first time and each chapter reveals a little more about the character. It's intriguing.

"Can I ask you a personal question?"

Jake raises his eyebrow. "Aren't all your questions personal ones?"

"No! I ask you regular questions all the time."

We stop to let a car go by before we proceed through the intersection. "Let's see. You've asked me what I write, when I started writing, why I don't write at home . . . I would say those are pretty personal."

I shake my head. "I would say that those are more conversational. For instance, a personal question would be—where do you go every night after you leave the writing room? Or, who is the man in the van? Those are examples of personal questions."

Jake turns to me with narrowed eyes. "Go ahead. Ask your personal question."

"No, I don't want to anymore. You're clearly not in the right frame of mind to answer. I'll save it for another day."

"All right, but try to intermingle it with non-personal questions. You know, like, what did I have for dinner last night. Or, where did I get this new T-shirt."

"Okay. Where did you get that new shirt?" I ask. I noticed it earlier. "Where *does* one get a T-shirt with a screengrab of a Wikipedia article about Lin-Manuel Miranda? The Gap?"

Jake laughs. "I work at a little T-shirt shop on Third Avenue. It's called NYTee. They can screen-print just about anything."

"Well, I like it. Even though my brother, the musical theater expert, would tell you that people who are still obsessed with *Hamilton* are unbearably cheesy."

"Who says I'm obsessed with *Hamilton*? For all you know, *Mary Poppins Returns* was a formative movie of my childhood."

That makes me giggle. "I do recommend the original book."

"Well, you can tell your brother that *In the Heights* and *Hamilton* were groundbreaking in their day—the casting, the storytelling, the use of a musical style that isn't usually taken seriously by Broadway types."

"I'll make sure to let Daniel know."

We reach the steps and stop. "Good night," Jake says. Shoving his hands into the pockets of his beige corduroys, he turns around and walks in his usual direction.

"Don't worry," I call out after him. "I won't ask where you're headed. In case that's too personal."

He turns around and smiles before he continues walking.

CHAPTER TWELVE

As Yoly and I leave the library on Monday night, I remember standing out here with my mom, waiting between two pin oak trees for Ernie to pick us up from story time. I would stare up at the long pointy oak leaves, willing them to change colors before my eyes. Fall would eventually fill the trees' thin limbs with vibrant scarlet. Every time I exit this building, I check the leaves of this grouping of trees. Even though fall is several months away, I still watch for any changes, looking forward to the appearance of the deep red hues and the memories they'll bring with them.

Ricardo has to work late, so Yoly suggests grabbing a quick dinner out. After three weeks of eating homemade sandwiches for lunch, I figure I can splurge a little, especially since the payment for my latest *Latina at Large* piece hit my account this morning.

At the restaurant, I go to the restroom and as I come back, I'm startled to see Yoly talking to Buck, who's standing next to our booth. I hang back and watch until he leaves.

"How do you know him?" I ask Yoly when I sit down.

Yoly takes a sip of iced tea. "Buck? He's a friend of Ricardo's. He runs a shelter for teens. He sometimes has referrals for Ricardo."

Whatever I was expecting to hear, it wasn't that. "I guess

that explains why he's always picking up very young people in that van of his."

Yoly swirls around the lemon in her iced tea. "Yeah, he's usually out every night, looking for kids who could use a safe place to sleep. If they're willing, he brings them back to the shelter."

I digest this information, feeling guilty for the assumptions I made about him. I still wonder what Jake's relationship is to him, but I don't feel like I can ask Yoly about that. Instead I ask, "Why wouldn't they be willing? The teens he finds? Wouldn't they be glad to have somewhere to go?"

Yoly shrugs. "Some people have had bad experiences in shelters. Had their belongings confiscated or stolen, been left open to harassment or assault, been forced to detox in unsafe ways. But Buck's shelter is small and specifically geared toward teens. Most unhoused teens have either run away from bad situations at home or been kicked out by their families, so Buck knows it's hard for them to trust strangers. His goal is to meet them where they're at. To offer help and resources but not shame them or pressure them. And mainly just to keep them as safe and as comfortable as possible, as long as they're not putting anyone else in danger."

The phrase *kicked out by their families* reverberates in my ears. "He sounds like a pretty good guy."

"He really is," Yoly says right before her phone starts going off with a bunch of texts. I watch her face as she bites on her lip and frowns.

"Anything wrong?" I ask her.

"Well, Ricardo just heard from our community network; there's a family that needs a place to stay tomorrow night. They're asylum applicants and they have a hearing the next morning. Their original plans for lodging fell through and they can't find anyplace else they can afford on short notice. Do you think you could ask Layla if you could spend the night at her place, just this once?"

A family? My first thought is that the studio is already too small for three people; how can an entire family fit? "Uh, sure. I'll message her."

"I'm so sorry. I hate to do this to you . . ."

"Don't be sorry. It's your place. It's your couch. I'll check with Layla right now."

Layla: Finally a sleepover! We're long overdue! Let me confirm with my parents.

I pick at my food, reflecting on everything I've learned in the last few minutes. When I first landed on Yoly and Ricardo's doorstep, I thought of myself as homeless. Giving myself that title seems so naïve now, when I think of people my age who are left to walk the streets of New York City, or this family that will be relying on Yoly and Ricardo's secondhand couch on the night before a hearing might determine that they don't belong here.

Layla messages again, starting with five angry face emojis.

Layla: I'm so sorry. My parents said no. They didn't give me a good reason, but said positively no. I'm so sorry that they're being jerks.

I feel a ball drop in the pit of my stomach. My face feels hot and red, and there's a stinging sensation behind my eyes.

Me: It's fine. Don't worry about it.

Layla: Hey, I'll use my emergency credit card and we can get a hotel and do a sleepover there.

Me: No. You would get in so much trouble.

Layla: I would definitely get in trouble. But it would be worth it!

Me: Really, it's okay.

Layla: I'm so sorry. We can still meet for yoga in the park on Wednesday morning, though! We should make that a regular thing!

Yoly reads my face before I tell her anything. "She said no?"

I shrug because I don't trust my voice. I try to keep this in perspective—I was *just* musing over how lucky I am in the scheme of things. But it's a reminder of how precarious my life still feels.

Yoly looks down at her phone and starts typing. A minute later, she announces, "Katie said you can stay with her. They have an air mattress they can blow up in her room." She looks up at me expectantly.

"An air mattress?" I've heard of a waterbed, but what on earth is an air mattress?

"Yeah, it's a plastic case that you blow up. People use it when they go camping and stuff."

"Are you sure it's okay with them?"

"Yeah, Katie is so chill. She said yes right away."

"But did she ask Jake?"

"I don't know. She doesn't have to—it's her place too. If you really don't mind, then it's settled."

It might be . . . *interesting* to stay at Jake and Katie's, but I don't think I'll mind. Getting an up-close glimpse of Jake in his natural habitat might satisfy some of the curiosity that's been tugging at me since I first asked him for laundry detergent.

The T-shirt of the day is Speedy Gonzalez with the word *Rápido* written across it. Jake's position is the same—on the writing room's fire escape, cigarette in place, little notebook open, stubby pencil moving quickly. I take in all the details as I settle at my cubicle.

I'm getting a late start after my dinner with Yoly, so I dive in. The first magazine I pitched to has turned down my story idea about charity recommendations for teens, but Victoria's contact there says I'm welcome to pitch something else. I really need that notebook with all my ideas. Without it, I feel stuck. I also need to pick a book for this week's *Latina at Large* piece and for the first time, none of the options on my long list of possibilities jump out at me.

My mind drifts to this morning's ChitChat post from Junior Vega. He started a new story today: *Viktor Trejo didn't wake up that day with an agenda to kill someone, but the particles in the air conspired to initiate a series of events that had no alternate conclusion.* That was it—the shortest paragraph he's ever shared—yet it's been filtering in and out of my mind all day.

I reflect on what Yoly has said about the limitations of the literary canon. Maybe I should rethink my approach to my book reviews. Maybe I could start writing about newer, more outside-the-box stories. I could write about how the internet and social media are helping redefine what a classic is, redefine what's considered literature. As uneasy as I am about writing that hasn't gone through an editorial process, there's also something powerful about writers connecting directly with readers, telling the stories they want to tell the way they want to tell them, not worrying about how they should be categorized or what they should be compared to.

Why not acknowledge that and point people toward some writing that I think is especially good?

I text Victoria a link to Junior Vega's latest post and pitch her my idea: an anti-classic book review. Vega's work is everything my usual suspects aren't—contemporary, genre fiction, short and easily digestible, unfiltered. And yet it's also everything that I think literature should be—riveting and thought-provoking. Plus, it might speak to someone who'd never in a million years pick up a copy of *A Tree Grows in Brooklyn*, no matter how glowingly I've reviewed it.

Victoria replies that she'll look at Junior Vega's profile and get back to me about my idea when she has a chance. **For now, just do one of your regular reviews for this week.**

I sigh, pick a book off my list at random, and start drafting.

My eyes are heavy and long for rest. Their exhaustion outweighs my desire to work more, and I start to pack up. Madeline, the only other person at the cubicles, has been typing at least a hundred words a minute since I got here, but now her writing sprint has come to an end and she's also getting ready to leave. She says goodbye to me on her way out. Glen is still asleep on the couch, and Jake is on the fire escape lighting up a new cigarette. I catch his eye. He doesn't smile exactly, but he does acknowledge me. I take my time putting away my laptop while he finishes his cigarette.

Jake climbs in over Glen and walks up to me. "Hi. Ready?"

How has it become so routine, a part of our daily pattern? I nod and follow him out. Glen's solitary figure is all that remains in the writing room as Jake turns off the lights.

He buries his hands deep in his pockets and walks alongside me. "Katie says you're crashing at our place tomorrow night," he says, almost as a question.

"I hope that's okay. Yoly and Ricardo are having a family stay with them. It's just for one night."

"Of course it's okay. I didn't always have a place to stay myself and had to rely on the kindness of others." He pauses mid-step and turns to me. "So, of course, whenever you need a place to stay, you're welcome."

"Thanks." His earnestness throws me off a little—not because he hasn't been thoughtful before, but because he so often masks his softer side with a dismissive demeanor. I'm not sure how to react to this more open version of him. I feel like I'm in uncharted territory. "Speaking of . . . having places to stay . . . I ran into your friend Buck again."

He nods.

"Yoly says he runs a teen shelter." This kind of strategy works with Katie. Feed her a few words and she opens up. It doesn't work on Jake. Only direct and specific questions prompt a response from him. "Have you known him a long time?"

"I practically lived at his shelter for a year or so, after my parents died. At first I was staying with my aunt and uncle. They really tried to take care of me; did a great job with Katie. But it wasn't for me."

"So you ended up on the streets?" It sounds more judgmental than I intend. It's just hard for me to wrap my head around.

"You wouldn't understand."

"Sorry." I know that our circumstances are completely different—yet I feel like I *can* relate on some level. He didn't have a home he could return to. And, while the building I used to live in technically still exists in all its imposing beauty, I am not welcome there. "I'm glad you found someone you felt safe around," I say to Jake, which seems to be, if not the right thing to say, at least not the wrong thing.

"Buck saved my life. He'd pick me up, wherever I was. Bring me to the shelter. Every night I knew, sooner or later, I'd see that van coming to take me home."

"And now you go with him in the evenings to help him?"

"Once in a while. Why are you asking me so many questions?"

"Sorry," I say again. I knew I was pushing it; I should've stopped after the first few answers.

"Just making conversation?"

Just curious, very curious. His life is an enigma. I want to figure it out, get to the core of who Jake is. Why? I don't know. "Yeah, just making conversation. Sorry. I know you hate that."

I may be imagining it, but I think I catch the barest hint of a smile on his face.

I respect his preference for a wordless walk, right up until we reach the stoop. He says his usual terse "Good night" before walking off in the other direction.

I sigh as I heave myself up the stairs. I won't give him another thought. Bed—or rather, couch—is all I want to think about. Tomorrow, I'll be sleeping on an air mattress in Jake's apartment.

CHAPTER THIRTEEN

Yoly has a mournful look on her face as I pack my messenger bag for my brief stay at Katie and Jake's place. I know she feels awful about asking me to leave for the night, but I understand. That family needs a safe place to stay tonight. Their hearing tomorrow is huge, and they deserve a chance to be rested, ready, and on time, without spending money they can't spare on a last-minute hotel room. "Yoly, I'll be fine. It's just downstairs, and Katie is so nice. Don't worry."

Her face relaxes. "Thank you, Maya."

I clean up the area around the couch and push my suitcase and boxes farther into the corner to make more room. Ricardo walks in, followed by a very young couple. They each carry a backpack and hold the hand of a small, thin boy. Ricardo speaks to them in Spanish, and Yoly joins the conversation.

Those backpacks may hold all their possessions. My recent arrival at this very same studio apartment seems a world away from what they're facing. At the time, it didn't seem like I had any choice but to stay here, but it was actually one of several options. I could've gone to live with Victoria; I'll always have a place to stay with Mom in Guatemala. This small family has nowhere to go but the tiny apartment of strangers. I don't know where they're from or what they faced back there, but dire circumstances must've driven them to come here.

Ricardo introduces them to me. I greet them in my imperfect Spanish and move out of the way so they can sit on the couch. The little boy perches on his mother's lap and buries his face in her neck. This family came to the US in search of the American dream. This is who Bernard Wright is afraid of?

I wonder how Teresa and Brenda and their mom are doing. I know Ricardo can't tell me much, but at a moment like this, not knowing what their next chapter holds for them feels unbearable.

"Thanks again, Maya," Yoly says to me as we move toward the door. "Come back whatever time you want in the morning. I think we'll all be up early. Their hearing is at nine." She hugs me good night, and I head downstairs.

I'm expecting Katie to open the door when I knock, but instead it's Jake. "Hey," he says, sounding almost friendly.

"Hey." I walk in and stand listlessly in the middle of the living room.

He scratches the back of his neck, and I scan his faded T-shirt. It says *Menudo* and has a picture of a group of five young guys. I'll have to Google it later.

"Katie just texted me," he says. "She went to get frozen yogurt with Lorenzo, and they're on the way back. Might be ten minutes."

"Oh, okay." Should I leave and come back in ten minutes?

"Come here, we can blow up the air mattress while we wait for her."

I follow him into Katie's room. It has a full-size bed, a dresser with a mirror, and a small shelf with a ton of toiletries and three different sizes of Caboodles overflowing with makeup. I'm reminded of Victoria's childhood bedroom, which was much larger than this but similarly dominated by cosmetics storage cases.

Jake gestures to a large vinyl or plastic object that looks like a heavy blanket. He stretches it out on the small area next to Katie's bed and crouches behind it. I watch him plug its attached cord into an outlet. With a whirring noise, the air mattress begins to inflate. He must sense that I'm tracking his every move because he looks up at me from his crouched position. I quickly look away and keep my eyes trained on the pink and baby-blue lids of Katie's Caboodles. The whirring stops, so I guess the air mattress is completely inflated.

"There you go." He gets up and steps around the mattress to get to the door.

"That's pretty cool. I've never seen one of those."

"You've . . . never seen an air mattress?"

"Nope." I sound like a spoiled girl who only sleeps on beds made of golden feathers.

"Are you fine to sleep on it?"

"Yeah, of course. Thank you."

"I'll get you a pillow and comforter." He returns with a navy-blue pillow and a red-and-blue plaid comforter. He can't seem to decide if he should hand them to me or put them down on the air mattress, so I take them.

"Thanks again for letting me stay here. It's sucking more and more that I don't have an actual place to live until the fall."

"You can stay here anytime, Maya."

I think that's the first time I've heard Jake say my name, and for whatever reason, it's everything to me right now. "Thank you," I say just above a whisper.

"Sorry!" Katie's voice bounces down the hall. She comes to

stand in the doorway. "I meant to be back earlier—Oh, good. You got the bed ready."

I'm still clutching the pillow and comforter to my chest, so I bend down and lay them at the foot of the air mattress. "Thanks for sharing your room with me."

She claps her hands. "It'll be fun! Let's make popcorn and get in our jammies and watch a movie."

Jake leaves the room without another word.

I take my bag into the bathroom to change into my lounge pants and sleeping tank. It feels so intimate to be in the bathroom Jake uses. I look at the two toothbrushes standing in a small plastic toothbrush holder, at the light blue towels on the rack, and wonder which items belong to Jake.

By the time I come out of the bathroom, Katie has filled a huge bowl with microwave popcorn and placed it on the coffee table in front of the living room couch.

"Here." Katie hands me the TV remote. "You find a good movie to watch. I have to FaceTime Lorenzo for, like, ten minutes. He needs some help on a scholarship essay question. Is that all right with you?"

"Of course. Take your time." Once she's disappeared into her room, I set the remote next to the popcorn and look down the hall toward Jake's room. His door is open.

I walk the short distance and knock on the frame. "Can I come in for a minute?"

He closes his laptop and swivels around in his office chair. "Sure."

I take a few steps inside. "Can I sit down?"

His eyes slide down the length of my body for a second. He quickly turns his eyes to the floor. "Yeah."

I sit on the edge of his bed and rest my hand on the dark

green bedcover. It's worn and seems old, but it's very soft. "Katie's on FaceTime with Lorenzo."

"That happens a lot. Despite him living directly over our heads."

"Can I ask you a question?"

He laughs and swivels in his chair again. "You always do anyway."

I smile at his accurate analysis. "Do you have any book recommendations?"

He sits up straighter. "Book recommendations?"

"Yeah. I write this weekly book review for my sister's magazine. It's been focused on classics, though I'm thinking of opening it up. Either way I could use some new ideas." I gesture toward his bookshelves. "What's your favorite book?"

He watches me carefully, almost as if he's unsure about my motivation. Finally he rolls his chair away from his desk and toward the wall by the door. He pulls out a worn paperback, stands up, walks over to me, and holds it out.

I take the book and scan the cover: *Bless Me, Ultima.* Rudolfo Anaya.

"It was my dad's favorite."

I pull my phone out of the pocket of my lounge pants. "I'm going to take a picture of it and look for it at the library tomorrow."

He slides back into his chair "You can borrow that copy."

"Was this your dad's copy?"

He nods.

"Oh, I can't then."

"He'd be glad to know someone else is enjoying it." His mouth relaxes into a smile I've never seen cross his face before, and it does something to my chest.

I place it gently on the bed beside me. "I'll take good care of it. Promise."

"Let me know what you think when you finish."

"I will. So, what are you reading right now?"

"*The Magician.*" Jake gestures toward a paperback copy of William Somerset Maugham's 1908 novel on his desk.

"Oh! I read that a couple of years ago." I shiver at memories of its dark themes. "Oliver Haddo is just pure evil."

"The purest kind."

"Do you enjoy that type of story?"

"I don't enjoy it. I just try to understand it."

I pull my feet up on the bed and wrap my arms around my legs. "You're trying to understand evil? I don't think that's possible."

Jake seems to weigh that for a moment and eventually nods. "I think you're right. And maybe it's not useful to try to explain it. But sometimes I still want to—like maybe if I can understand it, I have some measure of control over it, or something."

He experienced evil up close. Someone crashed into his family's car and left without even a thought of who remained in their wake. Any evil *I've* seen firsthand cannot even compare.

"Let's find you something happier to read." Hopping off the bed, I walk over to one of his bookshelves and scan the contents. There's a lot of newer fiction, including some young adult novels—a reminder that Jake is only slightly older than I am. My eyes snag on several of Yoly's favorites that I also remember liking, but they're all pretty somber in tone. "Have you read all of these already?"

"Most of them."

I brighten when I see a well-loved title. "How about some Jane Austen?" I pull *Pride and Prejudice* off the shelf.

He shakes his head. "That's the kind of book you only read one time."

"Or eleven."

"You've read *Pride and Prejudice* eleven times? I think you need some more hobbies."

"Maybe, but I'm a sucker for a happy ending." I wave the book at him, playfully urging him to take it.

"What good is a happy ending if real life isn't like that?"

"We're talking about literature, not real life. Reading can be an escape."

He crosses his arms. "I prefer literature that's based on reality—what the author experiences, what they're feeling."

"Well, I prefer literature that imagines what life could be like if it wasn't full of limitations and expectations and tragedy."

"You've read *Pride and Prejudice* eleven times and you've never picked up on the fact that it's *about* limitations and expectations?" Jake says beneath a smile.

"Sure, but it's about overcoming them! Austen didn't agree with the societal rules of her time and place. In her world, you married your financial and social equal. Marrying outside your class was basically unthinkable. But in her books, people marry who they fall in love with, despite the social implications. She was writing about what she hoped, dreamed would one day be a reality."

"Is that why she never married?" Jake asks.

"That's my theory." I set the book on his desk. "Technically, she was engaged for one night, to this rich guy named Harris Bigg-Wither."

Jake snorts. "You're making that up."

"I'm one hundred percent serious. Engaged for one night,

woke up the next day and broke it off. Saved herself the trouble of marrying without affection."

Jake raises his eyebrows but otherwise keeps a straight face. "Or the trouble of answering to the name of Mrs. Bigg-Wither."

"I doubt a slightly goofy name would've mattered to her if she'd actually loved the guy."

"Hmm. So you think names don't matter?"

I'm not sure how to respond to that. Is he making a jab at my surname—the one that tells everyone I come from wealth and privilege, the one that tells them nothing about me as a person?

Katie pops her head in. "Ready? Sorry about that. Lorenzo was freaking out about this scholarship."

"That's okay." With the Anaya novel in hand, I follow her out of the room but turn around at the doorway. Jake is watching me, and I smile at him.

Sleep evades me much of the night as I try to find a way to get comfortable on a bed filled with air. Every time I shift or roll over, the sound of my body rubbing on the vinyl jolts me awake, and I worry that it's doing the same to Katie. Adjusting my body to different positions only pushes the bulk of the air from one side of the mattress to the other.

I don't see Jake in the morning. When I head to the bathroom to get dressed, his door is open, but he's not in there; nor is he in the living room.

I try to be quiet as I return to Katie's room. Katie is asleep on her stomach, covers kicked onto the floor, her feet dangling over the side. I leave the air mattress inflated on the floor, not knowing how to empty it or how it's supposed to be put away.

I pull a sticky note out of my bag and scribble a thank-you, which I stick on the mirror so Katie won't miss it.

When I get back to Ricardo and Yoly's, the apartment is empty. The family needed to be gone early for the hearing, and Ricardo and Yoly are probably at work already.

I revel in the comfort of the couch my body has become accustomed to over the last several weeks. I'll take this lumpy piece of secondhand furniture over a plastic mattress filled with air. My back sinks into the contours of the now-familiar cushions.

I have a few minutes before I need to get ready to meet Layla for yoga in the park. I open ChitChat, scroll past Layla's selfie with her Prada yoga mat, block yet another suggested post promoting Bernard Wright, and read the next installment of Junior Vega's new story. *When you're a monozygotic copy of the boy you shared a room with your entire life, there is a bond that can't be broken by earthly matters.* And that's it for today. I'll have to wait until tomorrow to find out what happens to these twin brothers.

Towering ginkgo trees frame the entrance of Central Park. More of them welcome me along the wide pathway as I leave the cacophony of traffic behind. A pair of runners dashes past me, weaving around a woman with a jogging stroller, her child's arms stretching out in the air.

Another woman pushing a stroller approaches me from the opposite direction—and waves as she comes closer. "Maya! Maya."

I don't recognize her until she's just a few feet away. Lisa Piccola has been my father's personal assistant since I was in elementary school. She's a tiny woman with long, gray-streaked dark hair. "Lisa! Hello."

She steps away from the stroller and gives me a hug. "Maya, I haven't seen you in forever. You stopped coming by the office."

I stopped a long time ago, when I grew weary of witnessing Dad in boss mode. He yelled at his employees and demeaned them, often in front of others, without ever voicing even the smallest apology. No task, it seemed, could be completed to his satisfaction.

But I don't say this to Lisa. We don't speak ill of Dad outside the family. "I know. School has just been so busy, and I'll be starting college soon."

"That's wonderful. I'm sure your dad is just so proud of you."

Nope. And she knows that, because she's seen him at his worst. I guess the paycheck must go a long way toward making up for the behavior she has to deal with.

"Who's this little one?" I point to the stroller.

"This is my granddaughter, Patty." She pulls up the sun visor so I can get a good look at her.

"Hi, Patty." I wave at the little girl, who seems to be about two.

"I retired this spring to take care of Patty full-time," Lisa tells me. "My daughter works on Wall Street, and she had a hard time finding good, reliable care."

"You retired? I didn't know that. My dad is probably lost without you."

She forces a smile. "He's doing just fine, I suspect. I trained my replacement. She's young and eager to take on a lot. She's doing great—has even stopped calling me with a million questions like she did the first few weeks."

"I can't believe you left. I can't imagine that place without you." Lisa knew everything that went on at that company.

Lisa squeezes her lips into a tight line. "Yeah. It was getting to be a little too much."

I nod, remembering late nights when I would walk past Dad's home office and hear him barking orders at Lisa over the phone. I'm tempted to ask what the last straw was, but that feels too nosy. Retirement looks good on her, and she probably doesn't want to think back to work.

"It's so good to see you, Lisa. And your granddaughter is adorable."

"She's a lot of fun. She keeps me young. We come here for a long walk almost every day."

"Hopefully I'll run into you again soon."

"Take care, Maya. Give my love to your mother." She gives me a final wave as they take off again.

I wave goodbye and speed up so I won't be late to meet Layla.

CHAPTER FOURTEEN

As I approach the front door of the writing room building on Monday evening, a teen girl comes down the stairs. I take in her uncombed blond hair, reddened eyes, blistery complexion, and ragged clothes. Her smell matches her appearance. I look away.

"Where's Jake?" she asks. "They said he isn't up there."

"Um, I don't know. Maybe he's at his other job. He'll probably come by later."

The girl comes closer to me. "Well, I have to talk to him. It's very important."

"Maybe you can check back in a little while." I grab the doorknob to go inside.

"No, it has to be now. He owes me ten bucks. Do you have ten bucks?"

I open the door, fighting an urge to bolt up the stairs. "No," I say honestly. I never carry cash.

The girl grabs my arm. "Please. I'll pay you back. I promise. He owes me. You can get it from him when he gets here."

"Sorry, I have to go."

I don't see it coming, but I feel it: the girl hits me with something hard. The jagged edges of whatever it is tear at the skin on my cheek. I try to grab her arm so she doesn't do it again, but she pulls my bag off my shoulder and runs down the street.

I wince in pain but run after her. My life is in that bag; I can't let it go.

The girl crosses heavy traffic and keeps running along the opposite sidewalk. I dash toward the end of the block, headed for the crosswalk, and collide with someone. The impact jars me and I stumble.

"Hey, what's the hurry?" It's Jake.

I keep running. "Your *friend* stole my bag!" I call over my shoulder as I cross the street.

Jake outruns me about three seconds later. He's right behind the girl as she darts down the stairs to a subway stop.

I reach the bottom of the subway steps in time to see the girl hurdle the turnstile and run onto the train just as the door's closing. Jake's about to jump over the turnstile too, but the train is already moving. The girl watches through a window, clutching my messenger bag.

I let out a shriek of frustration. "There goes my bag, my laptop, everything!"

Jake comes toward me. "I'm sorry." For the first time, he notices my face and reaches out to wipe a streak of blood dripping down my cheek. "Did she do this?"

"Yes, but I'm fine. I don't care. I just want my bag."

"What did she hit you with?" he asks as he wipes his bloody hand on his shirt.

"I don't know. A rock, maybe?"

"We've got to get this looked at. Let's go."

"No, I've got to get that laptop back. I can't afford a new one right now. Plus it has so much of my work on it—"

"Don't you have your articles backed up?" he asks.

"Some of them, but not everything I'm working on. I do a lot of my brainstorming and drafting in my notebooks, which are also in my bag. And that bag . . . it's special."

Jake reaches into his back pocket for his cell phone. "Let me text Buck. He can be on the lookout for her. He might know where she's headed, maybe even where she'll go to hock it."

"Hock it?"

"Yeah. She'll take it to a pawnshop." He asks me for a description of the bag and what's inside, swipes out a quick message on his phone screen, and turns back to me. "I've asked Buck to check a few places and keep me posted. Please, can we go get you checked out?"

"I'll be fine. It's just a surface-level scratch. Nothing's broken. I'm not concussed or anything."

"At least let's get some ice on it."

We walk up the stairs to the street, and Jake hails a cab.

At our building, he takes my hand when I get out of the taxi and keeps holding it as he leads me inside.

We end up in his room. I sit on his bed, and he brings a first aid kit and an ice pack. He puts some ointment on my scratch and covers it with a Band-Aid. Finally he holds the ice pack up to my eye. "I'm so sorry about this."

"It's not your fault; you're not the one who mugged me." I glance at him with my unobstructed eye. "She said you owe her money."

He sighs and sits down on the bed next to me. "Well, that's not true. I've *given* her money in the past—everything from cash to gift cards for restaurants. But I found out she was selling the gift cards for half the price to get money so she could get high. It's really tough to see. Buck's brought her to the shelter sometimes, but she tends to get violent with the other people there. Definitely not the case for everybody using drugs, but that's how she's been."

"Is that how you know her? Through Buck?"

"Yeah. He's tried to help her, but it's a long hard road to recovery once you're dealing with that kind of addiction, and nobody else can walk that road for you."

I take the ice pack off my face because it feels too cold.

Jake pulls out his cell phone. "Buck hasn't texted back. If you're okay on your own, I can go look for your bag myself. I have some ideas about where she might take it."

"I appreciate that." I get up from his bed. "I appreciate *all* of this," I say, handing the ice pack to him.

"It's the least I can do. I take full responsibility. If she hadn't been looking for me, this wouldn't have happened."

I say goodbye and leave his apartment, trying not to wince at the pain.

Pain reliever. Notify credit card company. Two things to do and then I can lie down, close my eyes, and pretend this never happened.

But it did happen, and I may never see my bag again. The beautiful bag that connected me to Mom, bridging the three thousand miles that divide us.

When Yoly sees my face, she flips out. Explaining what happened only intensifies her worry. "I knew I didn't like you going to that writing room. I told Ricardo, I don't think Maya should be going there every night. Ay ay. When your mom finds out, she's going to kill me."

"She's not going to find out. Yoly, I'm fine."

"I'm sorry, Maya. Did you call the police?"

"No. I mean, I don't think that would help anything."

She sighs. "I agree, but you're handling this more calmly than I would. You've gotta be pretty shaken up."

There's no denying that. I've never had anything like this happen to me before. With my new independence comes the necessity of taking care of myself and being more aware of my surroundings. Today was a failure on that front. My father would certainly have a good laugh at my naiveté. And then he would tell me how disappointed he is in me for letting my guard down, letting myself get taken advantage of.

I try to push aside the thoughts of what Dad would say, but they're replaced with Victoria's warnings about how unsafe New York is and her urgings that I move out of this city. I wish I could call Mom and tell her what's happened, but if she knew about this incident she'd be overcome with worry and probably tell me I shouldn't be going to a strange apartment building.

Yoly takes my chin in her hand and turns my face from side to side, trying to see how bad the damage is. "What if she comes back to the building?"

"She won't," I say even though I'm nowhere near sure about this. The fact is, I don't want to feel afraid of going to the writing room. It's become a haven for me, a place where I feel centered, and I don't want to lose that.

I remind myself that the woman wasn't targeting me directly; she didn't know anything about me except that I was entering the building where Jake spends a lot of time. It's hard for me to wrap my head around what her life must be like; I know only a sliver of her story. But I do know that her showing up there was a desperate move, and that her taking my bag was even more desperate. I just have to hope that she won't feel the need to do something like that again.

I must've fallen asleep because the next thing I hear is a soft knock on the door. I sit up on the couch and look at my phone; it's late. Yoly and Ricardo must be in bed.

I open the door to find Jake holding my laptop bag. "Sorry it took so long."

"You got it back! Where'd you find it?" I open the bag quickly. My wallet's gone, but that's no surprise. The laptop looks undamaged. The notebooks are all there.

"Buck found one of her friends who said she always takes her stuff to this place on Columbus. Most pawnshops won't buy anything from her; they know it's all stolen. But this place always takes whatever she brings. So I went there. The guy said she'd just brought it in."

"Thank you so much!" I clutch the bag to my chest. I've been worried about the laptop, about the articles, but losing the bag felt like losing a part of my mom. I run my hand over the woven blue and green diamond shapes, which remind me that even though we're in different corners of the universe, we are still connected on this path.

Jake steps back, his hands in his pockets. "That bag is special to you?"

I look up at him. "Yeah, my mom gave it to me."

His worried expression relaxes into a smile. "I'm so glad you have it back. Is anything missing?"

"Just my wallet. I already canceled my credit card, and I didn't have any cash in there. Guess I'll just need to get my ID replaced."

He reaches into his back pocket and takes out his wallet. "I'll cover the cost of your duplicate license. What's the fee, like twenty dollars?"

"No, that's okay."

"Maya, I have to."

"No. I owe *you* money. How much did you have to pay to get this back? I know they didn't just give it to you."

"No way. You're not paying me back for that."

I smile. "All right then, we're even. Thank you for everything." I sling one arm around his neck for a quick hug . . . but stay there. He wraps his arms around my waist.

After a moment he pulls away. "I'd better let you rest. Sorry you didn't get any work done today."

"That's okay. I'll work extra tomorrow. Meanwhile I'll take this as a sign from the universe to back up all my files. In several places." I force a smile, which he almost manages to return. "Thanks again."

"G'night, Maya."

The next morning, I'm on the couch resting, as Yoly instructed me to do before she left for work. Even though pitch letters and my latest book review are calling my name, I set aside these adult worries for the moment. I feel like being the mythical lazy teen Dad keeps telling me about. I scroll through Chit-Chat—Layla holding coffees for some executives while wearing a cute outfit, with all the right filters; Lucinda on a yacht in the Mediterranean—until I find the latest Junior Vega paragraph: *Viktor's brother, Marcus, didn't grow up seeing people as potential threats at worst and liabilities at best. That was Viktor's department. Marcus was a trusting boy whose smile reached out to anybody who came within his sightline.*

Once I'm caught up on social media, I pick up *Bless Me, Ultima*. I'm close to finishing and try to take good care of the thin pages as I turn them. They're covered in handwritten notes that seem to get more enthusiastic the deeper into the book I get. There's one line that's highlighted, underlined, *and* framed by hand-drawn stars.

There's a knock on the door, so I pull myself off the couch and comb my hair down as I walk toward it.

Jake stands there holding a napkin-covered plate in one hand and a paper bag in the other. "I came to see how you were doing. Hope that's all right."

"Sure. I'm feeling much better." I cross my arms over my chest because I'm not wearing a bra under my thin white T-shirt, but there's no way to make up for my cutoff sweats. I could've probably done a better job at taming my hair as well.

His eyes instinctively go to my bruised cheek. I look horrible—I know that. "I brought you some breakfast."

"Thank you." I'm about to reach for the plate, but it occurs to me that he doesn't seem in his usual hurry to get away. "Do you . . . want to come in?"

"Sure, for a minute."

He takes the plate over to the table and sits down in the chair across from it.

I take the opposite chair. "This looks delicious." I tilt my head to peek at what's under the napkin: a buttery bun covered with powdered sugar.

"It's my mom's egg-and-cheese breakfast sandwich. She used to make it all the time."

I want to dig in, but I'm worried I'll end up with a face full of powdered sugar. I take a careful bite and am quick to wipe my mouth. "Mmm. This is so good."

"It's my favorite breakfast." He hands over the paper bag. "So, I've mentioned the T-shirt shop where I work. I made this for you."

I open it and pull out a light gray T-shirt. It's screen-printed with a black sketch of Jane Austen and her signature beneath her picture. "Wow. Thank you. This is really cool. I love it." I hold the T-shirt out in front of me to take in all the details. Registering *his* shirt, which I've seen before, I ask, "So, who or what is Menudo?"

He laughs. "They were a Puerto Rican boy band back in the day. My mom was a fan growing up, and my dad got her this shirt."

"That's cool. It's like you carry a piece of your parents around with you."

"Yeah—it's so worn, I'm worried it can only withstand a few more washes before it just falls apart."

"Well, thank you for making this shirt for me. That was really nice."

"I'm glad you like it. And I've started rereading *Pride and Prejudice*. So far it's pretty good the second time around."

I press my T-shirt to my chest and grin. "I told you! It holds up!"

He laughs. "Yeah. I don't think I'll be challenging your record anytime soon, but it's worth revisiting."

"And I've been reading *Bless Me, Ultima*. I like it a lot. I'd like to feature it in my book review for my sister's magazine." It was published in 1972, which qualifies it as a classic by my standards.

"Yeah? What do you like most about it?"

"The symbolism, probably. It gives me a lot to think about. I've been reading some of the notes in the margins—are those yours or your dad's?"

"My dad's. That's one thing I love about reading his books. He's marked them all up, and I get to kind of know what he was thinking when he read them."

I grab his dad's book off the coffee table. "I know you said this is your dad's favorite book. Is it yours too?"

"Nah. I sort of have a love-hate relationship with it."

"Why?"

"I love it because he loved it, and I hate it because of how it describes tragedy."

"Like in this bit here?" I open the book to the page with the ultra-highlighted quote and hold it out to him.

He nods. "Yep. I've read that book so many times trying to figure out what he loved so much about that line."

It's a reflection on overcoming the hard things that happen to you through human fortitude. "It's very hopeful," I say. "Uplifting."

He turns his eyes away from the page. "It's bullshit."

"How is it bullshit?"

"Suffering doesn't exist to make us stronger or to teach us lessons or to help us prove ourselves. There's no grander meaning in it. It just happens. It's random—or it's on purpose, inflicted deliberately, by people or by systems. But it's not a plot point you can just convert into something good and then move past."

I absorb that for a few moments. "Do you think your dad felt differently?"

Jake shrugs. "He was a freaking optimist. Glass-half-full kind of guy."

I immediately regret asking the question. His dad died in a terrible, random, senseless way. For Jake, that probably outweighs anything his dad believed while he was alive.

Then again, if Jake didn't want me to ask uncomfortable questions, he could've just not loaned me the novel or not told me about its significance. "Why did you suggest I read this?"

He looks up at me and then back down toward the floor. "I wanted to know what you thought of it." His eyes float up to meet mine. "The boy in the book—Antonio—he says that the tragedy could not defeat him, but sometimes I feel like all tragedy *can* do is defeat us. What do you think?"

His eyes search mine, and I don't have anything profound to offer. It's not like I'm an expert. My current problems are minimal compared to what Jake has faced, compared to what others endure. In the past week alone, I've crossed paths with multiple people who live in a much crueler world than I can even imagine.

All my life, Dad has told us that hardships will build character and strength, so he's sought to manufacture obstacles for us. The implication is that if I can't meet those challenges on my own, I'll somehow be a failure. If I feel defeated by *my* predicament, how can I expect someone else to overcome a real tragedy?

"I don't know." I wish I had a better answer.

CHAPTER FIFTEEN

On Tuesday night, after Jake walks me home from the writing room, I watch his retreating figure through the small square window of the building's front door. As usual, he's headed away from the apartment to some mysterious destination. He told me he helps Buck "once in a while," so what is he doing the rest of the time?

I open the door slightly and peer around it, just in time to see him turn the corner. I step outside and take the steps two at a time, holding my bag closely so it won't jostle at my side.

When I reach the end of the block, I push my back against the wall of the nearest brownstone. Slowly, I peek around the corner, fully expecting he'll be right there to catch me. He isn't; I can see him still walking, about half a block ahead. He stops, watches for traffic, and crosses in the middle of the street. I stay frozen, my back against the wall. Moving even an inch would surely attract his attention.

I'm not even sure why I'm following him. It's beyond simple curiosity; it feels like a need to know.

I hazard another glance, and he's hailing a cab. He is quickly picked up and almost out of sight. The cab hits a red light and stops abruptly. Thank goodness for New York City stoplights. I step out into traffic and am able to wave down my own cab.

The driver looks into his mirror and catches my eyes. "Where to?"

This is something I never thought I'd say. In fact, it's so outrageous that I wonder how the driver will react. "Can you please follow that taxi that's three cars in front of us?"

"You got it."

It surprises me that he doesn't hesitate or question my motive, like he tails other vehicles on a daily basis. He follows Jake's taxi, but not too closely.

"Boyfriend cheating on you?" he asks.

"What? No, nothing like that."

"Sorry. Don't mean to pry."

After that, he's mercifully silent. My cab stays three or four cars behind Jake's. Deep red brake lights indicate his cab will be coming to a stop. It does, right in front of a bar.

"Want me to wait here?" the driver asks.

"Yes, please." I watch as Jake exits his cab and walks toward the bar's entrance.

The building has small windows framed by discolored wood. On the door is a neon sign with an image of a bottle being poured into a martini glass and another sign that says *Roxie's.* Jake leans against the panel of windows, lights up a cigarette, and takes several deep puffs.

"Are you getting out here?" the cab driver asks me.

"No. Let's wait a few minutes and then can you please drive me back near where you picked me up?"

"Whatever. It's your coin." Yep, another expense to dent my account balance. Luckily I just got paid for this week's *Latina at Large* piece, so I won't have to dip into my library paycheck, which I'm supposed to be saving for this fall's student housing.

I watch Jake a few more minutes. What is he doing here?

Is he meeting someone? Why would he drive out here to go to a seedy bar? These kinds of bars are all over the city. You don't have to take a cab ride to go to one.

He takes one last puff, squashes the cigarette with his shoe, and goes inside. I want to be the proverbial fly on the wall inside that bar, but I can't risk being discovered. Is it the same place he goes every night? Why would they let a nineteen-year-old in? Maybe he has a fake ID.

I ask the driver to take me back, and as we drive away, I realize I'm not any closer to answers.

The next day, I'm exhausted. I'm grateful that there's still coffee left in the pot Ricardo started. Before even thinking about eating, I drain an entire cup and read the end of Junior Vega's most recently published short story. It took me a while to get my hands on the magazine it's in; I put a hold on it at the library weeks ago. A text from Victoria interrupts me but proves thematically appropriate.

Victoria: I checked out Junior Vega on ChitChat. Quite a following he has!

Me: What do you think of me doing an article about his work?

Victoria: For the classics book review?

Me: Yeah, as a sort of spin-off from what we tend to think of as a classic.

Victoria: Hmm, seems like a bit of a stretch. How about making it a whole separate article? Maybe twice the length of one of your book reviews? I'd pay you double your usual rate. How's that sound?

Me: Um, is that a trick question? It sounds ideal.

Victoria: Go for it. Send it to me when you have it, and I'll slot it in. If it gets good traffic on the website, we can talk about shifting your regular book review in that direction too. Meanwhile, any luck with your other pitches?

Ugh. I haven't followed up with the person who rejected my first pitch but invited me to try again. I know there are interesting ideas in my brainstorming notebook that I can draw on. I just need to go get it.

Before I can respond to Victoria, a FaceTime call comes in from my brother. "Daniel! How are you? I miss you."

"Hey, Mayita. Miss you too." His black hair is slicked back with a generous amount of gel—part of his look for the cruise performance. It's so nice to see his face, animated with enthusiasm as usual. "I've been wanting to call you, but it's been tricky with the time difference and our schedule, plus sometimes we don't have service."

"How's the show?"

"So much fun. We've only got about a month left, and then we'll be back home. I can't wait to see you."

"Me too. And how's your boyfriend?" I don't know Adam. He and Daniel met on the tour, and they've only been dating a couple of months.

"Good. He's from New York too, so we'll be heading back together. He's lined up a gig apartment-sitting for a friend who's going on tour, a studio out in Inwood, through the end of the year. You'll have plenty of time to get to know him."

"I can't wait to meet him. Have you talked to Victoria?"

"No. I'm going to call her next. Sorry neither one of us was there for graduation. I bet that was a bummer."

"Yeah, quite the bummer."

"Have you seen Dad since you left?"

“Nope.” I haven’t so much as had a text from him for days. I’m tempted to tell Daniel about *Charlotte’s Web* and the health insurance and every other petty thing Dad’s done to me. But that wouldn’t fix anything. “I’m going to stop by his place in a bit, actually. I have to pick up a notebook.” I make the decision as I’m saying it. I should go this morning. Might as well get it over with. “Hopefully I won’t run into him.”

I tell Daniel I don’t want to see Dad, and the logical part of me doesn’t. But there’s always a small, irrational part of me holding out hope that my father will be different this time. That he’ll pull me into his arms, tell me he’s proud of me, and be the parent I’ve always wanted him to be.

We talk for a little longer, about the show and the beautiful places the ship has visited. I love that he’s experiencing this freedom, away from Dad and everything that kept him tethered to a life he didn’t want. In some ways, Dad was harder on him than on Victoria and me combined.

After breakfast, I clean up and still have enough time to swing back home—I mean, to my dad’s place—to grab that notebook before my shift starts. I decide to wear the Jane Austen shirt Jake gave me, for luck.

Anxiety filters through my entire body as I approach the building I called home for so many years.

Marcus, the doorman, brightens as he recognizes me. “Maya! Hello. I haven’t seen you in a long time. You’re off at college?” He opens the door as I come to a stop in front of him.

“College is starting soon.” I keep my answer vague. I know my dad brags to his business associates—people he sees as his equals—about not giving his children handouts, but I don't know how much of that filters down to people he considers beneath him. I wonder how someone like Marcus would view my situation. Would he pity the poor neglected daughter of a multimillionaire, or would he feel a certain satisfaction in knowing I'm no longer cocooned by privilege?

"Well, good to see you," he says. "Don't stay away too much."

I smile and wish him a good day before I head to the elevator.

I've pushed the *12* in this elevator so many times, but today feels different. I'm not coming home, to my room, to a place where I belong. This is not my button to press, not anymore.

The doors open on the twelfth floor with the *ding* as familiar as the voices of my family members. In front of our apartment, I automatically enter the four-digit key code into the keypad above the doorknob.

It doesn't work. Dad must've changed the code. I knock instead.

Melinda opens the apartment door, and shock flashes across her face. "Maya. My Maya." She pulls me in for a hug, grasps my arms and holds me out so she can get a good look at me, as if we've been apart for years. I take her in the same way. She's wearing her trademark khaki pants, light blue button-down, and pale yellow cardigan. Her grayish-brown hair, as always, is in a tight bun. "How are you?"

"I'm good. How about you?"

She frowns and hugs me again. "I miss you. I worry about you."

Melinda has been with our family since just before the divorce. She was here for the worst part of my parents' marriage, when each day started and ended with loud arguments that sent Mom crying into her bathroom. Dad always had the last word, even if it was an insult delivered through gritted teeth to the closed bathroom door.

"I've missed you too." The worry is also reciprocated; she's basically alone in this gloomy apartment, devoid of kindness or joy. "I'm doing fine. I came by to pick up a notebook."

"And how is the place you're staying? With your friend?"

I reassure her that I'm fine, and she releases me after one more hug.

I go past the front room, which is hardly ever used. I was never allowed to be in there with my friends. Dad has no friends, just business acquaintances whom he usually meets in his home office. I look at the ivory-colored leather couches and wonder when someone last sat on them.

I approach the hall leading to my bedroom, grateful that the door to Dad's home office is closed and hoping I can grab my notebook and be gone before he even figures out I'm here. I pad quietly past the door and am almost to the corner when it opens.

By reflex, I turn. Two more feet, and I would've been around the corner and out of sight. By turning around I've called attention to myself. I look up, prepared for his foul mood and a disappointed diatribe, but it isn't his face I see.

It *is* a face I recognize—one I've only recently become acquainted with. Bernard Wright.

The man I've seen too often on Julissa's tablet and my Chit-Chat feed, spewing hateful words, stands right in front of me. My voice fails me as I stare at too-dark brown hair that doesn't match the age of the weathered face. Definitely a dye job to try to look younger, but it just radiates fakeness.

His wrinkles relax into a smile as he nods at me and says, "Afternoon." He continues down the hall, and I hear him say, "So good to see you again, Melinda. Always a pleasure."

"You too, Mr. Wright. Let me show you out."

Good to see you again? Always a pleasure? How does Melinda know this man and why is he in our home? I'm stuck in place, unable to move. A quicker retreat would've led me to my room before Dad peeks his head out of his office.

"Maya? I didn't know you were here." He walks toward me, sleeves rolled up, a drink in his hand.

"I came to pick up a notebook I need. Why was that man here?"

He glances behind him. "Bernard. He's a friend."

"A *friend*? Dad, have you heard the things he's been saying? Disgusting, racist things—"

With a snort, he drains his glass. "Racist? Is that the word all the kids are using these days to refer to things they don't like?"

"Dad, look him up. He says terrible things about immigrants, about how they're going to replace white people." What was the term Brady used? "Great replacement" theory, I think.

"And?" He walks back into his office to pour another drink.

I follow him to the drink cart. "And it's kind of disturbing!"

"Don't be such a nitwit, Maya. Look around." He makes a sweeping gesture with his glass. "He's right. There are illegals coming over the border, being flown or bused right into New York. Pretty soon there will be more of them than there are of us."

"Them? Us? Do you hear yourself?" Which one, in his eyes, am I?

The landline phone on his desk rings, and he waves me away. "Let yourself out, will you? I have to take this."

I don't move. I can't move. "Dad, you do know that you married an immigrant and that you have three kids who are children of an immigrant."

He's already picking up the phone. He barks into it, "Hold

on a minute" and puts his hand over the receiver so he can respond to me. "Your mother came here the right way, didn't sneak in across the border. But you'll notice, she's not even an American. She doesn't love America; she left the first chance she got. The people coming here aren't Americans. They don't love this country like those of us who've been here for generations."

My head is spinning. What does loving America even mean and what does it have to do with anything? "Dad—"

He puts his hand up, starts speaking into the phone, slides into his desk chair, and swivels away from me.

I haven't said exactly what I want to say to him, but I'm pretty sure it wouldn't make any difference if I did.

I snatch my notebook from my room without pausing to look around and head back toward the front door. I want to stop to ask Melinda what she knows about Bernard Wright and how often he's been here, but more than anything, I feel the need to just get out of here.

When I come up the steps to the library, my heartbeat still thrums as rapidly as when I came face-to-face with Bernard Wright. I can't quite catch my breath, and I'm not sure if it's because I jogged over here or because the sight of Wright's snide face is seared in my mind.

Yoly. I need to find Yoly. I need to tell her what happened, try to make sense of it all.

She's in the breakroom, leaning against the counter with a cup of tea.

"Yoly." I grab her arm because I just need someone to hold on to. "I went home—to my dad's—and Bernard Wright was there."

She puts her tea down on the counter. "White supremacist Bernard Wright?"

"Yes. Dad said Wright is his friend, and I was like, do you know the kinds of things he says, but he didn't care. He was dismissive of everything I said. I don't understand, Yoly. How can he be friends with a racist? My dad is not a racist."

Yoly gives me a little shrug. "Have they been friends for a long time?"

"I don't know. I should've asked Melinda."

"And this is the first time you've seen him hanging out at your home?"

"I've never seen him before." I slide down onto a chair at one of the breakroom's tables. "Maybe my dad doesn't know that Wright's thinking of running for governor."

Yoly looks at me and twists her lips like she wants to say something, but she doesn't.

I keep talking, as if I'm trying to convince her of something. "It doesn't make sense that my dad would support what this guy stands for."

With a sigh, Yoly says, "I think it does. He's probably afraid of losing his power."

"My dad?"

"Yes. He knows Wright will support policies that will keep him wealthy."

"But why does he care about money so much?" I'm starting to sound a bit desperate. "He already has millions and millions of dollars."

"Maybe it's less about the money itself," says Yoly, "and more about being at the top rung of the ladder in our society. Feeling like he's superior to other people. Feeling like he has control and the rest of us don't." She shrugs. "That's my best guess. I have to get back to work, but let me know if you want to talk later." She grabs her tea and is out the door.

I still have a few minutes before my shift starts, so I stay in the breakroom, alone, trying to collect my thoughts. I decide to FaceTime Victoria, and she answers right away.

"Maya, how are you?" She's in her office, wearing her glasses and half-looking at a computer screen.

"Are you busy?"

"Never too busy for you." She takes off her glasses and turns fully to her phone screen.

"Remember that guy I was telling you about?"

"Jake, the overly formal weirdo?"

"No, not Jake. Bernard Wright, the guy who's thinking of running for governor."

"Oh, yeah. I looked him up. Loathsome dude."

"Well, I went home—to Dad's place—and Bernard Wright was there, leaving Dad's office, and he acted like he'd been there before. He told Melinda that it's always a pleasure. Dad said he was a friend and then made a ton of excuses for him. Said I'm a nitwit for thinking Wright is racist."

"He called you a nitwit?"

I shrug because it isn't the first time.

Victoria makes a disgusted noise in her throat. "I hate him so much. I wish you would just come here. I don't want you anywhere near either of them."

"What do you think Wright was even doing there?"

Victoria chews on her lip. "I don't know. Whatever it is, I don't like it. Are you feeling okay after running into him?"

"I think so. It just felt really shocking in the moment. I want to know why Dad considers this guy his friend. I've heard so many bad things about him; I've heard his ideas from his own mouth."

My dad is not a racist. How can he be when he married a woman from Guatemala and has three brown children?

Yoly's twisted lips when I told her I didn't think my dad could support a racist remain vivid in my mind. She didn't seem to believe me. What does she think of my dad?

What do *I* think of my dad? I know he loved my mother, started a life with her, had children with her. But he never really embraced her culture. He went to Guatemala a few times when they were first married, but he didn't usually come with us on our annual summer vacations to visit Mamá Juana and the rest of my mom's family. Victoria's memories of that one summer visit stand out because they're so unusual.

Dad never took the time to really learn Spanish. When we were little, Mom took a few years off work to stay home with us and we spoke Spanish all day long, but when Dad came home, we knew we had to switch to English. As the years went by and Mom went back to work and we were all in school, there was less Spanish at home. Little by little my fluency dwindled to the point where it's now choppy and imperfect.

And then came the day he put an embargo on travel to Guatemala. None of us were allowed to go—until Mom decided she would go even if it meant leaving me behind.

"There's no point in trying to understand people like that," Victoria tells me. "The best thing to do is keep your distance. And be careful."

"Of Wright?" I ask, thinking it's highly unlikely I'll cross paths with him again.

"Of Dad," she says.

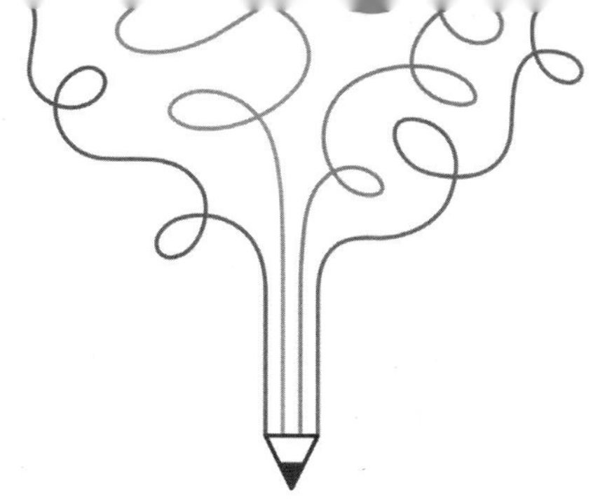

CHAPTER SIXTEEN

I enter the writing room and set my heavy bag at my feet. A quick glance at the fire escape shows Jake writing in his notebook. I watch him. Deep furrows in his forehead, brows drawn together in concentration. I envy the pencil in his hand; it knows the words that flow from his mind. I want to know what he writes, what he feels.

He scratches his right arm under his sleeve; I notice he has a square patch there. He looks up and sees me. A smile forms on his lips, and the tight wrinkles around his eyes dissolve. He might actually be happy to see me. He keeps his gaze on me, and I'm drawn to the fire escape.

I've never ventured out there before. It's his sanctuary, where he goes to get away from everyone. His inviting smile encourages me, though. Barely disturbing Glen's slumber, I climb over the couch and open the window.

"Mind if I come out for a second?" I ask.

He slides over, making room for me on the small platform. There isn't much space, but I squeeze in.

"I just wanted to say thank you again for the shirt. It fits perfectly. As you can see." I gesture awkwardly at myself, wishing I'd thought of something less ridiculous to say. I just really want to be out here with him.

He looks down and nods. "I'm glad."

I want to ask what he's been writing. His small notebook is on his lap, turned down; it's not for my consumption.

I'm starting to wonder if I should just go right back inside when he clears his throat.

"Katie said you really liked her arroz con gandules at Sunday dinner."

"It was delicious. She's a great cook."

"She's great at lots of things. Anyway, I wanted to tell you about this place I've been to that has the best arroz con gandules, even better than Katie's. It's up on 125th Street. I could give you the address if you ever wanted to go."

Give me the address? What is he talking about? "Thanks," I say cautiously. "That . . . would be great. I . . . hope I can find someone to go with me, though. I hate eating alone."

He thinks for a moment. "It's kind of hard to find. Want me to just show you sometime?"

He has a funny way of asking a person out on a date. Probably doesn't do it very often. He's not the type to flirt with someone on a whim. But he's playing it cool, so I try to do the same. "Sounds good."

"How about Friday?"

"Yeah, that works." Definitely a date, right?

One side of his lip comes up in a tentative half-smile before his eyes dart to the ground. He fiddles with the spiral of his notebook, scratches the square patch again.

How do we follow that up? I reach for something casual to say. "Nicotine patch?" I ask, gesturing to his arm.

He shrugs. "I'm trying to give up smoking. The patch is driving me up the wall, though."

"Worth it if it works, I guess."

"I guess so." He fiddles with the spiral, his eyes still downcast. "It's only been a few days, so I hope I can stick with it."

"Good for you. What made you decide to quit?"

He shrugs. "City's getting strict. It's hard to find anywhere to smoke these days." He looks up at me, stopping all his nervous movements at once. "Besides, I don't want to smell like cigarettes when I ask if I can kiss you."

His eyes hold my gaze. I feel tiny pricks all over my body. The shivering up my spine and the gnawing in my stomach confirm that this is what I've been wanting to hear.

I lean in, closing the tiny space between us. I shut my eyes and bring my lips to his. Feeling his lips intensifies the surges coursing up my spine, and I shiver despite the harshness of the sun's rays. His gentle kiss strengthens with each second. I bring my hands to his face, taking in its texture.

He pulls away slightly, catching his breath. He leans back against the railing, one hand over his knee and the other smoothing my hair as I press myself against him. The traffic below us is now more audible; I must've blocked out the noise while we were kissing.

There's no need to speak—and Jake, being a man of few words, probably prefers it that way. I feel the soft, soothing movements of his hand on my hair and close my eyes to take it all in.

He clears his throat. "I'm probably keeping you from your work. You didn't come to the writing room to sit out here with me and waste your time."

"I don't consider this wasting time."

"I'm glad." He looks down at his lap as an embarrassed smile comes to his lips. "I was just thinking about you when you showed up."

"Really?"

"Yeah . . . Is that okay?"

"You don't have to ask my permission for your thoughts. But, for the record, it's very okay with me." I finger the gold cross hanging from his neck. "So, are you a church boy?"

He snickers. "Nah. My dad was. This is his chain. I like to keep it close to my heart." He ticks his head toward the window. "Want some company inside while you work?"

"I'd love that."

I hate to relinquish the privacy of the fire escape, but I definitely won't mind sitting next to him as a writing buddy. I follow as he crawls through the window and over Glen. He walks to an empty table and holds out a chair for me.

I take the seat and open my laptop. He sits next to me, leafs through his notebook, and starts writing with his stubby pencil.

"What are you working on now?"

He stops writing, smiles, and shakes his head. "Shh. Glen's sleeping."

I roll my eyes. "He sleeps through everything."

Glen stirs on the couch and turns onto his other side.

"See that? You almost woke him."

I give up. I pull out my notes on *Bless Me, Ultima* and work on drafting this week's book review. With all the upheaval of the past few days, I haven't had time to start the anti-classics article that Victoria approved, so I figure I'll get to it next week. Jake writes quietly alongside me for nearly an hour.

I pause in my work and stretch my arms. Next week's review is nearly finished. Pretty good considering how distracted I've been by my proximity to Jake. I turn to face him. He's looking down at his notebook, but smiling.

"Katie and I made some crockpot apple cobbler earlier," he says as we get up from our spots and head toward the door.

"Want to come over and try it? She was going to take some to Lorenzo's but hopefully she left us a little."

"Sure, that sounds great." We smile at each other. My new goal is to elicit as many smiles from him as I can.

He slides his hands into the pockets of his jeans and keeps up a steady stride. I grip the strap of my messenger bag, as I can see there's no chance of him trying to grab for my hand. Maybe handholding isn't his thing or maybe it's extremely too early for that.

At the apartment, Jake says, "Katie's still upstairs at Lorenzo's. They're doing scholarship applications."

The entire place smells of sweetness. I follow him into the kitchen, where he turns the crockpot off and takes off its lid. "Looks like she did leave us some." He takes out two bowls and spoons the cobbler into them. "You want some ice cream?"

"Mmm. That sounds delish." *Delish*? I sound like a middle-aged cooking YouTuber. He doesn't seem fazed, and hopefully he won't hold my awkwardness against me. I hold my dish out as he takes a large spoon and slides a scoop of vanilla ice cream on top of the cobbler. While we eat, I'm spared from making any other cringey comments.

He leans on the counter, one foot propped against the wall behind him, and I stand slightly in front of him. The only sounds in the room are the clinking of spoons. I don't know why conversation feels so impossible right now. Even my go-to bits of small talk fail me.

I'm trying to think of something to say—about Katie, about the cobbler, about anything—but nervous energy fills the room, and I'm coming up empty. Jake slides his empty bowl onto the counter.

"I really want to kiss you again," he says, but makes no

move to do it. He looks at me and then at the floor.

I put my bowl down next to his, place my hands on either side of his waist, and lean in just a little until he meets me in the middle.

His lips feel cold from the ice cream, and his kiss is firm. He moves his hands up my back, one rubbing between my shoulder blades while the other one squeezes my waist. I push myself against his chest so his back is completely flush against the wall. The kissing intensifies, so unlike our nervous, unsure movements from a minute ago. Nothing about Jake is unsure now.

The door opens, and Katie comes in. I pull away from Jake, but he keeps one arm around my waist.

"Hi, Maya," Katie says, a smile playing on her lips. "I don't know if you two should be in here unsupervised."

Jake snickers. "Leave the parenting to me, Katie."

I smile but wonder what she thinks of me kissing Jake.

"Don't mind me, I'll be in my room." She walks away, still smiling.

Jake's eyes are laser-focused on the floor. His hand is still on my waist, though, so I lean into him, staring straight at the gold cross that hangs from his neck.

He turns his head to look at me. "Sorry we were interrupted."

"That's okay," I say, trying to hold his gaze. I keep leaning my body against his. His other arm goes around my waist, and he kisses me again.

"I really like kissing you." He allows me to see a different kind of smile, one I like more than any of his others. It's shy, tentative. I think I can fall in love with that smile.

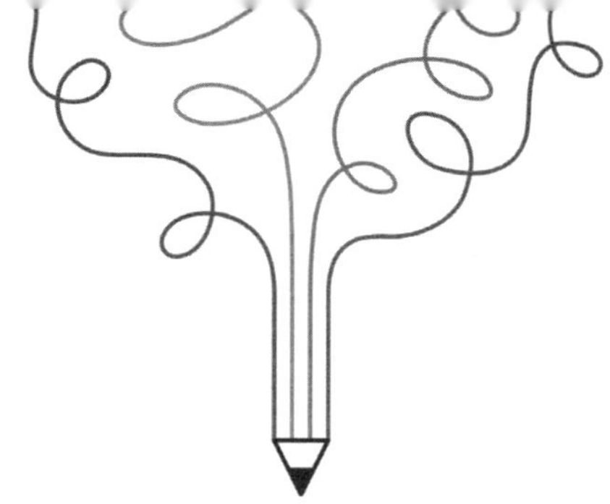

CHAPTER SEVENTEEN

We're in a cab headed to 125th Street. Jake and I are sitting about ten inches apart because even though we were very close last night, in the light of day, neither of us can quite figure out how to recreate that closeness. We steal glances at each other as the driver navigates through traffic up town. The humidity of the city air has followed us into the cab and this, coupled with the delayed sunset that summer brings, creates a heat that the AC can't handle.

"So, this is a Puerto Rican restaurant we're going to?" I ask.

"Yeah, the couple who owns it moved here from Puerto Rico about thirty years ago. I hope you like it."

"Katie says she wants to go to Puerto Rico one day."

"Yeah, maybe one day we'll go. I think my parents would've liked that. What about you—do you think you'll go to Guatemala soon?"

"Yeah, I really want to. I haven't seen my grandma in a long time, and I really miss my mom."

Jake reaches across the seat and covers my hand with his. He smiles and kind of winks. I can't tell if it's a cute, flirtatious wink or if the sun just got in his eye. Either way, the gesture adds to the heat my face already feels.

He asks me what I remember about Guatemala, and I tell

him about the beautiful beaches, the cities nestled in the central highlands, and the majestic volcanoes. The slight awkwardness between us fades as we talk.

The cab stops in front of La Boriqueña. The writing on the glass storefront is faded by years of sunlight. A man walks out, and an aroma of spices wafts out behind him. Jake pays the cab driver—and freezes. Just freezes.

I take a step toward the door of the restaurant, but Jake's feet are adhered to the cracked sidewalk.

His eyes follow a stream of cars going in the opposite direction of our cab. Without warning, without a word to me, he takes off running.

I follow him, trying to catch up, but he's moving so quickly that only the blur of light blue from his Menudo shirt is visible.

After covering a block or so, he stops. His hands go to his knees as he stares at the traffic ahead. He straightens and puts his hand on his chest. He's forgotten all about me.

I jog to catch up to him, dodging a woman pulling a cart. "Jake."

He doesn't turn toward me. He leans against the brick wall of the nearest building, his chest heaving as if he's drowning in the humid air. His eyes are wild.

I grab his arm and try to get him to look at me. "Jake! Are you okay?"

His eyes widen as he seems to notice my presence for the first time. A woman with graying dark hair in a tight bun comes out of the corner store holding two canvas shopping bags. When she sees Jake, she pauses and puts the bags down at our feet.

"¿Qué te pasa, mijo?" When Jake doesn't respond, she turns to me. "¿Qué le pasa?"

"No sé." I shake my head.

"Está teniendo un ataque de pánico."

A panic attack? She's probably right. Jake is having a panic attack, and I have no idea what to do about it.

The woman puts her hands on Jake's shoulders. She talks to him in Spanish, telling him to take slow, deep breaths. She tells him to close his eyes, and she counts as he breathes in deeply through his nose and exhales through his mouth. He focuses on her instructions the entire time.

Once he starts to breathe normally, she squeezes his hands and asks him what his name is.

"Jacobo," he tells her.

"Yo me llamo Sandra. ¿Jacobo, estás bien ahora?"

He nods. "Sí."

Sandra pats his shoulders once more and gives him a small smile. I thank her for her help as she picks up her bags and moves along.

"Sorry," he says without looking at me.

I grab his hand. "Are you okay? You scared me." I want to ask him a dozen more questions, but mostly I'm worried. "Should I call Katie?"

"No. No, I'm fine. No need to bother her. I think I should probably go home, though. I'm sorry I ruined our date."

"That doesn't matter. I'm just glad Sandra came along and was able to help you. I had no idea what to do."

He squeezes my hand and turns to me. "It wasn't your responsibility. I'm really sorry."

"You didn't do anything wrong," I tell him.

I flag down another cab, and Jake crawls in, with me right behind him. He runs his gold cross along its chain over and over, his body shaking slightly as if the AC is on full blast.

I want to put my arms around him, to steady his shaking limbs, but he's staring blankly out the window. I don't know if he wants to talk to me or even wants me here. The silence in the back of the cab feels as stifling as the heat, accentuating the honks of cars around us.

At home, we stop in front of his door. "Do you want me to come in?" I ask, hoping he'll say yes.

"That would be really nice. At least until Katie gets back. She and Lorenzo went to the movies."

In his room, he picks up a hoodie that's been draped across his chair, pulling it over his head and flipping the hood up. "I think I should lie down."

He stretches out on his bed, and I join him, leaving a little space between us. He's stopped trembling, but his face looks flushed, and drops of sweat bead his forehead.

Quietly, he says, "It was the Pontiac Aztek."

"What?"

"The yellow Pontiac Aztek. That's what triggered my panic attack. It's the second time I've seen a car exactly like that. Well, actually the third."

I adjust the pillow under my head and reach out to take his hand. "Why did it cause you to have a panic attack?"

"It's the same model of car that ran into us, that killed my parents."

"Oh, I'm so sorry." I squeeze his hand.

"We were coming home from camping upstate. Katie was asleep, and I was reading a book in the back seat next to her. Then this car ran a red light. It happened so fast, you know, and it was getting dark by then, but I noticed the car. That image of a bright yellow Pontiac is seared in my mind." He touches my fingertips with his free hand.

“I’m so sorry.” I touch the pads of his fingers, line my fingers up with his and move to interlace them.

“The second time I saw it was in front of a bar one night.”

“Roxie’s?”

“How do you know?”

I shouldn’t have said it. Why would I admit to mild stalking on our first date? “I’m sorry, Jake. I followed you one night because I wanted to know where you were going.”

“Really?”

“Yeah, I shouldn’t have done it.”

His brows knit together. “No. You shouldn’t have.”

“I’m really sorry. I let my curiosity get out of control. It was a violation of your privacy and I would never do it again.”

He sighs. “I can’t be mad at your crazy if you’re not mad at my crazy.”

“Don’t call it that. You had a panic attack.”

He slowly runs the fingers of his free hand along the chain of his crucifix. “After it happened, I started going out at night, convinced I could find that car again. I was so mad at myself for not seeing the license plate at the time. If I had, I could’ve told the police and they could’ve tracked down the driver. So, I thought if I could find that car, I could let the police know. It wasn’t realistic, I know, but once I started looking it was hard to stop. And then, one night last year, I saw a yellow Pontiac Aztek in front of that bar. That’s when I had my first panic attack. Someone thought I was having a heart attack, so they called 911. I ended up at the hospital, and I never got to see who the car belonged to. I kept going there every night to see if they would come back. I know it’s stupid, but I felt like I had to do *something*.”

“That’s totally understandable.” I squeeze his hand in mine. “It must be so scary, though—thinking you’ve seen it.”

"Yeah. And this time, I was also scared that I'd end up in the hospital again. That didn't exactly make the experience less traumatic last time."

I nod. "It all sounds really, really hard."

"It is. It's exhausting. I just can't let go of this pain I carry around everywhere. Now that I can finally afford therapy, I'm on a waiting list to see a counselor, but it might still be months before I can actually start sessions."

I bring his hand up to my lips and kiss it.

He scoots closer to me and lifts his hand to my cheek. "Thank you for being here for me."

I pull myself against him, looping my arms around his neck, and he draws me even closer as his hands go to my back. I lean my head against his chest; his heartbeat beneath the thickness of his hoodie feels fast, erratic. I don't know if it's the lingering effects of his panic attack or the nearness of our bodies. We lie in the quiet darkness of his room until the key turns in the front door and Katie makes her presence known.

CHAPTER EIGHTEEN

In the predawn hours, I sit on the chair by the window. Ricardo and Yoly turned in ages ago, but I haven't been able to sleep. I keep replaying tonight's events. It scared me—Jake's inability to catch his breath, how he lost control of his body. I didn't know how to help him, and I feel so thankful that Sandra came along and knew exactly what to do.

Jake told me he feels like tragedy is bound to defeat us. What if his tragedy—the death of his parents—does defeat him?

I finally drift off on the green chair, and that's how Yoly finds me in the morning.

"I hope you didn't sleep there all night. You're going to be so sore."

I stretch my legs out and pull myself to my feet. I already am sore. But I tell Yoly, "I'm okay."

"Ricardo's still sleeping, and I'm starving. Want to help me make omelets?"

That's just about the last thing I want to do, but I follow her to the kitchen counter because she rarely asks me to help her with food prep.

I wash some tomatoes for her and dice them how she showed me, slowly making each cut and wondering how on earth chefs on TV manage to do this with such speed and precision while holding extremely sharp knives. I tell Yoly what happened last night.

"Is Jake all right now?" she asks.

"He seemed calmer by the time we got home. I'll check on him later."

She nods. After a pause she asks, "So, you going to dinner with Jake—was it a date? Are you two dating?"

I feel myself flush. "It was a first date. I mean, it was supposed to be. We didn't actually make it to the restaurant."

She listens while whisking the eggs. "And how are *you* doing? That must've been unsettling for you."

"I just wish I'd known how to help. If it happens again, I'll try to do what that kind woman did for him."

Yoly purses her lips. "Feeling responsible for someone else's mental health struggles is a lot to take on, especially at your age."

Annoyance surges through me. She's not my mom, or my sister. And there's a reason I'm not telling *them* about last night. "I don't feel *responsible*. I just care about him!"

"I know, I know. But you haven't known him that long, and you're both really young, so . . . try to take things slowly."

"Okay," I say, because the last thing I need right now is to get into a fight with Yoly.

After breakfast, I go downstairs to check on Jake. Though I don't know his whole work schedule, I'm pretty sure he's home most mornings. I should probably text first but I'd rather see him face-to-face. Something like anticipation—or trepidation—creeps in as I knock on the door.

Jake is wearing his Roberto Clemente jersey. I know whose jersey it is now because last time he wore it, I googled number 21 for the Pittsburgh Pirates. Clemente was a Puerto Rican baseball player who died in an airplane crash while he was delivering relief supplies to victims of an earthquake.

Jake's gold cross hangs in the V space of his jersey, and I want to reach out and touch it like I did the other night, but I know we're not there in our relationship yet.

"Hi," I say.

"Hey." I know what the face of someone who is happy to see me looks like, and this isn't it.

I hoped he would invite me in right away, but he's still standing in the doorway, and all of a sudden, I'm asking for laundry detergent again. "Can I come in?"

He moves away from the door and gestures with his hand. "Yeah, of course."

"How are you today?"

"Doing better. I'm sorry I ruined our night, ruined our date."

"We can try again another night."

Jake twitches his lips. "I don't know. I'm kind of in a messed-up place right now, and I don't want to bring you down with me."

"You're not bringing me down."

"I really like you, but I don't like what happened yesterday, and that I brought you into it. It's not fair to you. You didn't sign up for that."

"You had a bad night. We all have our bad days. I'm in a messed-up place right now too. Sleeping on my friends' couch, kicked out of my home . . ."

"It's not the same, Maya. My parents are dead, and you have no idea how that's affected me. You only got a glimpse last night, and I promise, you don't want to be around for more."

I get a tight feeling in my chest, as though I'm still chasing him down the street the way I did yesterday. Why are people always putting themselves out of my reach?

I try to shrug off that thought. "You really don't have to worry about it. *I'm* not worried about it. Let's just put it behind us for now, okay? I came by to see if you want to walk to the writing room with me." Maybe working on his fire escape will shift his mood along with his focus.

Jake lets out a deep sigh but moves further into the room. I can't tell if this is a small concession or if he's retreating from me even more.

I aim for a light conversational tone, hoping to entice him into talking about something other than his angst. "I want to start working on a new article, about Junior Vega and his vengeance lit. Have you heard of him?"

Jake scoffs and aggressively runs his fingers through his hair. "Yeah, I've heard of him. Some third-rate social media reject."

I keep my voice neutral instead of reacting to his foul mood. "I actually think his work is really interesting. Even though it's not what I'm normally into at all."

"It's just a bunch of tired, violent tropes remixed to seem less like the trash they are."

There probably isn't a single sentence I could say at the moment that wouldn't provoke a volley of verbal arrows from him. He's determined to unleash his anger on something, anything. "Well, we're both entitled to our opinions. I'm writing about mine."

"Go ahead if you want to squander your time on garbage."

He walks over to the counter and picks up a few envelopes, as if junk mail is a top priority all of a sudden. "I don't think I'm going to go to the writing room today. You can go ahead. There's some stuff I need to do around here."

"Well, I don't have to go either. We can hang out here."

Jake tosses the envelopes aside and finally looks up to meet my waiting eyes. "I think it's better if we just stop things before they really get started."

He says it so abruptly that all I feel is blank shock. "What? But—why?"

"It's not fair to you to bring you near the dysfunction that is my brain right now. I thought I was doing better, but yesterday proved I'm not."

So we're back to that. His words are simple and straightforward, but it feels like there's so much more beneath the surface. I can't tell what he's really thinking, what's really driving him to talk this way. "Well, don't I get a say?"

"You get to decide if you still want to be my friend after all this."

"Friend? You didn't kiss me like you just want to be friends."

"I'm sorry." He sinks down onto the couch and drops his head down into his hands. "I'm so sorry."

I absolutely did not see this coming. How do you know, in the moment when you're doing something glorious like kissing a boy whose touch makes your whole body shiver, that it will be the last time you'll experience that feeling? You don't. *I* didn't. When I was on Jake's bed, his arms pressed firmly against me, his entire body aligned with mine, I assumed it was the beginning of something. How can it already be the end?

"Jake, you don't have to push me away—"

"I'm not. But I do think it's better if we're just friends right now. If you want to be my friend, then I'm happy about it. If you don't want to be anywhere near me, then I understand."

"None of the above. I want to pick up where we left off last night." I point toward his room.

"I never should've let that happen. I was in a bad place."

“That makes me feel really good, thanks.” I walk out and slam the door behind me, running up the steps.

Sadness piles onto anger as I sink down on the couch. I clutch my pillow to my stomach. This feels like a breakup even though we weren’t officially together. My only breakup was sophomore year when Matt Blinkman moved to England for his father’s job. That didn’t feel anything like this. It was like reaching the satisfying end of one chapter while looking forward to the next one. This is like being blindsided by a twist in the middle of a book and not knowing how you’re going to even keep reading. I’ve already been left stranded by every member of my family. Being pushed away by Jake is one more rejection—one I don’t know how to bounce back from.

CHAPTER NINETEEN

It's Monday morning, and I want to call in sick to work. All weekend I've been afraid to leave the confines of the studio apartment for fear that I'll run into Jake. Yoly and Ricardo have left for the day, and I've taken my sweet time getting ready. I press my ear to the door to listen for noise coming from the stairwell. Nothing. Slowly, I open the door and peek across the hall toward Daisy and Lorenzo's door. Nothing. I pop my head out and find the stairwell empty. I pad down the stairs without running into anyone. I close the front door behind me and almost make it to the bottom of the stoop before I spot Katie walking up the sidewalk. We see each other simultaneously.

"Hi, Maya," she says, a tentative look on her face.

"Hi. How are you? How . . . How's Jake doing?"

"He's fine. I'm sorry things didn't work out between you two. I really wanted them to. You guys looked cute together the day I walked into the kitchen."

"Yeah. I thought he liked me."

"He does. He really likes you. He just doesn't want to drag you into what he calls his mess." She puts the word *mess* in air quotes. "But he's been working really hard on himself; maybe he'll feel differently after he's had a chance to process what happened the other night. Just give him time."

I force a smile, not sure whether to be hopeful or skeptical or both. "I'll try."

After what happened with Jake, the writing room is ruined for me. I *could* still go and do my work and ignore his presence on the fire escape, try not to think about how the fingers holding his stubby pencil once interlaced with mine. I *could* very well sit at a cubicle and not ponder the taste of his lips. But more likely, those thoughts—already at the forefront of my mind—would be amplified the minute I walked into any space he occupied.

So today after dinner I settle myself at Yoly and Ricardo's tiny table with my laptop, hoping to finish a fresh round of pitch letters and churn out a book review for this coming week. I'm seriously tempted to just pick *Little Women*, which nobody could accuse of being overlooked or forgotten but which I have to revisit for the library book club anyway. My brain is so fried that I don't think I can do justice to more than one book right now. And the anti-classics piece will have to wait awhile longer—*not* because of what Jake said about Junior Vega's work, but because I need to be clearheaded when I write about it.

I've just started to tune out the background noise of Yoly and Ricardo's conversation when Brady and Julissa turn up. Each of them holds a bottle of wine and wears a weary expression.

"Open this. We're going to need it," Julissa tells Ricardo, shoving her bottle in his direction. "He just announced."

Ricardo takes the bottle to the kitchenette and searches for a corkscrew. "Wright's officially running for governor?"

"Yep."

Brady puts the other bottle on the counter. "Reinforcements

for when that one is empty." They both sink onto the couch with Yoly.

"He's already getting national coverage," says Julissa as she accepts a full glass of wine from Ricardo. "Mostly because he's raked in so much campaign money already. And we still have no clue where he's getting that funding."

"Can't the state election authorities investigate that?" asks Yoly. "Find out if he's getting sketchy donations from one or two super-wealthy people?"

"They're really slow with this stuff," Julissa says. "Technically, Wright hasn't even missed the deadline to report his donors. I'm sure he will, because most candidates do. But since it's so common, there's no guarantee anyone will look into it."

"Unless there's a public outcry over it," Yoly suggests. "If the issue was getting a lot of attention in the press . . ."

Julissa shrugs, which sloshes the wine in her glass. "Any investigation would still take a long time, with no guaranteed consequences. But yeah, public outcry would at least be an inconvenience for Wright and could hurt his campaign."

I've tended to stay out of their conversations, but now I feel the need to speak up. "Um, so . . . I saw Wright last week, at my dad's home."

Julissa looks up at me, like she's seeing me for the first time. To her I'm probably just a random girl whom Yoly and Ricardo took in out of pity like they've done for so many others. "You met Bernard Wright?"

I explain who my father is.

Julissa's eyes widen. "Is your dad involved in Wright's campaign? As an advisor? As a donor?"

A week ago, I would've said no way. But now I hear Yoly's words: *It's about feeling like he has control and the rest of us don't.*

I've always thought he used to love my mom. Used to love me, when I was little. But maybe that was only because back then, our lives orbited his.

I've always told myself he wanted his kids to grow into independent adults, but maybe kicking us out was just another way of controlling us.

I've been telling myself that he's not racist. That he must not realize what Wright's truly like or that Wright is eyeing the governor's office. That he already has more than enough of what he wants most.

Those are the stories I've been telling myself. They're not my father's real story.

"I don't know," I tell Julissa honestly.

Julissa leans forward on the couch. "Anything you can find out, Maya—anything that could be a clue about your dad's role—that would be a huge help. Voters deserve to know how Wright suddenly became such a donation magnet, how he went from being some obscure member of the state assembly to being a contender for governor. So far the major media outlets aren't taking an interest in where his money's coming from, and nobody else has the resources or the access to get answers."

"Well, I don't exactly have access either," I say. I can't imagine that my dad would voluntarily offer up a single ounce of information to someone he considers a nitwit.

"You're still able to visit his home, right?" Julissa takes the bottle Ricardo has set on the coffee table and pours herself another glass of wine. "I mean, obviously don't do anything reckless. Don't, like, steal his personal laptop or anything like that. But if you just *happen* to notice something—a file that's open on a screen, a printout that's sitting on a desk—that could be a start."

I nod slowly. "I can keep my eyes open."

"Are you sure, Maya?" Yoly asks.

No, not really. I've never done anything like this before—never in my life done anything behind my dad's back. But I do want to know what his connection to Wright is. I have to know.

"I can try."

The next morning, I'm up early. In about an hour, Melinda will be headed to the meat market. That's her usual Tuesday schedule.

I call Mitchell MedTech and ask to speak to my dad. His new assistant patches me through when I tell her who I am.

"Maya? Why are you calling me at the office instead of on my cell?" he asks by way of greeting.

"I just thought it was easier, in case you were in a meeting or something." Obviously I can't say that I wanted to make sure he was at the office and not at home.

"Well, what is it?"

"I might stop by tomorrow. I have to pick up my passport."

"Why do you need a passport?"

"Mom wants me to visit this summer before school starts."

"In Guatemala? She has got to be out of her mind."

"What do you mean?"

"Don't you listen to the news, Maya? Guatemala is not safe. Everyone is leaving to come here. Haven't you seen the migrant surges at the border?"

"Oh, you mean the migrants you keep saying have no right or reason to be here? Those migrants?"

"Their country, their problems to solve. You're not going. If she wants to see you, then she should come here."

I'm not even sure if I am going to visit Guatemala this summer, but this is too galling to absorb without pushing back. "You don't get to tell me what to do anymore. I'm an adult, remember? Isn't that why you kicked me out?"

He heaves a deep sigh. "Are you still upset about that? Today's kids have no appreciation for what their parents and grandparents have done. I am trying to teach you how to make your own way in the world, Maya. All kids want today is handouts. They don't actually want to work for anything."

I don't have time to get into a pointless debate with him. "Look, Dad, I have to go, but I'll come over tomorrow to pick up the passport." I hang up before he has a chance to disconnect the call.

I told him I would come by tomorrow so he won't suspect that I'm actually headed there right now.

Melinda embraces me and tells me she's so happy that I've come by again. I join her in the kitchen while she cuts up some fruit. She updates me about her son's promotion at work and her granddaughter's upcoming first birthday. I tell her about some of the classes I'll be taking at Columbia and about the recent pieces I've written for Victoria.

"Melinda, that man who was here last time I came by—Bernard Wright? Why was he visiting Dad?"

"Oh, Mr. Wright. He's a business associate of your dad's, I think."

"But he's a politician too, right?"

Melinda spears a piece of pineapple with her fork. "Yes, upstate, I believe."

"But why was he here?"

"Oh, you know I don't eavesdrop, Maya."

Fair enough. You don't keep a job with the Mitchell family by being indiscreet. "He's running for governor, you know."

"Yes, yes, I think your father mentioned it."

"Have you heard the awful things Bernard Wright has said?"

Melinda gives me a puzzled look. "No, what do you mean?"

"He talks about immigrants replacing white people and not wanting to let immigrants come here."

"That's strange. Well, I don't really like to get into politics, you know. They're all the same to me." She stands up and rinses the cutting board in the sink. "I have to get going soon. I'm supposed to pick up some of your dad's favorites from Pino's."

"Sure, you go ahead. I'm going to stay here for a few more minutes. There's one more notebook I couldn't find last time I stopped by, and I really need it. What's the new door code? I can lock up when I leave."

She hesitates just a moment before telling me the current code, and I can tell Dad's instructed her not to give it to me.

I listen for Melinda to close the door behind her. Once she's gone, I go straight into Dad's office.

He never keeps his office door locked because he believes that his forceful command to stay out of it is more solid than any lock you could buy. Until today, that's been true, but today I don't care. I go right in.

He's obsessive about order. The solid oak surface of his desk has only his computer on it. The adjacent shelves hold business books; his prized first editions and other collectibles are in the book room, also not locked.

I sit at his chair and face the door. How many times have I stood on the other side of this desk, facing my dad? All three of us have been summoned, throughout our childhood, to this office to weather his wrath—lectures, scoldings, or demands about something that we were to do or stop doing immediately.

I open the largest drawer of his desk. The contents are sparse—only a few envelopes and papers. But there's a campaign flyer showing Bernard Wright's smug face. He's standing in front of some trees, probably upstate where he's from. His hand rests on a holster with a gun at his waist. Below that flyer, there are others—all slightly different, like they're mockups, options from which someone would choose a favorite.

There's also a small, pale blue opened envelope. Inside is a thank-you card from Lisa Piccola and a picture of her and Dad at her retirement party.

His computer is password-protected and probably firewalled better than a federal agency. This might be all I can obtain from his office, but Lisa might be able to provide more answers.

And the flyer samples are all the confirmation I need that Dad is heavily involved in Wright's campaign.

Before I leave, I go into the book room. I shouldn't call it *the* book room; it's actually *his* book room. Most of *my* books are in my room on my Belle shelf. Only one of mine is housed here.

This room has its own thermostat to maintain the precise temperature needed to preserve the antique pages. Glass doors on the bookcases keep dust out. A basket holds white gloves because no one is allowed to touch these volumes with bare hands.

If I took *Charlotte's Web* out of its temperature-controlled environment without wearing gloves, he'd explode with anger. But it is *my Charlotte's Web*. It was a gift to *me* on *my* birthday. So I open the shelf where it lies and transfer it into my bag.

CHAPTER TWENTY

I call Victoria on my way to the subway. "So, you remember me telling you about Bernard Wright?"

"Your white supremacist?"

"He's not *my* white supremacist."

"Well, he's in your current state of residence which you are refusing to leave, so you just have to own him."

"Whatever, Vic." I put my finger in my other ear to drown out the sound of the cars passing by. "Anyway, I think Dad is playing a big role in Wright's campaign for governor. He might be a shadow donor, or something like that—contributing money in sketchy ways." I'm thinking of what Julissa said last night: *The major media outlets aren't taking an interest.* "Can you talk to some of your connections, see if a journalist can look into it?"

There's a long pause. "Maya, what does that have to do with us?"

It's a fair question from someone who's spent the last seven years distancing herself from Dad as much as possible. Part of me does feel like I have no business concerning myself with Dad's dubious activities—and even less business getting the press involved. That's not what we do in this family. We keep our grievances private and put on a brave face for the rest of the world.

"You said yourself—this is where I live. And if Dad's secretly working to get this guy elected, people should know about that."

Another pause from Victoria. "I can mention this to my friend Miranda. She's a news assistant at the *Times* who works with Jill Shields."

"And Jill Shields is a journalist?"

"She's a Pulitzer Prize-winning investigative reporter. You've never heard of her?"

"Sorry to disappoint you," I say dryly. "But yeah, that sounds good. Thanks. I have to get to work but I'll check in later."

I disconnect the call and shove the phone in my bag as I clatter down the steps of the subway station, trying not to think too hard about what I've just done.

Halfway through my shift, my phone rings with a 212 number. I let it go to voicemail while I finish shelving a cart of books. I listen to the message once I'm in the breakroom eating a granola bar.

"Miss Mitchell, this is Jill Shields from the *New York Times*. I have a few questions for you if you can get in touch at your earliest convenience . . ."

Why does she want to talk to me? I only have a few minutes left in my break and I'm tempted to just let this lie. But curiosity wins. I call her back.

She answers right away—I must be catching her on a break of her own.

"Um, hi, this is Maya Mitchell . . ."

"Hello! Your sister, Victoria, said it was okay to call. Did she tell you who I am?"

"Pulitzer Prize-winning investigative reporter."

She laughs. "Yes. Thanks for returning my call. I wanted to see if we could set up a time to meet and talk about what you know about Bernard Wright's connection to your father."

"Me? I don't know anything."

"Well, Victoria said you met Wright at your home."

"I wouldn't say *met*—I just ran into him. He'd been there talking to my dad." An instinct from my years of working on the school newspaper kicks in. "This is off the record, by the way."

"Of course, I understand. But I think there may be a bigger story here, and you may have some insight into it. Could we arrange a time to meet? Off the record until and unless you decide otherwise."

Against my better judgment, I tell her I can meet in Central Park right after my shift.

The afternoon ends with this month's meeting of the classics book club. We go around the room discussing *Little Women*, with each person posing a question that the others respond to one by one.

When it's my turn, I ask everyone to share which sister we most relate to. "I first read it when I was twelve and have always related most to Jo," I say. "I guess I consider myself a writer, so I can understand Jo from that perspective. But when I read it this time, what I related to most was Jo's struggle between duty to her family and duty to herself to live a meaningful life."

I pass the time to Concha, who's seated next to me, but I have a hard time concentrating on what anyone else is saying.

I'm thinking of the resolution of the book, when Jo lets go of the parts of herself that cause the most trouble and embraces a stable, fairly conventional life. I used to think of it as a happy ending, similar to the endings of other books I love, like Austen's novels and *Anne of Green Gables*. The kind of ending I always wanted for myself. Now I'm not sure what I want, but I do know my story isn't going to be so tidy.

I'm a little late to my meeting with Jill Shields. I pick up my pace as I walk along the tree-lined path. I've now googled her, so I know what she looks like—long, dyed-blond hair, late forties—and I see that she's already on the bench where we agreed to meet. She obviously did the same reconnaissance on me, because she waves as she sees me approach.

"Hi." I sit down on the bench next to her.

"Hi, Maya. I'm Jill. Thank you so much for meeting with me. Do you mind if I record our conversation?"

"Uh, go ahead."

"You are the daughter of Robert James Mitchell, owner of MedTech. Is that correct?"

"Yes." The question seems overly formal. Between that and being recorded, I feel like I'm under oath or something.

"You met Bernard Wright at your home? Did your father introduce you?"

"No—he was leaving my father's office, and I ran into him in the hallway. He just said a polite hello, and that was it."

"Do you know how the two of them know each other?"

"No. Our housekeeper said that they're business associates, though. I also know that my dad has copies of different campaign flyer prototypes for Wright. I saw them on his desk." It all sounds so innocuous when I say it out loud. Maybe I'm blowing this out of proportion, inviting scrutiny of my dad's actions for no reason.

But Jill says, "Did you know that your father has donated to Wright's state assembly reelection campaign?"

"No. He doesn't really tell me what he does with his money."

Jill pulls a tablet out of her bag. "He gave the maximum amount that an individual is legally allowed to contribute to a statewide political campaign. The New York State Board of Elections has a database that shows contributions. It's publicly available information. But here's what I find really interesting: When someone makes a political donation, they must disclose their employer. And if I do a search for Mitchell MedTech, I find hundreds of employees who've donated to Bernard Wright." She shows me the search results. "Every one of these people has given the maximum allowable amount."

I take the tablet from her and scroll. The names blur past me, and I don't feel as if I'm taking them in at all until my eyes snag on one. "Lisa Piccola is on here."

"Who is that?"

"She used to be my dad's assistant. She's retired now, but I ran into her the other day." Does she actually support this hateful man? It's hard for me to imagine, but I guess you don't always know people as well as you think you do.

I scroll back up through the list, looking for other names I recognize. "That's weird."

"What?"

"Ernie Esposito. He's my dad's driver. That's a lot of money for him to donate to a political campaign. His wife is sick, so I assume he has medical bills. Why would he spend so much money on something like this?" I know he's generous; he picks up flowers for his wife once a month and has bought me a ten-dollar scratch-off for every birthday since I was ten. But it seems out of character for him to donate to the political campaign of a candidate from upstate.

"That's what we want to find out," Jill says. "I can send you this link and you can look through the list more thoroughly when you have time. See if you recognize any other names that seem odd to you. A custodian? A low-level assistant? I want to see if there are any other low-paid workers who are also making these large donations." She takes the tablet back and asks for my email to send me the link.

"What does this mean?" I ask.

"Well, I have to ask myself, why would these folks be donating so much money to a state assembly campaign? Especially when Wright's interest in higher office wasn't widely known until very recently."

I mull that for a moment. "You think they've been . . . pressured to make those donations? Like, coerced? By my dad?"

"I don't know. It's possible that he gave them the impression it was a condition of keeping their jobs. It's also possible that he reimbursed them for these donations with equivalent bonuses, so that he could, in effect, give more money to the Wright campaign without it all being attached to his name. I'll need to find out more before I can determine if this is a story, but I think it could be a big deal. It'd help to be able to talk to an insider who could give me more information."

"I'm not an insider," I say quickly. "My dad barely speaks to me."

"I understand. I'm thinking of Lisa Piccola, actually. Do you have her contact information?"

"No . . . but I did randomly run into her at the park not long ago. She says she takes that same path almost every day."

"Can you try to reach out to her?"

"How? I just told you I don't know how to get ahold of her." Nervousness bubbles up in the form of irritation. "Isn't that *your* job, figuring out how to get in touch with people?"

Jill twists her lips and reaches for a cardholder from her bag. "I can find out how to contact her, yes, but she might be more willing to engage with me if she's heard about me from someone she trusts first. Can you try to run into her again? Maybe you can walk by the same path where you saw her, around the same time?"

What have I gotten myself into? When I had the idea to get a journalist involved in this situation, I didn't expect to be recruited as her unofficial assistant. I want to say no, that I've already gone out on a limb by meeting with her and that I shouldn't become further involved.

Instead, I say, "Will Lisa get in trouble over this?" I don't understand enough about campaign finance law to gauge whether Lisa may have broken it by going along with whatever Dad's scheme is.

"I can't make any guarantees," Jill says gently but firmly. "All I can say is that, if something like this comes to light, people who have the courage to come forward and tell the truth about it tend to fare better, overall, than people who actively try to cover it up."

That doesn't exactly reassure me. But I give her a half nod.

Jill hands me her card. "If you do see her, please tell her to call me. I would really like to talk to her. Meanwhile, I'll keep in touch with you."

I don't know if I want her to keep in touch with me—to

interrogate me further about Dad, his political involvement, and the donations of his employees. This whole ordeal is starting to feel like a shroud that I want to take off me.

But can I stand by and do nothing while my dad potentially takes advantage of his entire workforce for his own ends? While he ignores laws and ethics to prop up the campaign of a despicable man?

I wish I could say that this has nothing to do with me, but that would be a lie. Now that I know about it, I can't just bury my head in the sand and ignore it.

CHAPTER TWENTY-ONE

The first thing Victoria says after I've updated her is "You don't have to be involved in this, Maya."

"A little late for that," I say as I perch on the front steps of the apartment building after work. My bag sits in my lap; I can feel the weight of *Charlotte's Web* inside.

"I just mean, Jill Shields can do her own legwork. You don't owe her anything."

"She's not asking for much. *I* don't have to be a source because I don't have any truly sensitive information. All I have to do is convince Lisa to talk to her."

"Still—what if you approach Lisa and she goes straight to Dad? If Dad finds out you've been talking to a reporter, he'll be beyond furious."

It's not like this hasn't occurred to me. "I don't think Lisa would do that. She wouldn't want to get me in trouble with him. And someone has to hold him accountable for what he's done. He bullied his employees into going along with his scheme to get this guy elected. Can you imagine him telling people like Lisa and Ernie they had to donate money to Wright? They would've felt like they had to do it or they would lose their jobs."

"Yeah." Victoria's voice drops. "I can't imagine all the stuff he's made Ernie do over the last few years. People feel like they have to do what he says or he'll get back at them. Which is why I'm worried about *you*."

"I can take care of myself," I say. I don't add, *I've been doing that for a long time, because I haven't had a choice.*

Layla can't make it to yoga on Wednesday morning, but I go to the park anyway, hoping to run into Lisa Piccola on her daily walk with Patty.

I choose a bench for my stakeout and wait. I see over a dozen strollers amble by, but none of them carry little Patty.

I'm still a half hour away from my shift starting, but sitting here watching every passerby is tedious, and I'm tempted to give up, to head to the library for the sanctuary of air conditioning.

My eyes rest on a pair of young girls meandering by. The older one in braids pulls along a younger girl in lopsided pigtails, whose finger points at a nearby butterfly. They're following a woman in yoga pants whom I assume is their mother. She talks on her phone while pushing a chunky stroller with one hand. Maybe it's the girls' ages or their proximity to each other that makes me think of Brenda and Teresa.

The memory of those sisters, eyes filled with fear, all alone, worried for their mother, is never far from my mind. Those helpless and harmless girls are among the people Bernard Wright rails against. He hates their presence in this country and in this state, hates their very existence. If his hate is harnessed to power, he'll be able to enlarge the target already on the backs of people like Brenda, Teresa, and their mother. The thought keeps me planted firmly on this park bench, waiting for Lisa Piccola.

Not long after the yoga pants mom and her kids pass me, Lisa pushes a stroller in my direction.

"Lisa!" I dash toward her. Should I pretend it's a coincidence that I'm running into her, or do I tell her I've been waiting for her? I don't know. I should've thought it through before this moment. "Hi."

"Maya, it's so nice to run into you again."

I wave at Patty, who has one thumb in her mouth and the other one in her ear. She gives me a half wave with the fingers near her ear. "How are you and Patty doing today?"

"Great. We're headed to the playground."

"Do you have just a minute to talk, or can I walk with you to the playground?"

"Sure—she can walk with us, right, Patty?"

Patty nods and waves at me again.

I walk alongside the stroller, doubts about what to say tumbling in my head. "I've been wondering . . . Did you know that my dad supports Bernard Wright for governor?"

Lisa stops suddenly and stares at me, which earns her a grunt from Patty. She starts pushing again, picking up speed. "Why do you ask?"

"A lot of people are interested in how Wright has so much money. He's just a state assemblyman, yet he's gotten a huge influx of campaign donations over the past few months, starting *before* he got into the governor's race."

"How would you expect me to know anything about that?" Lisa says in a harsh voice I've never heard her use.

"Sorry, Lisa. I'm just trying to find out if Dad has donated to him, and I thought you might know since you worked for him for so long."

"Maya, I told you that I retired. I'm not his assistant anymore."

"I know that, but I also know how much you took care of for him for a long time. Lisa, Bernard Wright would be really bad for New York. Do you want Patty to grow up in a state where the governor is racist?"

"Maya, if you're trying to convince me not to vote for Bernard Wright, I don't think now's a good time to have that conversation—"

"There's an investigative reporter from the *New York Times* looking into Wright's campaign," I rush on. "They know that most of Mitchell MedTech's employees donated the maximum allowable amount to Bernard Wright's campaign, including you. They have all the names. Including yours." I pull out my phone and scroll through the list Jill showed me. There is Lisa Piccola with the maximum contribution next to her name.

Lisa stops the stroller, and Patty immediately protests. "That's confidential. How do you have that?"

"It's not confidential. It's public record. Anyone can do a search by employer. Hundreds of Dad's employees contributed the maximum donation to Wright. Why do you think that is?"

"I don't know." Lisa says the words in a clipped manner and squeezes the handle of the stroller.

Patty starts kicking her feet, trying to get Lisa to move again. I feel bad for hijacking Patty's stroll with her grandmother, but I can't just let this drop.

"Why did you donate this much of your own money to Bernard Wright?" I press. "Is this really a man you want to be our governor?"

Lisa pulls her eyes away from me and kneels in front of Patty. "Why are you asking me all of these questions?"

I've done plenty of interviews for the school paper. Mostly, they've been cordial. I've never done an interview that felt outright hostile before, but this could be headed that way. And it has nothing to do with Lisa's granddaughter getting antsy and my delaying their playground time. Lisa has information. She knew everything about the company, transferred every call to Dad. She has to know more about this than she's letting on.

"Because the reporter wants to talk to you for the article," I say. "She wants to know why every one of these MedTech employees donated the exact same amount, which just happens to be the maximum amount they can donate."

At Patty's insistence, Lisa stands and starts pushing the stroller again, and I follow.

"You're not in trouble, Lisa. She just wants to talk to you." I pull out Jill's card and hold it out for Lisa.

Lisa doesn't take it.

"She just wants to ask you a few questions. You can remain anonymous. Please think about it."

"I have to go." She grabs the card and takes off at an increased speed.

I let her leave because I can tell she's done talking to me, and I really don't know what else to ask her. This is not the kind of story I'm used to chasing. Questioning hesitant sources who are probably hiding something is not where I see my career going. I'm relieved that my part of this is done. The rest is up to Jill Shields.

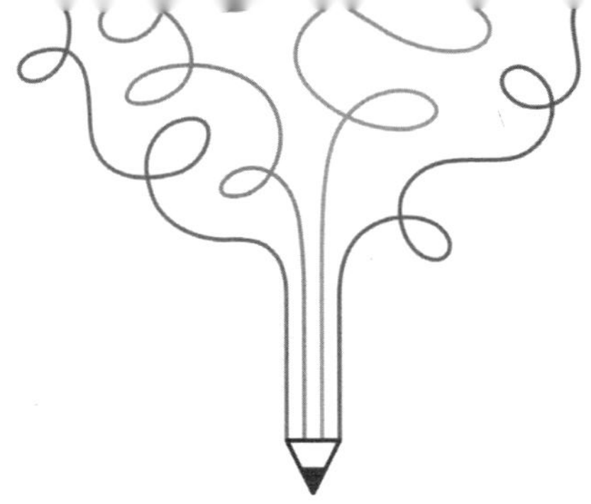

CHAPTER TWENTY-TWO

A week goes by. No word from Jill Shields. I try to put her out of my mind. Along with a lot of other things.

Like Jake. It's almost impossible not to think of him, but every time I do, my heart hurts. I've avoided the writing room and instead doubled my efforts to get writing done at the apartment. It's been slow going, and I've still made no progress on the anti-classics article.

On the second Saturday in August, Layla invites me to check out another yoga class with her—this one in Morningside Park near me. I meet her in the Garment District first. She wants me to help her choose fabric to make into curtains for her new place in Virginia, where she'll move this fall. She'll be studying interior design, and she's practically completed a master's thesis already, if there is such a thing for that field.

Trailing Layla around her favorite fabric store requires an immeasurable amount of patience. Thankfully, today I'm in a patient mood. Spending the day with Layla is a welcome distraction from Jake's withdrawal and Dad's questionable actions. Layla has offered a sympathetic ear regarding Jake, but I don't broach the topic of my dad until we've already looked at well over thirty bolts of fabric on each of the floors of this store.

Layla's been my best friend for years and knows more about

Dad's casual cruelty than anyone else outside our family—and the people who work for him. Yet I still hesitate to go into detail. It puts her in an awkward situation with her own parents, who feel they have to stay on his good side.

Still, I decide she needs to know about the situation with Wright, since it could affect our entire state. As I explain, she tears her eyes away from the fabric long enough to gape at me.

"Maya! I am so sorry. I can't believe your dad is involved in something that shady. Like, why? He's already comfortable. He'll stay comfortable no matter who wins some random election."

Comfortable is the term families like hers and mine use instead of *way richer than anyone could possibly need to be.*

"Power," I say, feeling the truth of Yoly's suggestion more fully now. "It's not just about him having everything he wants—it's about other people having so much less. That's what gives my dad a sense of satisfaction. Knowing that other people are struggling because they're not him, because they're not like him."

"I really am sorry," Layla says. "But that's *wild* that you got the *Times* to investigate. If it all comes out in the open, maybe he'll stop giving that Wright guy money."

"I hope so," I say, though I doubt it will be that simple, even in a best-case scenario.

"Well, I promise I won't tell anyone it was you and Victoria who tipped off the reporter." She studies some pale violet fabric. "What do you think of this color?"

It's the perfect color if it means we are done for the day. "It's really pretty. Do you want the same color for a bedspread?"

"Yes, but maybe a darker shade with a simple pattern . . ." An alarm goes off on her phone. "Oh! Almost time for us to get to Morningside. Let's stop at your place and change into our yoga clothes before we head to the park."

"Oh . . ." I'm already wearing my yoga clothes under my regular outfit. I assumed she was too. "Are you sure you wouldn't rather, um . . . ?" What, change inside a coffee shop restroom? That would not be Layla's style.

"I've been dying to see the place." She hustles me along to get her fabric cut. "You haven't even posted any pictures of it!"

Layla's never been inside Yoly and Ricardo's apartment—nobody from my old life has. I swallow back an instinctive sense of self-consciousness. The studio is nothing to be ashamed of. "Well, you can see it now," I say. "Let's go."

Lorenzo, Katie, and Jake are all sitting on the stoop, and we can't very well go up the stairs without greeting them. That would go against eighteen years of "tienes que saludar" training embedded in me by my mother.

"Hi, Maya!" Katie is the first to speak after taking a lick of a bright red popsicle.

"Hi, everyone. This is Layla. This is Katie, Lorenzo, and Jake." I point to each one as I introduce them to her.

Her eyes land exactly where I expect them to. "You're Jake?"

He nods, scratching his arm just under the nicotine patch, his eyes on the popsicle he holds. "Hey."

"We made paletas," Katie says. She holds hers out for me to examine. "Strawberry banana with honey. Go get them some, Jake."

A minute later, he's back with two more paletas. He gives one to Layla first and meets my eyes as he hands the other one to me. Our fingers touch when I take it from him.

"Thanks." I take a lick, and I'm immediately transported

to the last time we shared a cool treat—and the feel of his cold lips on mine.

"You made these?" Layla asks Katie.

"Yeah, we just blend the strawberries and bananas like a smoothie, and then we pour them in a mold and put them in the freezer."

"Thanks for sharing. Layla and I have to go now." I grab her by the shirt and pull her up the front steps.

Once we're in the apartment, I sink down on the couch. Fabric shopping with Layla always exhausts me.

"This place is adorable," says Layla. "And he's so cute, Maya. Like, really cute."

"I know, I know, but he just wants to be friends."

"I saw the way he looked at you. He does not just want to be friends. Trust me."

I'm torn between hoping Layla is right and knowing Jake has set a boundary I shouldn't cross. I don't want to be like Dad—ignoring what someone else asks for, what someone else says they need, just so I can get what I want when I want it. No matter how hard this is for me, it's not my place to push back on Jake's feelings.

On the other hand . . . he did say he would like to be friends. So maybe that's the next chapter for us.

On Sunday afternoon, I pace back and forth in front of the writing room's building. Chipped paint—faded from the sun, weathered from the rain—stares back at me. I hadn't noticed the cracked paint before, a longtime effort to mask the aging of a century-old building. Other times, I've hurried inside and up the stairs to the writing room. Today I hesitate, working up the nerve to go in.

The wind whips through my hair as I stand there contemplating. I pull my hair back, wrapping it around my hand.

This doesn't seem like the right approach. I should've talked to Jake by now, rather than pretending we weren't living in the same building with just a floor separating us.

But I'm here, so I take the steps slowly and stop again in front of the door to the apartment. My heart hammers against my chest as I reach for the doorknob that I've turned over a dozen times before. The door opens.

It's Glen. I almost don't recognize him; this is the first time I've seen him awake. He doesn't know me, but he nods as he heads toward the stairs.

The open door gives me a glimpse inside. No one is in the quiet room. I step in. Jake is on the fire escape, writing. He's wearing a sweatshirt with the hood up, but he isn't smoking. His pencil moves at top speed on the small notebook in his hand. I watch him for a few moments, until he looks up. His eyes lock on mine, but his face has no expression.

I stand there, smiling tentatively at him, not making any effort to move forward. He climbs over Glen's vacated couch and comes toward me.

"Hey," he says.

"Hey. How are you?"

He shoves his hands into his pockets. "All right. You?"

"Fine."

I see a bouquet of flowers on the counter, and for a split-second I think they might be for me.

How truly arrogant of me. *Friends.* He said he wants us to be friends. Besides, Jake Canales does not seem like the kind of guy who gets a girl flowers. He's more of a T-shirt gifter.

"I'm sorry . . ." we both start.

"You have nothing to be sorry about," he says, eyes on the floor—their favorite view. "I'm the one who made you feel uncomfortable."

"It's not your fault. You were being honest with me, and I appreciate it. I just needed some space. Being here, looking at you on the fire escape, would've just made me think about kissing you." I flash another smile so he knows I'm saying it lightly. "Hard to concentrate, you know."

He laughs and finally drags his eyes up to meet mine. There is so much pain behind them. "I'm sorry. I bet you came by to work."

"Yeah, but I also wanted to see how you were doing." I reach for his hand and give it a squeeze. "I'd like to take you up on your offer of friendship, if that's still on the table."

Jake squeezes back and lets a soft smile grow on his face. "It's absolutely still on the table."

"Glad to hear."

He clears his throat. "Well, your favorite cubicle is open." He points to the cubicle by the door where I usually sit.

"Thank goodness. I don't know how I would've coped otherwise." I put my hands on the back of the chair, squeezing. My eyes inadvertently go to the bouquet on the counter, and he notices.

"It's my mom's birthday," he says quietly. "I'm taking flowers to her grave today."

"That's really sweet."

"Would you come with me?"

His question surprises me. "Are you sure you want me to go?"

"Yeah, if you're up for it. If you have time. It's in Jersey City. We would have to take the bus."

I've never been on the bus. Still—"Yeah, I'd like to come. What about Katie?"

"She went with my aunt and uncle this morning, but I had to work."

"Are we leaving right now?"

"Yeah, if you're free."

We take the subway to the Port Authority. I've never been inside this massive building. If Dad didn't like me to take the subway, I was definitely not allowed to board a bus. And I can kind of see why. The fabric-covered seats probably never get cleaned and have seen the bottoms of thousands of people. Jake chooses one, and I slide in next to him. This is how normal people transport themselves every day; they don't have an Ernie to take them to their destinations in luxury vehicles.

"This is my first time on a city bus," I tell Jake once we're seated and have started our journey.

"For real?"

"Another byproduct of being my father's daughter. He had a huge list of things we weren't allowed to do."

"Well, I love riding the bus. I can't imagine living in a city where you have to drive your car everywhere you go. It seems like such a waste of time. On public transit, your time is yours. I've done so much writing on the bus and the subway. You can just kind of push everything else away and focus on your pencil. And then before you know it, you're at your destination. You don't have to worry about traffic, speed limits, where you're going to park. It's perfect."

The bus rattles its way into the Lincoln Tunnel, the harsh

lights accompanying us through the stretch of pavement and tile walls.

I sit back and relax against the seat. "It is kind of cool. Strangers coming together, headed in a shared direction with diverse purposes, all experiencing the same thing at the same time."

"Sorry you had to go your whole childhood without this experience of common humanity."

I laugh, glad to feel us slipping into a conversational groove. "My mom would probably say the same thing. She wanted us to have a regular childhood, but my dad wanted to live like rich New Yorkers. So, like, one day he would host these thousand-dollar dinners for his clients, and the next day I'd be at a soup kitchen volunteering with my mom."

"Your mom sounds cool."

"She's very cool." I tell him the same story I told Katie about how my parents met. "My mom is a very smart woman, so I don't know how she fell for . . . that. Or kept falling for it over and over again, long enough to have three kids with him."

"I'm sure she saw something in him," Jake says.

"He's a super charming guy. He can charm just about anyone until he doesn't want to anymore, and then he's the complete opposite of charming."

Jake raises his eyebrows. "Well, you don't have to worry about that with me. No one has ever accused me of being super charming."

I smile and think back to the day I met Jake. He was neither talkative nor pleasant, but something drew me to him. It was the way he carries himself. He isn't trying to impress anyone, yet there's a dignity about him—and an honesty. For as much as he keeps to himself, he's never lied to me. He's the same person on the surface as he is inside: a little rough around the edges, but with a generous heart.

Daylight greets us on the other side of the tunnel, and we keep chatting while the bus heads into New Jersey. After it exits the highway, it makes over a dozen stops as it weaves its way through the Jersey City streets. Once the bus reaches our stop, we walk about ten minutes to the cemetery, still talking easily—about his recent shifts at the T-shirt shop, about my review of *Bless Me, Ultima*, about whatever comes to mind.

We enter through a black wrought-iron fence and head straight toward a towering stone cross. Following a wide path with gravestones on both sides, we pass the massive cross and reach a cluster of trees. Jake stops in front of twin flat headstones. He takes the rubber band off the stems of his bouquet and puts it into a vase that's already here, full of water and long-stemmed daisies. He arranges his bouquet among the existing flowers and sits down cross-legged in front of the graves. I lower myself to the ground beside him.

Jacobo Canales, Sr. His father. *Carmen Vega.* His mother. I sit silently beside him. I want to reach out and take his hand, offer him a small semblance of comfort, but I don't want to interrupt his thoughts, his communion with his parents. Quiet companionship is all I can offer.

"My dad started an herb garden on our fire escape when I was little," he tells me. "It was in a planter box, and we planted basil, cilantro, parsley, oregano . . . It was my job to water them and break off pieces as he needed them when he cooked. Being on the fire escape at the writing room helps me feel close to him, you know, to remember those memories. Sometimes when I'm sitting out there, it's so damn hot, but it reminds me of planting that little herb garden with him."

I imagine little Jake out there with his herb garden. Little Jacobo Junior, since his dad was Jacobo too.

Junior. *Junior*. I look back at the headstones and then at Jake and then back to the headstones. His mother was Carmen Vega.

I take a sharp intake of breath as the realization dawns.

Jake's eyes shift slightly toward me, for only an instant. He traces the edges of his dad's headstone in soft deliberate movements, taking in the rough texture of the stone.

"You're Junior Vega?" I say quietly.

He turns his eyes upward with a nod of his head. "Yeah."

"You're amazing."

"Whatever."

"I'm serious! Your writing is amazing, and I'm not the only one who thinks so. Your followers agree."

"I don't have any followers. That's Katie. She started the ChitChat account; she's the one who runs it."

"My point is that people love what you write, Jake."

"Well, I guess that's good because I hate it."

"Why?"

He unfolds his legs and stands up. "It comes from a place of hate. I hate the person who killed my parents and left them for dead on the side of the road with their two kids stuck in the back of the car. I channeled that into my writing and for some reason, people enjoy reading it."

"I'm so sorry, Jake." I stand too. "Now I get why you reacted the way you did when I mentioned that I was going to write an article about the Junior Vega stories. I won't write it if you don't want."

"I don't want to tell you what to do, but I really would rather you didn't." He shakes his head and starts walking toward the exit. "I wrote those stories because I had so much anger inside and I needed to find a way to let it out. Writing was a way to leave my anger on the page. It helped a little. Then Katie found my notebooks and submitted some of my stories to lit magazines. I didn't even know she was doing it until something got accepted for publication. I was so mad at her when she told me. I hadn't meant for anybody else to see it. It's my private ugliness; it's not art, not the kind of stories I want to share with the world."

I walk alongside him, our feet moving in tandem on the pavement toward the exit. "What changed your mind?"

"I haven't actually changed my mind, but the extra money doesn't hurt, you know? Katie wanted to move to the city so we could live together for her last year of high school, and anything I can earn with the writing helps cover the rent for our apartment. She basically made that happen."

"Wow. Katie. That surprises me."

He laughs and shakes his head. "She's a force. She made up the pen name because she knew I didn't want anyone to know I was writing that shit. Then she started this ChitChat account, posting a paragraph of my writing each day to get people wanting to read more. Before I knew it, the account had like a zillion followers, and little by little the money from the follows and likes and shares started to add up. Plus, companies were offering us deals to endorse their special pens and notebooks and whatnot. Katie handles all that. It's pretty much the reason we can afford our place."

"Well, I think you're both really impressive. But I'm sorry you feel . . . self-conscious about the stories you write."

"Yeah, I just feel like I have better stories inside of me, stories that aren't only about rage. I've been changing up my style, trying to move in a new direction. I'm almost done with a novel draft, so we'll see how that goes."

"That's really cool," I say. "And brave. I'm sure your parents would be proud of your writing—all of it."

He shrugs, clearly unconvinced.

"I guess what matters most is that *you* feel good about what you're working on now. But for the record, I think everyone we know would be very impressed by Junior Vega."

At this, he rolls his eyes but also smiles a little. "I've actually been thinking maybe I'll give Katie permission to tell Lorenzo. It's been killing her to keep a secret from him. I just know that the minute Lorenzo knows, Daisy will know, and the minute Daisy knows, the whole neighborhood will know."

"There are worse things than being a local celebrity," I say, which coaxes a chuckle out of him.

"Yeah, being a ChitChat celebrity is *way* worse."

We leave behind the peaceful, verdant surroundings and head toward the clamorous city street.

"Thanks for talking to me about this," I add. "I'm sorry for getting us off track. I didn't mean to detract from your visit."

"I actually wanted to tell you. I'm glad you know now. I don't like keeping secrets. And I know you've always been very curious about what I write." He says this with a smile.

"Very curious. Or, as you might say, nosy."

He takes one last look behind us, gazing in the direction of the side-by-side headstones. "Thanks for coming with me. I'm glad I didn't come alone."

Jake brushes his fingers against mine, and after a moment he takes two of them in his hand.

By the time we're back on the bus headed home, he's taken my whole hand in both of his and holds it in his lap. I guess we're friends who hold hands now? But I don't push; I let him take the lead.

CHAPTER TWENTY-THREE

Back at our building, we stop in front of Jake's door.

"Want to come in?" He opens the door and holds it for me.

"Um, do *you* want me to come in? Last time I was here, that was not the impression I got."

"I do want you to come in, but only if you want to."

I walk through the open door and can't decide if I should sit on the couch or just stand in the middle of the room.

"Want to sit?" he asks.

Sitting it is, I guess. I drop my bag on the floor at my feet, and we settle on opposite ends of the couch.

"So, what else have you been up to since the last time I saw you?" he asks.

"Why are you being so nosy?"

He laughs and replies with my words from one of our earliest conversations. "I'm just trying to make conversation so this isn't awkward."

"What is wrong with silence? Why do people always think they have to be saying something?"

He laughs again and turns his body to face me. "I've missed you. I didn't mean for you to stop coming to the writing room."

"I know you didn't. It was just difficult being around you. I felt that rejection so hard."

"I wasn't rejecting you, Maya. There isn't a single aspect of you that I would ever reject." He looks right at me. "I was rejecting the idea of being together. The way I am right now, I don't belong with you, because you shouldn't have to deal with my problems."

"Deal with? You say that like you're an unruly toddler."

"That's how I felt the night of our date. Like a child having to ask for help. That's not the kind of relationship I want with a girlfriend."

A girlfriend. Well, I knew Jake wasn't the casual fling type. Still, I feel the impact of that word—the weight of a hypothetical relationship—and not in a bad way.

"So . . . you're saying you only want to be in a relationship where you never have to ask your girlfriend for help with anything? You know that doesn't exist, right?"

He shrugs, eyes drifting at the ceiling.

"Have you ever had a girlfriend?"

"No."

"Well, I've had a boyfriend. And there were times that I asked for his help, like reaching a high shelf at the Strand. And there were times he asked me for help, like giving him the answers on our calculus test."

Jake laughs and peels his eyes off the ceiling. "You gave him answers on a calculus test?"

"Yeah. He had a really pretty face, but he was kind of dumb."

"Why did you break up?"

"He moved away. What I'm trying to say is that when you're with someone and you care about them and you trust them, it's okay to be vulnerable in front of them and let them be there for you, let them help you. You did that for me. When I showed up at your door that night last month, I had no other place to stay. That was a very vulnerable moment for me. As a rich girl, I've never had to worry about something like that."

He grunts; I can tell he doesn't think this compares with his baggage, and he may well be right. But it feels big for me—it feels like something I'll always be carrying around.

"You made me feel at home, made me feel safe. And I let you do that for me, and it was hard, but that's okay because I learned that you are someone I can trust."

"Of course I am. Always."

"I'd like to be that for you too, if you'll let me."

Instead of answering directly, he says, "I finally was able to start seeing a therapist. We've only had a couple of sessions but they've been good. She says I might be afraid to let people get close to me because deep down, I believe I'll end up losing them. She says it's important to work on getting past that."

I want to be able to promise him that he'll never lose me—not the way he lost his parents, at least. But I can't promise that. I can't control the future, can't predict how the story will end or even how many chapters will be tinged with tragedy. All I can be sure of is the present.

"Well, I'm not going to try to talk you into dating me." I reach out for his hand and take it in both of mine. "But just know that I want to be there for you, like I want you to be there for me."

"Okay." He shifts closer to me, pulls his hand out of my grasp, and brings it up to my cheek. He leans in, and this time I wait for him to come all the way to me. He touches my lips with his for a soft, tentative kiss. I kiss him back, wrapping my arms around his neck.

"So does this mean that I'm out of the friend zone?" I ask him jokingly.

"You can be in whatever zone you want to be in as long as it means I get to keep kissing you." He moves my hair back over my shoulder and kisses my neck.

I run my fingers across his chest, outlining the triangle of the Puerto Rican flag on his hoodie. He leans back, and I rest my head next to my hand on his chest. Both of his arms come around me.

"What if your father doesn't approve of me?" Jake says out of nowhere. "Like, I'm just some guy who works at a T-shirt shop. He probably wants some Ivy League frat boy for you."

"It doesn't matter what he wants. He always wants the wrong things. He threw away the best thing that ever happened to him—my mom—and keeps reaching for more money, more influence, more . . . I don't even know. I don't have to live my life according to his priorities anymore. All that matters is what I want, and I want you."

He kisses my forehead. "And I want you."

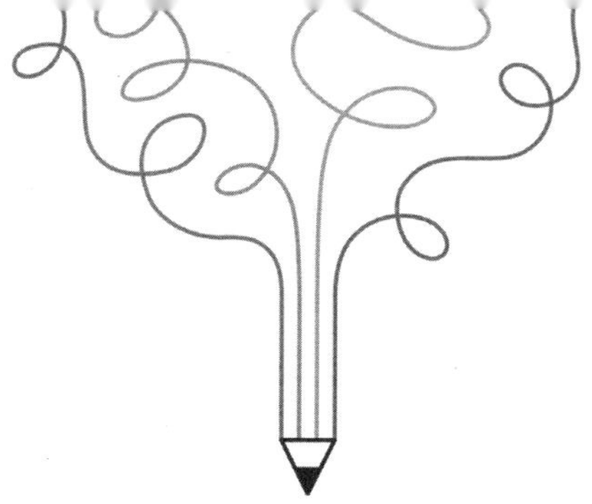

CHAPTER TWENTY-FOUR

I've missed going to the writing room. I'm there every day of the next week, working on book reviews and more story pitches. On Saturday, Jake isn't scheduled to work at the T-shirt shop, so we spend the whole day together, simmering black bean soup and swapping books at his apartment before we head to the writing room.

My freelance workload is picking up. I finally got good news from one of the teen magazines I pitched; they'll pay me to write a short article about nonprofits in the city where teens can volunteer, so I work on drafting that. I'm also starting another pitch, for a piece I want to call "The New Summer Reading List"—a top-twenty roundup of recommended reading for high school students. Absent from this list will be obvious choices such as *To Kill a Mockingbird*, *The Great Gatsby*, and *The Catcher in the Rye*. Instead I'd like to spotlight young adult novels that showcase great writing *and* that I think will speak to teen readers. I got the idea from seeing all the YA books on Jake's shelves, right alongside literary legends of the past. I haven't read that much YA myself, but I know Yoly will have a ton of recommendations to help me get up to speed.

Jake is a hand holder after all, I've discovered. We keep our fingers loosely intertwined as we walk home in the evening. It's strange to think back to the nights when we barely talked on these treks. Car horns and the swoosh of tires accompany us on our walk as always, but tonight they serve as only a backdrop for our voices.

I tell Jake that I'm still planning to write about anti-classics and highlight more recent works that get overlooked in favor of the "literary canon," but I assure him that I won't mention his writings if he'd prefer I didn't. "Maybe when your book eventually gets published, you'll let me review it."

"Maybe," he says. "You can read the draft now if you want."

"Yes, I want to!"

"It's different than the Vega stuff. It doesn't follow the same formula. I don't want my stories to be about that anymore. The stuff that Katie's posting right now—it's almost a year old, but she knows that's what gets the views, so she keeps posting it. I let her do whatever she wants with the account because we need the money, but eventually all that vengeance lit crap will dry up because I've stopped writing it."

"Well, I'm here for it, all of it. I still don't think you should be ashamed of the vengeance lit—it's really compelling. It totally changed how I think about literature, actually. But I'm also excited for whatever you try next."

He releases my hand and slides his arm around my shoulder, and I wrap mine around his waist.

My phone buzzes with an incoming call right when we reach our front steps, and I sit down on the stoop to answer. It's Dad. I let it ring two more times while I take a deep breath and compose myself. Jake sits on the step behind me, and I lean back against his legs. "Hi, Dad."

"Maya. I'm reviewing your classes before I authorize the tuition payment. You're going to have to change some of these."

"What? What do you mean? My schedule is all set." Thanks to dual-credit classes and AP tests in high school, most of my core requirements are done, and I chose my first-semester classes months ago.

He laughs that laugh I've known all my life, the laugh that denigrates you without a word. "Romantic Poetry? Early American Literature? What the hell kind of classes are those?"

"They're English classes I need for my major."

"What the hell is your major?"

"*English.*"

"English is a language that you speak, not a major. Literature is a hobby you may have, not a major." The volume of his voice increases with each sentence. "You need a major that will lead to a career. I know we've had this conversation before."

Jake caresses my shoulder. He can probably sense the tension in my body—and hear most of what Dad is saying.

"Dad, my major is English. Then I'll get my graduate degree in journalism."

"That is a waste. I'm not paying for you to waste your time reading books. You read books in your free time. You get on the business track so you can take over MedTech eventually. God knows it won't be Victoria, throwing her life away on that inane magazine, or your brother singing and dancing on a cruise ship. No."

"Dad, you can't pick my major for me."

"I can if I'm paying for it. You're going to take Financial Accounting, Marketing Management, Macroeconomics, Statistics. Change your classes, send me the schedule, then I'll authorize your tuition payment." He hangs up.

I lower my head to rest it against Jake's leg, and his arm comes around me. I've tried to be strong ever since the day Dad had Ernie dump me in front of this very door. But this is too much. Tears I don't want to hold back anymore pour out.

Jake shifts down to my step and takes me in his arms. I cry into his chest as he rubs my back and repeats, "I'm sorry. I'm so sorry."

Eventually, I pull back and wipe my eyes. I look at Jake and force a smile. "Well, that's my dad for you."

"I'm so sorry he's doing this to you."

"I don't know what I'm going to do," I admit, my voice shaky. "I don't want to take those classes, but I don't have the money to pay for my tuition."

"What about your mom?"

"She's been helping me a lot already. And he screwed her in the divorce, so she doesn't have much money."

"Are you going to call her?"

"Not right now." I wipe my face with my sleeve and turn away from him. "I don't want her to see me like this. I'll try to get ahold of her tomorrow."

"Maybe he'll change his mind."

I laugh. "No chance of that. Robert James Mitchell doesn't change his mind. He doubles down."

"I'm so sorry, Maya. I didn't know it was this bad."

"Yeah, and it's not just the classes. There's so much more I'm finding out that makes me question everything about him." I tell him about how Dad denied there was anything wrong with Bernard Wright's racism. "And now a reporter from the *Times* is investigating him. He may have pressured a lot of his employees to donate to Wright's campaign, then reimbursed them with bonuses or something to make up for it. He's all set on getting this guy elected, and I still have no idea why."

Jake frowns, digesting everything I've told him. "I'm sorry

that there's so much going on with your dad and that Wright guy. I did see a video clip of Wright the other day—he seems beyond shitty. But what are you going to do about your classes?"

"I don't know. I really don't know." I smile feebly at him. "Sorry to ruin our night." What started out as a lovely evening stroll has disintegrated, along with possibly my entire future.

He reaches out to stroke my hair. "I'm sorry about what your dad said. The way he talked to you—it isn't right."

"That's been pretty much my whole life."

"I think I understand now why you said Victoria hates your dad."

Victoria. There's an idea. I draw myself out of his embrace. "I should give her a call. Maybe she'll have advice for me." Victoria is always the voice of reason. She is the "dazzlingly clever" one, after all.

"Want me to stay with you while you talk to her?"

"No, you go on in. Thank you for being with me tonight, though. It means a lot."

He kisses my forehead. "Always."

"Hey, girlie. What's up?" She's in her running clothes, and I'm afraid I've disturbed her workout.

I'm trying to be strong, but the tears reemerge.

"Hey, what happened?"

"It's Dad. He wants me to drop all the classes in my schedule and sign up for econ and statistics and all these business classes. He says if I don't, he won't pay for tuition."

"That pendejo."

"Victoria—"

"Don't defend him! Look how he's manipulating you, just like he always did with Mom. If you give in now, you will always be giving in. He will own you. Don't take his classes. Don't do anything he wants. You might have to take a year off—keep working and save up. You can apply for financial aid and scholarships for next year. I'll help you. We'll figure out a way."

My heart sinks into my stomach as I think about postponing college for a year. Everything I've imagined for myself is slipping away, and there doesn't seem to be anything I can do about it. "I can't believe this is happening. I'm supposed to start classes in two weeks! I'm supposed to move into student housing! I'm supposed to be on Columbia's health plan! I can't live in the dorms or get student health insurance if I haven't paid the tuition!"

"Maya, I don't want you to freak out. We'll find a way to fix this."

"I *am* freaking out!" Asking Yoly and Ricardo to keep hosting me indefinitely would be a huge imposition. Finding someplace affordable to rent on such short notice might be impossible. Crashing with Daniel and his new boyfriend at the Inwood studio they'll be apartment-sitting, commuting more than an hour to my library job and sharing space with a total stranger, would be technically doable but probably challenging for all of us . . .

"Look, let's bring Mom into the call. We'll brainstorm solutions to look into, and then go from there. Okay?"

I want to scream that it's not going to be that simple. But Mom's face is already popping onto my screen as Victoria brings her in.

"Mis dos hijas. ¿Cómo están, muchachas?"

At the sight of my mom's face, I burst out crying again because she should be here with me right now. I should be able to collapse in her arms until the tears subside. Instead I'm sitting alone on the steps of this apartment building.

"¡Mija! ¿Qué pasó?"

Victoria fills Mom in on my conversation with Dad.

"Hijo de su madre. Are you going to change your classes?"

"No!" Victoria and I say together.

"Well, did you apply for any scholarships?" Mom asks.

"I didn't think I'd need any!" I sob. "I thought it would all be paid for. He let Victoria go to journalism school! Why not me too?"

Victoria scoffs. "*Let* is a stretch. Once he found out about the jewelry I sold and realized I wasn't going to just do his bidding, he stopped paying my tuition too. I had to cover the rest of it myself with the money from the jewelry, the jobs and internships I got, and some scholarships and loans."

The implication hurts: I wasn't smart enough to see this coming and plan for it. I've never been the dazzlingly clever one.

Mom covers her face with her hand and rubs her eyes. "This is all my fault."

"Mom, no," I say instinctively.

"I left you kids with nothing. Nothing at all. And he has all the power over your future, Maya."

"We'll figure something out," Victoria says firmly. "Maya, I was lucky; I was able to pay off my student loans, and now I've got some money in savings—"

"No, Victoria. I won't take your money."

"Maya, listen. We can make it happen. It will all work out."

I sigh. "Let's talk tomorrow. I need some time to think."

"Before you go, I have to tell you both something," Victoria says. "I heard from my friend Miranda today. She works for the reporter who's been writing a story on Dad—Mom, you remember I mentioned that to you when we last talked?"

"Of course. What did she say?" Mom asks.

"The story is coming out on Monday, and according to Miranda, it's worse than we thought. There are the campaign finance violations of reimbursing his employees with bonuses in exchange for them making donations to Wright, but there's more."

I should probably feel something—shock, unease—but I'm numb right now. I feel so detached from my dad and everything he's done. Still, I dutifully ask, "What else?"

"Turns out Dad created shell companies to funnel money to political action committees, and they've given Wright a lot of money—way more than Dad's legally allowed to donate under his own name. Between that and coercing his employees to donate, he could be in a lot of trouble."

Mom shakes her head. "He'll buy his way out of it. He always does."

We agree to talk tomorrow and say goodbye. My heart hasn't stopped slamming against my chest since I heard Dad's voice on the phone. I close my eyes and try to take a few deep breaths to calm myself. I feel like I'm falling apart, and it's more than just the financial worries. If it were simply a lack of money, I would focus on the numbers and figure it out. But this is a fracturing of something much bigger.

Parents are supposed to provide protection, support, love. All my life, Dad's offered them or withheld them depending on his whims. And all my life, part of me has believed that if I can just prove myself to him, he'll decide I'm worthy of a steady supply. If I can just win at the game he's set up, playing by his twisted rules. If I can just exceed his expectations, again and again and again.

He treats our relationship like a business deal, and I thought I could cope with that. But that deal was supposed to include one privilege for me: four years of college tuition. And now he's threatening to withdraw that too.

His support—and his funds—have now been directed elsewhere, to the campaign of a racist politician. He bribes and coerces his employees to support a man who vilifies immigrants with the same brown skin as his children. He would rather prop up someone who openly hates people who look like me than give me the one thing I thought I was guaranteed under the terms he set for his parenting.

My first instinct is to double over and cry some more, but I restrain myself. It's not what Victoria would do. At a very young age, she devised a plan to free herself from Dad. She created a solution to her problem, and I can too. I have to.

CHAPTER TWENTY-FIVE

Jake makes his first appearance at Sunday dinner at Daisy and Lorenzo's. When he and Katie walk in with their covered dishes, Daisy is the first to greet him.

"So you're not too internet-famous to join us?"

Everyone laughs, as his identity has become common knowledge throughout the building. This morning, Daisy accosted Yoly on the stoop to tell her what she'd heard from Lorenzo, who'd heard it from Katie, who'd finally gotten Jake's permission to share the secret. Yoly's definitely the most star-struck; everyone else just thinks it's kind of funny.

"That's Katie's account," Jake says. "She's the one who's internet-famous. Your future daughter-in-law, Daisy."

Katie gives him a playful shove as he puts his dish down on the counter.

Daisy turns furrowed brows to Jake, then Katie, and then Lorenzo, who puts both hands in the air as his mom declares, "Very far in the future, because Lorenzo still has medical school after college." She points at him with her wooden spoon.

"We're not getting married, Mom!" Lorenzo protests.

"Look what you've done," Katie says to Jake. "I think I liked it better when you didn't come to Sunday dinner."

"I know someone who disagrees with you." He walks over to me, puts his arms around my waist, and kisses my cheek.

"Daisy, tell them no kissing in the apartment," Katie says.

Daisy stirs a pot on the stove. "If they're not related to me, I don't care."

"Jake," Ricardo says, "Yoly and I wanted to ask you something. We've been working to spread the word about how Bernard Wright would be bad for New York."

"Bernard Wright?" Lorenzo asks, his head swiveling toward Yoly. "That dude showed up on my ChitChat feed. He comes off like a *Batman* supervillain. I didn't think he was for real at first until I looked him up. He is batshit."

"Lorenzo, language!" Daisy shouts from across the apartment.

"Sorry, Mom, it's just a fact. I can't wait to vote against him."

"Exactly, and that's why we want to ask you a favor, Jake," Ricardo continues. "The *Times* is about to publish an article about one of his campaign's biggest funders . . . but obviously not everyone reads the *Times*."

I told them about the article last night, after I found an email from Jill Shields in my inbox giving me an official heads-up about it—and after we talked over my predicament, which gave me some ideas for how to move forward.

Yoly picks up where Ricardo left off, asking Jake, "Would you be willing to post a video about Wright? Like, just one video; we don't want to take over your platform. But you can reach a lot of people who don't read the newspaper. Everybody needs to know."

I stiffen. Letting the neighbors in on his secret identity is one thing; putting a face to the pseudonym for the whole internet to see would be something entirely different. I wish Yoly and

Ricardo had run this by me before approaching Jake about it.

Jake doesn't seem offended, though. "Yeah, I hear you. Of course I'd like to help, but it's Katie's account." He looks at his sister.

"I think it's a great idea," says Katie. "And you should be the one speaking, Jake. People are going to want to hear directly from you."

"They don't know me, not really."

Katie puts a hand on Jake's arm. "They know your words; they care about your words. They'll trust what you have to say."

Jake looks over at me, worry overtaking his face. "What do you think? Isn't the article going to be mostly about . . . ?"

"My dad? Yeah." I'm aware that this conversation has completely hijacked Sunday dinner, that everyone's watching me. I try to sound brave. "You should do it. People need to know about Wright, *and* about my dad's involvement with him."

"That would be a good angle for the messaging," Ricardo says. "The more Mitchell sees his name attached to Wright, dragged through the mud, the more likely he is to pull back some of his support."

The way Ricardo refers to my dad by his last name, just as he refers to Wright, jolts me. It's still my last name too.

Jake looks at me again, and I nod at him. He has a large audience. If he can reach some of the young people who follow him, it could make a difference.

"Okay, let's do it. Get your phone, Katie."

Katie puts down the plate of lumpia she'd been munching on. "Right now?"

"Why not? Let's just go for it."

"Can you record it now but wait to post it?" Yoly asks. "The *Times* article is coming out tomorrow morning. Can you post after that? I'll text my friend Julissa—she can send you some relevant video clips of Wright to include."

Katie nods, pulling her phone out of her back pocket. "I'll record it now, edit it tonight, and post it tomorrow. Should I go get my ring light?"

"Katie, I couldn't care less about the lighting," Jake says.

"Time out!" Daisy puts her hands up to form the letter T. "Can we please sit down and eat Sunday dinner like God intended and then you can film your little TikTok dances afterward?"

"It's not a TikTok dance, Mom," Lorenzo says.

"I don't care, Lorenzo. You're not going to make an internet video while my pancit sits there on the table getting cold. Come on, everyone, get a plate."

We all comply and form a line in front of Daisy, who serves everyone a generous portion of pancit. Jake and I sit on the love seat in the living room.

"Are you sure you're okay with doing this?" I ask him quietly.

"I mean, I'm not necessarily *excited* to do it, but I'm up for it if I can help in any way."

"And are you ready for the whole world to know your identity?"

Jake laughs. "The whole world?"

"You know what I mean."

"Yeah. Now that I've talked it over with you, I do feel . . . less embarrassed by it. Like, I did write those stories from a place of anger, but anger's part of the human experience. And if my words moved people, connected with people, maybe that's not something I need to hide from."

"Sounds like the therapy is working," I say and we both chuckle.

"I'm just worried about *you*," he adds after swallowing a mouthful of pancit. "About how this stuff with your dad could affect you."

I don't let myself hesitate. "People need to know that my dad is doing something illegal and unethical, and that he's doing it to benefit a hateful man. He's hurt a lot of people, for a cause that'll hurt even more people. Why should he get away with it?"

"Well," Jake says, "I'm going to follow your lead here. How about you help me script out what I'm going to say in my video? You can make sure I get the facts right and don't overstep."

I smile at him. "You want me to be your editor?"

"More like my cowriter, I guess."

"Deal."

We finish eating Sunday dinner like God intended and help Daisy clean up. Afterward, I grab my ideas notebook from the studio and join Jake and Katie in their apartment. Sitting on the couch with Jake, I write down a few notes. "First, you can introduce yourself. Then say a little bit about Wright . . ." I jot down the main bullet points and hand the notebook over to Jake to take a look. We go back and forth a few times, tweaking wording so that it'll sound as natural as possible and be easy to follow.

Jake takes a seat on a stool at the counter. Katie aims the phone and tells Jake to start.

"Hi, I'm Jacobo Canales, aka Jake, aka Junior Vega. Thank you to everyone who has followed me here. The reason I'm making this video and finally showing my face is to let you know about something happening here in New York, where I live. There's a man running for governor named Bernard Wright. Here are a few examples of what he'll bring to the race."

"Here's where I'll put in the clips Yoly was talking about," whispers Katie.

"So that's his deal in a nutshell: racism and anti-immigrant nonsense, dialed up to eleven. And his campaign has raised a lot of money." Jake glances over at me, just briefly. "Some of his donations are connected to Robert James Mitchell, founder of Mitchell MedTech, who may have violated campaign finance laws to funnel money to Wright. You can read more about that in a *New York Times* article published today. Wright talks a lot about immigrants supposedly being criminals, but it looks like he has no problem with laws being broken for his benefit. I love New York, and I don't want a man like this to be our governor. I encourage all of you to learn more, spread the word, and get involved, so that everyone knows what's going on. Elections are still a year away, but the time to start paying attention is now. And by the way, any money I get from likes and shares of this post, I'll be donating to Votemos Todos, a group that helps Latine voters make their voices heard. I've linked to their website in my caption, so please check them out and chip in if you can."

That last bit was my idea. My research on charity groups has paid off.

"Great, Jake," Katie says. She checks her phone. "I got Julissa's video clips. I'll finish putting this together tonight."

I walk over to Jake, who's still on the stool. He puts his arm around me, and I rest my chin on his shoulder. "That was great," I say into his ear. "A lot of people will know what's going on because of you."

"Because of *us*," he corrects me.

Layla texts me, sending a picture of the progress on her curtains. I haven't seen her since our shopping trip more than a week ago, and we haven't checked in since I told her that Jake and I are back together.

Her previous text—**Told you he was still into you! I could see it in his eyes!**—hovers above the photo she's just sent.

I consider telling her about the latest developments with my college situation, but I decide to wait until I have a plan in place. I've spent the last twenty-four hours researching my options, and I know none of them include "Layla's family bails me out."

Before I turn in for the night, I sit on the steps of the apartment building to call Victoria. Usually she drives the conversation, asks the questions, gives me advice or suggestions. This time, I dive right in with my ideas.

"So, first off I was thinking about why I even applied to Columbia. And I think it was mostly because of Dad, and not necessarily because that's what I wanted. You know, it's prestigious. That was important to him. I don't think it's that important to me that I go there."

"Are you sure?"

"Yeah. I mean when I got accepted, of course I was happy. And I've been excited to go there, but I think I would be happy going somewhere else that I could afford."

"There's always UCLA."

"No. Stop, Victoria. There are other schools right here. Instate tuition is a fraction of what UCLA would cost. I'm going to apply for the winter session. There might be scholarships I can get. In the meantime, I can keep working at the library and writing, saving up everything I can . . ."

"But where will you *live*?" she demands. "You were supposed to move into student housing in September. If that's off the table—"

"I've talked that over with Yoly and Ricardo. They're about to move into a bigger apartment in this building; they were planning to sublet their studio. So they've offered to sublet it to *me* until I get something else lined up."

Victoria's already protesting. "You can't possibly afford the rent in Morningside Heights!"

"I've been saving up to pay for housing anyway. This'll be tight, but I can manage it for a few months." Along with a government health insurance plan, phone and internet bills, transport costs, groceries, and miscellaneous household supplies. I've done the math and it *almost* works, especially if I can land some more freelance writing jobs. "Besides, I owe Yoly and Ricardo for the three months they've let me stay with them for free. This way I can pay them back to some extent."

Victoria doesn't look totally convinced, but she nods. "Well, that's at least the start of a plan. And I can open a savings account for you that Mom and I can add money to. Between us, we can handle this. We don't need him anymore."

I want to protest, to refuse to take her money. But I remember what I told Jake about being able to rely on people who care about you. She wants to help . . . and I think I want to let her.

CHAPTER TWENTY-SIX

Victoria FaceTimes me first thing Monday morning. "Did you read it yet?"

"No. Did you?"

"Let's read it together."

We stay on FaceTime while we skim the article silently. An anonymous former employee is referenced and quoted, and I wonder if it's Lisa Piccola. Did she end up meeting with Jill and giving her some of this information?

"This is so bad," Victoria says when I'm halfway through. "So, so bad."

Jill ends the article by predicting that the New York election authorities will investigate Dad—probably a self-fulfilling prophecy, since her reporting is going to draw a lot of attention. It'll be harder for the authorities to look the other way now. I switch back over to FaceTime so I can see Victoria's face. "Do you think he could go to jail?" I ask her.

"Eh, I doubt it. You heard Mom. He can buy himself out of anything."

"It's got to catch up to him sometime."

"We can only hope."

Is that what I hope—that Dad will to go to jail? I don't know. I've never actively wished harm upon him. He is, after all, still my father. But if he did something this unethical, shouldn't he face consequences?

Victoria changes the subject. "So, I got your latest book review and it's good, but what happened with that other idea you had—Junior Vega and the ChitChat posts, the anti-classics one?"

"Oh, yeah. I'm not going to do it."

"Why? I thought it was a good idea. I've even been checking that account every day."

"So . . . it turns out . . . Jake is Junior Vega."

Victoria stares at me with widened eyes. "Your Jake?"

"Yes, my Jake."

"Incredible. Then you've got an insider's view! Why don't you want to write about it?"

"He asked me not to. I'll still write about anti-classics, but I'll focus on other work."

"Whatever. Send it to me when it's done. So is this thing with Junior getting serious?"

"Maybe. We're taking things slowly. But he's been really supportive. He's even going to post a video about Wright on his account today."

"That could have a lot of impact." Victoria sounds impressed. "Smart move."

"Jake was worried about mentioning Dad's name and how it might affect me, but I told him I don't care."

"Good for you. I'm glad you didn't listen to me when I said this had nothing to do with us. You're shining a light on bad people. And yes, Dad is bad people. So don't let anything bring you down today, okay? If this derails or even just slows down the campaign of a racist, then that's a reason to celebrate."

After we disconnect, I push aside thoughts of Dad and Bernard Wright. There are college applications to complete and scholarships to apply for. I thought I'd finished with all this months ago, but I am starting my search over today.

I go to CUNY's website to figure out how to apply. Columbia is in the past for me. It was a dream, whether it was mine or just my dad's, that will never be realized, and I'm starting to be okay with that.

I find a couple of merit-based scholarships that might work for me. They require sending a portfolio of my writing, so I spend some time compiling my best pieces from the school newspaper and from *Latina at Large*. I take a quick break to shower and have breakfast and move my laptop to the table because slouching on the thrift-store couch has not been good for my back this morning. I'm almost finished gathering everything for the CUNY application when there's a knock on the door.

It's Jake. I pull him in and close the door behind him. My arms come up around his shoulders, and my fingers lock behind his neck. "Hey. I was wondering when I would see you today."

"Is now a good time?" He pulls me in and interlaces his fingers behind my waist.

"Uh-huh. I've got half an hour before I need to leave for work."

Jake bends forward to kiss me and pulls me in so tightly that I feel the buttons of his shirt against my thin tee. His lips on mine feel fresh and new every time, and I will never get tired of the feeling that runs through my whole body when he kisses me.

He pulls away and rests his forehead on mine. "I don't know if I could get through a whole day without kissing you."

"You won't have to." I grab his hand and lead him over to the couch to sit next to me. "I'll still be living right upstairs from you for the next few months, and hopefully by January,

I'll be able to start college somewhere nearby."

I fill him in on the plans I've formed over the past day and a half, from subletting this apartment during the fall to applying for other schools in the city. "With scholarships and student loans, I think I can pull it off. I'm not taking any money from Dad."

"That's awesome," he says, giving my hands a squeeze. "And you're feeling all right with not going to Columbia?"

"Yeah. That was always Dad's plan for me. I'm going to make my own plan for myself." I grin at him. "CUNY isn't as close as Columbia, but it's still only a subway ride away, if you need to get your daily kiss."

He smiles, but only halfheartedly. "That's good news. I'm sorry to have to follow it with some bad news."

"What's wrong?"

"Just a lot of comments on my video about your dad. I'm sorry."

I grab my phone off the coffee table and open the ChitChat app. I've been so wrapped up this morning that I haven't even seen the finalized version of Jake's video. I watch it before scanning the comments.

No surprise that a millionaire is funding a racist.

Isn't he married to a Latina? How can you be racist if you married a Latina?

It's called hypocrisy. For someone like this it's like breathing.

My feelings are mixed as I read comment after comment. I'm glad most people seem as outraged as I am by Wright's platform and my dad's involvement, but it's weird to see so much negativity directed at the name Mitchell. I share my dad's last name. It was given to me at my birth, and it's going to follow me the rest of my life.

"This is what we hoped would happen," I point out. "People are talking about Wright and paying attention to what he and my dad are up to. That's a good thing."

"I know, but it can't feel good to have people online talking about your dad, your family." He takes my free hand and puts it in between both of his.

"That's not your fault. My dad made these choices."

"Are you worried that he'll find out that you helped jump-start the *Times* investigation?"

"I'm not sure it matters whether he finds out about that. He's going to find out I don't support what he's doing. That's more than enough of a betrayal in his eyes. But I'm not going to just keep quiet about it."

And even as I say it, I make a decision. I need to repost Jake's video on my own feed. I tap the Share button, which will automatically route one cent from my account to Jake's. I immediately turn off the comment option on my repost, close the app, and set my phone down.

I don't want to think about my dad anymore. I lean into Jake and push him down on the couch. His smile widens with every inch he goes back. I lie on top of him, and he pulls me in for a kiss.

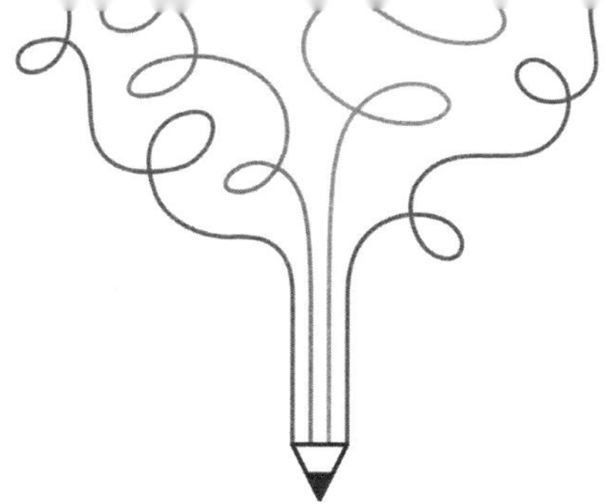

CHAPTER TWENTY-SEVEN

On the way home from work, Yoly turns to me on the crowded subway. "How are you doing with all this stuff about your dad? The story coming out, all the chatter online."

"I don't know. I guess I'm having to accept that Dad's turned into someone I don't recognize. Maybe that's who he's always been, and I just didn't let myself see it." From the minute I saw Bernard Wright in the home I grew up in, it felt like a completely different place. I know now that even if I wanted to, even if Dad would let me, I can't ever go back.

"I'm sorry, Maya. I don't want to pile on to what you're already dealing with, but I have to tell you that our community group is planning a protest outside the MedTech building this weekend. The goal is to get him to pause his financial support of the Wright campaign. Julissa thinks standing outside Mitchell's building, continuing to draw attention to his shady behavior, might make a difference. If your dad has to choose between his own business and reputation, and supporting Bernard Wright, he'll probably pick himself over Wright."

"How big of a protest?" I ask.

"We're hoping for a turnout of several hundred people. I'm sorry if it feels like a personal attack. It's not meant to be."

I shake my head. "I'm not my dad. I don't feel like any of

this is an attack on me. He's the one who did something wrong. In fact . . ." I think about Teresa and Brenda, who are a threat to no one, and their mom, who's just been trying to make a living and care for her daughters. "I want to come."

"Are you sure?" Yoly looks even more uneasy now. "There's always a chance the police could show up, even though this is going to be a nonviolent demonstration."

"I understand." Honestly, maybe I don't; I've been shielded from so much by my dad's wealth and privilege, by his whiteness. The stakes are probably higher than I can really process. But I know I can't just sit behind a locked door and let myself feel safe while people like those little girls are being attacked.

Yoly still doesn't seem on board. "What if the media picks it up—that Robert Mitchell's daughter is protesting outside his company headquarters?"

"I don't care. I hope the media does notice I'm there. I've cared what my dad thinks of me my whole life. Where has that gotten me?" I say it again for emphasis, inscribing the words in the air. "I. Don't. Care. Anymore."

At the writing room that evening, I join Jake out on the fire escape, and he pulls me into a kiss. I really like this new routine. It's about more than the stability of knowing I can count on someone. It's about the genuine smile that comes over his face in my presence and knowing I had a little something to do with that.

When we met, I was at the lowest point in my life, feeling so utterly alone, and he was in a bad place as well, carrying so much pent-up pain. I don't think that pain has diminished, but neither of us feels so alone anymore. We both have something that makes us smile each day, and that's worth a lot.

We exchange updates about our days, and I tell him about the protest tomorrow.

"Yeah, Katie and I are on the email update list for the community network now. We agreed I should make a second video, specifically about the protest. I would love your help scripting it."

Together, we draft the outline of what he'll say. He takes notes, then rehearses for me out on the fire escape. "You might remember the post I made a few days ago about Bernard Wright and Robert James Mitchell. This is a follow-up, inviting my fellow New Yorkers to a protest on Saturday. We're meeting outside the Mitchell MedTech building on Park Avenue at three in the afternoon. We have to come together to tell Bernard Wright and his financial backers that their racist, anti-immigrant sentiments are not welcome in our state. New York City has always been a city of immigrants, so there's no better place to launch a fight like this—a fight for fair treatment for everyone. A fight against people who lie and cheat their way into power. A fight to welcome and support the people who want to call this place home. Hope to see you on Saturday."

"It's good," I tell him. "I think your delivery really sells it. I bet a lot more people will be motivated to come once they hear from you."

"Yeah—some, maybe." Always so self-deprecating. "Are you sure you're okay with me recording that and posting it?"

"Yeah. I'm actually planning to go to the protest myself."

"Well, Katie and I will be there with you." He kisses me again before we go inside. We've both got work to do: he's finishing his novel draft, and I'm tackling the pitch for that summer reading piece. I haven't yet chosen the full list of books to spotlight, but I know I want to feature *Before We Were Free* by Julia Alvarez and *The Poet X* by Elizabeth Acevedo, so I can use those as examples in the pitch. We sit across from each other at a table, and he taps my foot with his, relaxing his lips into an easy smile I want to imprint on my mind.

The next morning I watch Jake's video, thinking about how we crafted each word together. I've used writing to convey meaning for as long as I can remember, but I'm new to creating this kind of message. I've helped Jake speak to more people than I'll ever meet in my life. I've helped him target my father, inviting those people to converge on Dad's building to condemn his actions. And I don't feel bad about it. It's the least I can do to fight the injustices he's invited upon our state with his support of Bernard Wright.

I share Jake's post on my ChitChat profile and send the link to Layla. I'm not exactly asking her to come to the protest, but I do want to let her know that it's happening. I didn't hear from her at all yesterday. I would've thought she'd at least check on me after the story came out. I can tell she's seen my message with the link to Jake's post, and I see the response bubbles appear on my phone. They go away and come back, but after five minutes, there is still no text from Layla.

I do get a notification, though. It's from Lucinda—who's liked my repost, shared it, and commented: **Wish I could be at the protest! Thanks for representing New York. Miss you, Maya.**

I get several more likes and shares, doubtless thanks to Lucinda's much more popular profile. Even though we're barely in touch anymore, my message has reached her. That gives me the tiny bit of the courage I'll need to face what's ahead.

On Wednesday morning, I finally hear from Layla.

Layla: Sorry for the late response. I saw your posts. Are you sure you want to protest your own dad?

Me: Yes. I have to do it. He's wrong. I have to speak up. I can't let his beliefs and actions represent our name.

Layla: He's gonna be so pissed.

Me: Nothing I do makes him happy. This will just be one more thing.

Layla: I wish I could come support you, but my parents would kill me.

It's not that I was expecting Layla to be a stalwart, arms-locked collaborator in this venture, but I was hoping she would at least say something more encouraging. On some level, I get it. She won't be impacted by this directly. Bernard Wright is not after her or anyone who looks like her. He's after people who look like me and like my mom. Even if Wright won the election, Layla's life would go on, uninterrupted. She has no skin in the game.

I get a call from Dad just as I'm about to leave for work.

"Maya. I'm outside your building. Come let me in."

I dash to the window and see one of Dad's cars come to a stop in front. Ernie gets out and opens the back passenger door. Out comes Dad dressed in a cobalt suit.

"I'll meet you outside," I say in a flat voice that surprises me. Maybe I'm in shock. But I'm not letting him into this apartment. I disconnect the call before he does.

He looks up at the building and shakes his head, barking some order to Ernie over his shoulder.

My first coherent thought is that he must've noticed that I took *Charlotte's Web* again.

But he could've just sent Ernie to retrieve it, like he did last time. Why has he come here himself?

I brace myself to face him in mere seconds. This overwhelming dread isn't new to me; it's been a part of interactions with my dad for most of my life. The anticipation is sometimes worse than the reality. Knowing that in just a few seconds, you could be left feeling like a piece of trash.

Even though I'm expecting to see him as soon as I step outside, it's still jarring to be face-to-face with him after all this time.

"So this is where you're holed up?" He looks around with unmistakable contempt.

"What do you want, Dad?"

He ignores my tone. "I heard about the protest you're planning. Did you think I wouldn't find out about it?"

"I just found out about it myself."

"You and your little friends need to call it off."

"It's not up to me."

"Well, whoever the hell is orchestrating it—tell them to drop it."

"People have a right to protest," I snap. "Whether you like it or not."

He takes a few steps forward and grabs my arm. "Listen. This is what you're going to do." He takes his other hand out of his pocket and points at me. "You're going to tell your friends to cancel the protest or you can kiss your tuition money goodbye."

"I already kissed it goodbye. I'm not taking your business classes, and I'm not taking your money. And I am not going to try to stop that protest. Actually, I'm going to join it." In all my interactions with my father throughout my life, I have never answered him back like this.

Dad's face is starting to flush. "I'm not fooling around here—"

The door of the building opens suddenly, and Jake steps outside. "Let her go."

Dad's eyes snap toward Jake. I pull away from his grasp.

"Who the hell are you?" Dad asks.

"Doesn't matter." Jake comes to stand by me and loosely holds my hand. "Are you okay?" he asks me.

"Yeah."

"I know who you are." Dad narrows his eyes at Jake. "You're that TikToker who's been telling lies about me." I've never thought of my father as someone who searches for his own name on social media, but that must be how he found out about Jake's posts, and probably the plans for the protest too. It makes him seem surprisingly small.

"Where's the lie?" Jake fires back at him.

Dad laughs "You are going to take those videos down and keep my name out of your mouth."

Jake shakes his head. "Nah."

Dad purses his lips and gives a slight nod. "Okay then. I'm going to find out every detail about you, and you're going to wish I'd never heard of you. Your choice." With a little shrug, he turns back toward the car. Ernie, who's been standing uncomfortably off to the side this whole time, opens the door for him, and Dad gets in.

After he closes the door, Ernie turns sad eyes to me and gives me an apologetic look.

As soon as the car drives off, I turn to Jake and bury my face into his chest. My whole body is shaking. He presses me tightly against him. “I’m so sorry,” he whispers against the top of my head.

“I’m the one who’s sorry. What he said to you . . .” I’ve taken Dad’s arrows all my life, but seeing his rage aimed at someone I love is so much worse.

“I don’t care,” Jake assures me. “What can he actually do to me?”

“I don’t want to find out. I hope it’s just an empty threat.”

CHAPTER TWENTY-EIGHT

On Friday, Jake and I head home from the writing room a little earlier than usual. We're only a couple of blocks from our apartments when Victoria FaceTimes me.

"Hey. Um. I wanted to talk to you. Do you have time?"

I stop mid-step, and Jake stops next to me. "Yeah—Wait. Where are you?" I peer at my screen to study the tree behind her. The thin branches look very familiar.

She turns to the side, moving her phone, and I see my apartment building right behind her.

"What?!"

I break into a run, with Jake right behind me. I scream when I see my sister standing right by our stoop. I grab her in a fierce embrace. "You're here! You're really here!"

"Surprise!" Victoria pulls back to look at me. "You look so good."

"You do too!" Her shoulder-length hair is pulled up in a ponytail. She's wearing jeans and a short-sleeved blazer. "Wow, Vic. What are you doing here?"

"I thought it was time to visit my little sister." She looks over my shoulder. "And her boyfriend. You must be Jake." Victoria, being an honors graduate of Mom's "tienes que saludar" class, extends her hand. "It's nice to meet you."

He takes her hand and nods a silent acknowledgment. I'm still tutoring him in this area.

"When did you get here?" I ask.

"Just now. Took a cab to my hotel and then the subway here."

"Are you going to see Dad?"

"He's going to see me, outside his building at tomorrow's protest."

"You're coming to the protest?"

"Yeah, I can't let you stand alone. We're in this together."

"I'm so glad you're here." I pull her into my arms again.

"Jake, you don't mind if I steal my sister away, do you? I'm only here for a couple of days."

"No, of course not. Good meeting you. I'll see you later, Maya."

I lean in for a kiss and he glances at Victoria before giving me a peck on the cheek.

Victoria convinces me to pack a bag and stay the night at her hotel. She picks the queen bed next to the window. Victoria always chooses first. It's been that way since we were little, when she would grab the first cookie straight out of the oven or the best seat at the movies. I hop onto the remaining bed. She kicks her shoes off and sits cross-legged, facing me.

"You doing okay?" she asks. "You're the one who's always held out hope for him."

I sigh. "You know how people sometimes say something is shocking but not surprising? That's how all this stuff with Dad has been for me. It's time for me to see him for who he really is instead of who I wish he was. And it's time for the world to see that too."

Victoria nods. "One hundred percent. And I hope *he* sees *us* out there tomorrow, front and center."

This feels odd—what we're about to do. Openly, publicly defy Dad. As much as we've seethed about him in private, we've always kept our grievances within the family.

The satisfaction in Victoria's voice hits me in a vulnerable spot. Dad's not the only one I've been resenting all this time. "You finally came back to New York because you wanted to see Dad humiliated," I say quietly. "You didn't come back for me."

First Victoria, then Mom, then Daniel. They each left Dad for their own reasons—valid reasons—but in the process, they left *me*. I was like the little duckling that couldn't keep up, struggling along through the rushing waters by myself while the rest of the ducklings never looked back. I've navigated so much on my own. Having Victoria here is wonderful. But I needed her here last month, last year, three years ago.

"I'm sorry I left you behind," she says. "I should've been here more."

"Yes, you should have. I know you had to get away from him, but you should've come back for me. It shouldn't have taken you this long to come back for me."

She gets off her bed and comes to sit next to me. Her arm goes around my shoulders. "I'm sorry. I was so focused on getting away from him, and then on staying away from him. I guess I didn't think about how it would affect you."

"I was all alone with him the last two years. Every disappointment, every angry thought was directed at me."

She cries into my shoulder. "I'm so sorry, Mayita. I will come back more often. I promise."

Her tears are contagious. Suddenly, we're back in the walk-in closet of her childhood bedroom, her arm around me, her hands pressed to my ears as Dad's shouts carry from down the hall.

Once we've cried ourselves out, Victoria retrieves a box of tissues from across the room. We both wipe our eyes and blow our noses and laugh at the synchronized sounds of it all.

"So. Tell me all about this Jake."

I roll my eyes, but honestly, I'm glad for the change of subject, and I couldn't have chosen a better one myself. "What do you want to know?"

"Everything! What's his deal? Like, why is he so frowny and allergic to eye contact?"

"That's how he is when you first meet him. You just have to get to know him." Suddenly I remember Dad threatening Jake and me the other day. My instinct is to keep that to myself, to not worry Victoria, but I remind myself that it's okay to lean on others sometimes. I bring her up to speed.

"Oh my god," she says. "I hope you told Jake to be careful."

"Careful how? What can Dad actually do to him? Jake's not a high-powered business leader or a politician or anybody important. Dad can't actually ruin his life." I'm saying it as much to reassure myself as to convince Victoria.

"Don't underestimate him, Maya. Be careful. Be vigilant. He can strike when you least expect it."

CHAPTER TWENTY-NINE

Katie and Jake's apartment has become our poster-making headquarters for the protest. Lorenzo distributes thin wooden posts to staple to posterboard, and Katie wields the staple gun. I sit at the coffee table trying to squeeze all my words on one poster. *Wright Is Wrong for NY.*

Ricardo and Yoly have gone on ahead to help Julissa and others set up. We're heading out at two to meet them. Daisy has taken a liking to Victoria and talks her ear off at the kitchen table as they work on their posters. There's a knock on the door, and Jake jumps off the couch to answer it.

"Daniel!" I yelp and run over to hug my brother.

"Maya." He picks me up and twirls me around. Victoria runs over from the kitchen and grabs him for a hug once he puts me down.

Daniel's brought his boyfriend, Adam, whom I'm meeting for the first time. He's almost Daniel's exact height, with black curly hair and a warm smile, and I would've loved to watch them perform as T-Birds in the cruise ship production.

"I can't believe you're here!" I tell Daniel. "I missed you so much."

"Well, hopefully we'll be here for a while. Adam has an audition next week for a show here in the city, and I'm doing a couple of open calls. If we can line up some local work, we should be able to stick around long-term."

"It'll be so nice to have you around. Both of you!" I make a hasty round of introductions.

Daniel smirks when I get to Jake. "So, you're the boyfriend, huh? Did Victoria already talk to you about your intentions and all that?"

"My intentions?"

"Yeah, you know, the talk that boyfriends usually have with the dad, when the dad's a normal dad and not a megalomaniacal millionaire who has to be protested and pressured and legally sanctioned into acting like a human being." Daniel slides to the floor and picks up a blank piece of posterboard.

"Well, uh . . ."

"I was kidding, Jake. If Maya trusts you, I trust you. You're cool with me."

"Ignore him," I advise Jake. "He's just trying to do big-brother stuff, making up for completely abandoning me on my graduation day."

"Maya, I'm sorry. I was in the middle of the ocean."

"I know. I'm just contractually obligated to give you a hard time."

Adam nudges Daniel. "Give her the graduation present."

"Oh, yeah." Daniel digs into a backpack he left by the door. "Here, Maya. For your new place." He hands me something wrapped in a brown paper bag. It turns out to be a set of four ceramic bowls. "They're hand-painted. I bought them in Greece."

I run my fingers along the patterns—white painted flowers on sky-blue ceramic with navy-blue outlines. Daniel was thinking about me while he was halfway around the world, picking out these bowls as a gesture of love, the way Mom was thinking of me when she got me my messenger bag in Guatemala. Meanwhile, Dad's apartment, just across the park, is filled with expensive and opulent possessions that seem meaningless to me right now. "They're so beautiful. Thank you, Daniel."

"I helped him pick them out," Adam says.

"And he's never going to let me forget it." Daniel shakes his head, running a hand through the waves of black hair that come down over his forehead.

"Thank you both. I really love them." I put the bowls back in the bag and turn to Jake. "Can I store them here until I officially move in upstairs?"

"Yeah, I'll keep them in our cupboard for you." Jake takes the package from me and puts it on the high shelf above the sink.

Victoria claps her hands to get everyone's attention. "All right, people, let's finish up these posters. We should be heading out soon." Typically enough, she's taken charge of this poster-making party in this apartment that is not hers for this protest in a city where she doesn't live.

Within the hour, we're approaching Dad's building on Park Avenue. I've been outside this building a hundred times. We've been in and out to visit Dad, to drop something off, or to join him for lunch. I know which elevator to take and every hallway that will lead me to his office. But today we won't be going inside. Today we're outsiders, and for the first time in my life, that doesn't feel like something to be ashamed of.

A large group is already assembled, and I can't see Yoly or Ricardo anywhere. Even though Victoria hasn't been in the city since she left seven years ago, she somehow is at the front of our little group. Leading is in her nature, and I guess we're all followers.

As we head deeper into the crowd, I get a text from Layla. It's a picture of her flashing a peace sign.

Layla: I brought some of my Previdial peeps to the protest. Turns out a few of them are real ones!

Me: Layla! Thank you for coming!

Layla: Of course. If it's important to you, then it's important to me.

Me: What about your parents?

Layla: They're gonna be pissed. But better to ask for forgiveness than permission!

A FaceTime call comes in from Layla, but it's hard to hear her with all of the peripheral noise. "Are you here?" she says.

"Yeah! So are Victoria and Daniel!" I pull Victoria into the camera's frame.

Layla screams and begins jumping up and down. "Let me see where you are. I'm going to come find you."

I move my phone around to let her see my location.

"I think we're just across the street from you. I'm coming."

We disconnect the call, and I scan the crowd for her. Film crews are set up across the street, and people are streaming toward Dad's building from two directions. A small group of young people—possibly students—walks in front of us, holding signs and chanting "El pueblo, unido, jamás será vencido."

Yoly and Ricardo come over with Julissa, and I introduce Victoria and Daniel to them.

"Thank you both for all you've done to help my little sister," Victoria says.

"She's awesome and has been a great guest. Even knows how to run the dishwasher and washing machine now." Yoly winks at me.

“I’m glad we could help, and it’s so nice to finally meet you,” Ricardo says. “We’ve heard a lot about you.”

“Uh-oh,” Victoria says. “I hope at least some of it was good.” This comment earns Victoria a slap on her arm from me.

Ricardo laughs. “Of course.”

Julissa pipes up. “Would it be okay if I took a picture of the three of you to put online? It could have a big impact.”

My instinct is to say that we’re not big-impact people. Take away our surname and there’s nothing notable about us. I write book reviews for a niche magazine, my sister runs that niche magazine, and my brother just finished playing an ensemble part on a cruise ship musical. I’m not even a particular fan of having my picture taken.

I glance at Daniel, who looks good in every photo he’s ever uploaded to social media. He gives me a shrug and a smile, camera-ready that fast. Victoria turns to me, a worried look on her face. She’ll squash this if I give her even a hint of uncertainty.

The truth is, it *will* have a big impact—Robert James Mitchell’s three children protesting outside his building.

Jake gives my arm an encouraging squeeze. He had the courage to drop the mask of anonymity when he urged his followers to pay attention to these issues. I need to do the same.

“Sure,” I say. “If you two are up for it.”

“Let’s do it.” Daniel puts his arms around us and pulls us in toward him.

Julissa takes a few pictures before someone else comes over.

“Excuse me, are you the Mitchell children? I’m with *New York News*—do any of you have a moment to talk?”

“It should be you, Maya.” Victoria gives me a little shove. “I can’t even vote in this state.”

Let Victoria take one for the team. She owes me. I push

her in front of me. "No, you're the oldest. And the dazzlingly clever one."

"What? I don't even know what that means."

"Just go!"

Victoria joins the reporter and cameraman who are waiting for their interview. Layla comes up behind me, squeezes me around the waist, and props her chin on my shoulder. I turn around to hug her.

This crowd around us feels huge—I'm bad at estimating, but I wouldn't be surprised if five or six hundred people are spilling over the sidewalk all along the block. Someone holding a bullhorn leads the crowd in chanting "Wright is wrong!" over and over again, drowning out the sounds of passing traffic. A few people approach the front door of the building and get pushed back by security guards blocking the entrance.

I've never been part of a protest. I've never had a cause, and I didn't go looking for one. I am here today because a hateful man walked past me in the home where my mother taught me that when we have more than we need, we give to those who need more. And her lessons to me about how to treat others in this world didn't match up with my father's actions. If I have to choose whether to align myself with my mother's compassion or with my father's greed, then the choice is easy for me.

I'm proud to be here, standing with friends who took me in when I had nowhere to go, with siblings who've protected me as best they can, and with a boy I think I'm in love with.

In this moment, I'm exactly where I need to be.

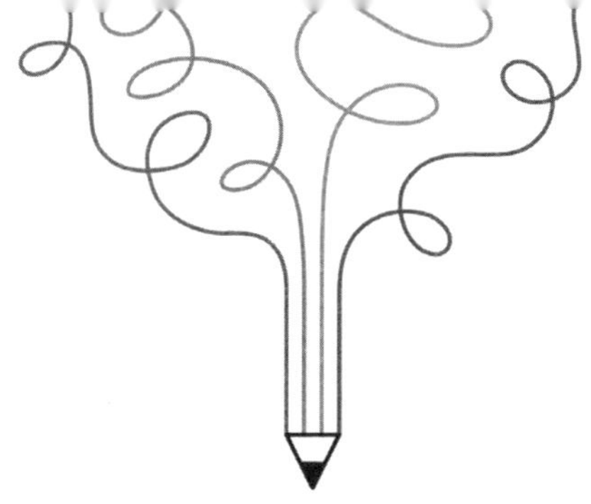

CHAPTER THIRTY

The protest wraps up early in the evening without anybody getting arrested, which I'm sure will be a disappointment to my father. A few hours later, Daisy convenes a special meal outside of our regularly scheduled Sunday dinners. She insists that I invite Victoria, Daniel, and Adam, and we squeeze into Jake and Katie's apartment because it's the biggest of the three.

Jake's the only one who's not here. I texted him thirty minutes ago, but he hasn't texted back, even though his short work shift ended almost an hour ago. It's not like him, and I worry that he might've had another panic attack.

Finally the door opens, and Jake walks in. His eyes land on me. "Hey. Sorry I'm late."

Daisy stands up to get him a plate. "I saved you some lumpia. Daniel was going to eat it all if I didn't put it aside for you."

"Thank you, Daisy. You're my hero." Jake comes over to me.

I stand up to hug him. "Everything okay?"

"Yeah, I stayed at work late talking to Tony." He turns to my siblings. "He owns the T-shirt shop where I work. I guess your dad paid him a little visit. He offered Tony ten thousand dollars to fire me."

"Damn!" Victoria slams her palm on the table. "Prick. I told you, Maya—I told you he'd make good on this threat."

Daniel puts his hand on my shoulder. "Ugh. So typical." Nobody bothers to point out that it's illegal. My dad has been getting away with—and may very well keep getting away with—much worse.

"Tony didn't take the money, did he?" I ask.

"He wasn't going to, but I told him he should."

"What?" Katie and I say at the same time.

"Tony has a lot of debt, and the shop needs some upgrades. I told him to take the money. I can find another job."

"But you love that place," I say.

"He knows a guy who runs a shop in Midtown. He's going to put in a good word for me."

I circle my arms around his waist. "Jake, I'm so sorry."

"It's okay. I mean, yeah, it sucks. I like working there. But I'll be okay. And at least Tony gets ten thousand bucks out of it."

"But it's not fair!" I burst out. Dropping my voice, I add, "It's not right that my dad keeps hurting and manipulating people I love."

"People you love?" He holds my gaze. The others may or may not be overhearing our quiet words. It doesn't matter to either of us.

"Yeah." My mouth dissolves into a smile. "Love."

"I love you too, Maya." He caresses my cheek and leans in to kiss me. "It's really okay. What matters is that you and I are together. If your dad really wanted to hurt me, he would make you stop seeing me."

"That's never going to happen. I'm done letting him tell me what to do."

Around us, the conversation has moved on. Everyone else is talking about Wright's campaign now.

"Wright's already publicly distancing himself from Mitchell," Ricardo is saying. "Which is reportedly pissing Mitchell off; word has it he's planning to pull his financial support from Wright—not because of the investigation but because Wright isn't going to bat for him."

Daniel snorts. "I'd love to see those two massive egos become each other's undoing."

"It'd make sense," says Victoria. "Neither of them wants this kind of scrutiny—from the authorities or from voters—and they'd rather blame each other than actually change."

Ricardo nods. "And if they fall out over this, it could have a snowball effect with other big donors. They're not going to want the authorities investigating *them*."

"Who knows," Yoly adds. "Wright might end up suspending his campaign."

"We can dream," says Ricardo with a sigh. "If nothing else, he may have less money to throw around, and he's going to have a hard time digging his way out of the negative coverage. The key will be keeping voters aware of his agenda, and keeping them invested in stopping it."

"In other words, lots more work to do," says Yoly with a sigh.

That's when Daniel's phone rings. "It's Dad," he says.

Victoria comes over to him. "Put it on speaker. You shouldn't have to deal with him by yourself."

Daniel nods and accepts the call. "What's up, Dad? You heard I was back in town and wanted to congratulate me on the run of my show?"

"Only if it means you're going to get a real job now."

Daniel has a smirk on his face because humor has always been his preferred method of dealing with Dad, but I can see the hurt under the surface. "Not likely. Anything else I can do for you?"

"You came all the way across the world to humiliate me today. My own son—the one who was supposed to carry on my name."

Victoria grabs the phone out of Daniel's hand. "You humiliated yourself by hooking up with a racist piece of garbage who has no business being a governor. That humiliation is on you."

"Ah, Victoria, so kind of you to join the conversation. You've all ganged up on me. Maya?"

I lean in over Victoria's shoulder. "I'm here too."

"A father's greatest disappointment. You spend your life working to provide for your family, and all you end up with is a trio of worthless traitors who turn against you the first chance they get."

"Aw, come on, Dad. Why are you trying to flatter us?" says Daniel.

Victoria elbows him in the side, and he covers his mouth to stifle a yelp.

Dad laughs dryly. "I hope you don't rely on your humor to make it in show business, Daniel, because the dearth in your wallet will be equivalent to the dearth of your talent. And Maya? I hope your T-shirt boy got his message. It's really just the start of a very bitter game that I am going to win eventually."

"You can't hurt us," I tell him. "We're not little kids anymore."

"The hell I can't, Maya. I still have all the power, and you'll see the brute end of it by the time I'm done with you."

"I don't know about that," Victoria chimes in. "Do the words *criminal charges* mean anything to you?"

"Cute, Victoria. You still don't understand the value of

money, do you? You might never understand. When you have as much money as I do, no one can touch you."

"It's going to catch up to you one of these days, Dad," Victoria says.

"It already has," I add. My heart is hammering so powerfully that I can feel it all the way to my ears. "You've lost everything of real value. The woman who loved you once—gone. Public respect—gone. Your three children—gone." I push the End Call icon on Daniel's phone, my whole body shaking.

Daniel and Victoria wrap me in an embrace. The shivering in my body releases a flood of tears that are more relief than anything.

Daniel and I tag along on Victoria's cab ride to the airport. We sit together in the back seat as we always did when Ernie shuttled us around: Daniel behind the driver, Victoria in the middle, me on her other side. My arm is intertwined with hers, and a rock sits lodged in my throat. I didn't realize how much I needed to see her, to feel like she was actually part of my world again.

"We're going to be okay," Victoria tells us. "He can't control us anymore. He's going to see that."

I rest my head on Victoria's shoulder. "I'm going to miss you, Vic. Promise you'll come back for Thanksgiving?"

"I promise. Maya, I'm so proud of you. So proud of both of you. The three of us—we're going to give new meaning to the name Mitchell."

I think she's right. I may not be dazzlingly clever or divinely beautiful or angelically good, but I have qualities I can be proud of, qualities I can nurture and strengthen. I'm happy with the person I'm becoming.

After we take Victoria to the airport, Daniel heads to an audition and I go to the writing room. I've still got an anti-classics article to finish, after all, plus that summer reading list pitch. And the editor at the teen magazine that accepted my charity story reached out to me after she saw the protest coverage. She pitched *me* an idea for an article aimed at first-time voters. I'll offer guidance on how to register to vote, plus tips for getting informed about candidates and issues.

Once Yoly and Ricardo move across the hall, I'll have their place all to myself and might not need to come here, but for now this still feels like a second home.

When I first stepped through this doorway, I felt so alone in the world. No matter what the future holds, I know I will never feel that alone again. Wherever I am and whatever happens, I will make a place for myself—and, with my words and actions, try to make a place for others too.

QUESTIONS FOR DISCUSSION

1. At the beginning of the story, Maya refers to herself as "homeless." How does her understanding of this term, and of her own and others' situations, shift over time?

2. How does Maya rationalize and make excuses for her father's behavior? How and why does this become more difficult for her as the story progresses?

3. Why is Maya skeptical of social media as a writing platform? Do you agree or disagree, and why?

4. Jake has kept his everyday life and his writing life separate. Why does he feel ashamed of his writing? What factors help him move past that shame and discomfort?

5. Maya often compares her life to her favorite novels. Is there a comparison that you find particularly apt? What about one that you disagree with?

6. What emotional role do books play in Maya's life? What do you make of her decision to take back her copy of *Charlotte's Web* from her father's apartment?

7. For much of the story, Maya tries to be as independent as possible and avoid depending too much on others for help.

Yet she witnesses many cases of people stepping up to support someone who needs a hand. What example of a character or characters helping someone else stands out to you? How does it affect Maya's perspective?

8. Maya dreams of eventually becoming a journalist and of having "the power of stringing words together to tell the world something." How does she end up doing this in unexpected ways?

9. In what ways does Maya consciously choose to be different from her father? How do these choices influence her personal relationships?

10. How does the writing room serve as an anchor for Maya? What places have felt safe and nurturing for you when you needed them?

ACKNOWLEDGMENTS

This book had a long journey. I started writing it over twelve years ago in a completely different genre, tense, and point of view. I am grateful for the gift of time. It took a long time for this book to become what it needed to be, for me to tell the story I needed to tell.

I am thankful to my parents, José and Cory Argueta, who left behind their native country of Guatemala in search of a better life for their daughters. They have always been selfless, generous, and kind. I'm grateful for their love. Everything I've done in my life is in hopes of making them proud.

Thank you to Ruben, Diego, and Omar for being wonderful sons and truly great people. I am grateful to have the honor of knowing you your whole lives, and I'm so proud of the men you have become.

My sister, Claudia, was my best friend growing up and the person I love to talk to most about writing. Thank you for reading everything I write. I always know that you will give me the feedback that I need to make my stories better. Thank you for introducing me to *Anne of Green Gables* the summer you came home from college. You are my bosom friend and my kindred spirit.

Thank you to the wonderful Librarypalooza committee and the amazing librarians at Northside, who are so supportive of my books and of all authors. What you do for students is so imperative. You put yourselves out there on the front lines, fighting for our kids and their right to read. I am so grateful to know you, and I am so happy every time I get to see you! Sheryl, Lucy, Zinnia, Jennifer E., Corey, Jennifer P., Kristen, and so many more—thank you! Thank you also to the wonderful librarians who run Teen Bookfest by the Bay. You work so hard to put on an amazing festival every year! I would like to send a big thank-you to all librarians for the important job they do for students and for having to pick up a fight against book-banning that should have never been foisted upon them.

A special thank-you to one Northside librarian who even shouts me out on morning announcements. Thank you, Jennifer Parker, for your support and enthusiasm and for making little stickers of my book. I'm so lucky to have you on my side. Thank you to everyone else at Cable who make it such a wonderful place to work.

Thank you to Kathy Green for believing in Millie from *Where I Belong* and helping that book make its way into the world—and for helping to carve a path for me to tell more stories. I am so fortunate to have you on my side.

A huge thanks goes to Amy Fitzgerald. This has been our third time working together. I'm so grateful for your confidence in me and for you championing my books. Thank you for making my books better with your edits. I am always happy to see your name in my inbox.

Thank you to the entire team at Lerner for the years of support and assistance. It is always a pleasure to see Kathleen at TLA. I love stopping by the booth! Thank you for helping me with the book-signings. A big thanks to Lindsay, Rachel, and Megan for all their work to promote my books.

Thank you to Elsa, my OG VT from CC, for flying with me to Utah three times. Being roomies with you is so much fun. Two Jack's Pizza for life. A big thanks to my San Antonio Storymakers friend and cousin, Tara. It's so nice to know that you're just down the highway from me. And thank you to my other San Antonio Storymakers friend, Evelyn, for shouting me out on Facebook and for being one of the best people I know. I am so glad you're just down the road from me.

Guadalupe García McCall, I will forever be grateful for that brunch at Texas Grounds where you listened to me talk about this book. I was stuck, and your wonderful suggestion was just what I needed to finish this book. I'm so happy to live so close to you!

I love being a writer in Texas because there is such a wonderful community of authors here who I run into at festivals, conferences, retreats, book launches, and other events. If I started a list of all the amazing kidlit authors who live in this great state and who I get to rub elbows with, it would take this entire page. I am so grateful to work among you all. I'm grateful to the Texas Institute of Letters community for bringing me into their fold, and for the important work that they do.

Thank you to my Musas hermanas. It is such a privilege and a pleasure to be numbered among you all. Our Texas retreats have been among some of my favorite writing experiences.

Thank you to all my family in New Jersey, Utah, Texas, and Idaho for all the love and support.

My biggest thanks goes to my husband, Nolan, who has been supportive from day one. I decided I wanted to get a book published in 2004. When I spent hours at the computer with no promise of publication, Nolan never questioned the time I dedicated to writing. He has been encouraging from day one and has supported my dream every step of the way. Thank you, and I love you.

ABOUT THE AUTHOR

Marcia Argueta Mickelson was born in Guatemala and immigrated to the United States as an infant. She is the author of several young adult novels, including *The Weight of Everything* and *Where I Belong*, a Pura Belpré Young Adult Honor Book. She lives in Texas with her husband and three sons.